"I MAKE YOU UNCOMFORTABLE," SAID DAPHNE. "I CAN TELL."

"Not at all . . ."

"You don't have to lie."

Wes was struck silent, like a chastized schoolboy. He felt that Daphne was very far away, and it saddened him unaccountably.

"I'm uncomfortable with a lot of people," he finally said. "Don't take it personally." He wanted suddenly to tell Daphne how he felt about her, to unburden himself of the guilt he felt. It was unthinkable.

He fell silent again. But she could heal him, he sensed instinctively, make him happy and whole as he'd never in his life been. He savored the possibility of loving her like a morsel of the most delicious chocolate, tasting it until every bit was melted away.

Yes, she made him uncomfortable, he wanted to shout at her. She made him crawl with desire.

ABOUT THE AUTHOR

To provide authenticity for *A Dangerous Sentiment*, Carla Peltonen and Molly Swanton spent a good deal of time tracking Hurricane Gloria, which battered the New England coast in the fall of 1985. The writing team of Lynn Erickson is already awash in research for their next Superromance, which will transport their loyal readers to Scotland and Greece in early 1987.

Books by Lynn Erickson

HARLEQUIN SUPERROMANCE

HARLEQUIN INTRIGUE

These books may be available at your local bookseller.

Don't miss any of our special offers. Write to us at the following address for information on our newest releases.

Harlequin Reader Service
901 Fuhrmann Blvd., P.O. Box 1397, Buffalo, NY 14240
Canadian address: P.O. Box 603,
Fort Erie, Ont. L2A 9Z9

Lynn Erickson

A DANGEROUS SENTIMENT

Harlequin Books

TORONTO • NEW YORK • LONDON
AMSTERDAM • PARIS • SYDNEY • HAMBURG
STOCKHOLM • ATHENS • TOKYO • MILAN

Published October 1986

First printing August 1986

ISBN 0-373-70231-0

Printed in Canada

This book is dedicated to Carol Mayhew Mays,
a descendant of Thomas himself,
whose help and many books on Martha's Vineyard
were invaluable, and to Jerry Friedenberg,
who provided me with information about
the Coast Guard stations on Cape Cod.

CHAPTER ONE

DAPHNE FARWAY tilted her head back and looked up at the nondescript concrete office building. Yes, this was it: 470 Atlantic Avenue. Practically on Boston's waterfront. Somehow she'd expected it to be more prepossessing, more imposing, more *something*.

She wiped beads of sweat from her upper lip and drew in a lungful of hot, muggy air. She glanced at her watch: 11:30 a.m. Time for her appointment.

The directory inside said merely U.S. Secret Service, fifth floor. Brady had worked here, she couldn't help but recall. The lobby, the directory, the chair and the elevator doors must have been as familiar to him as his own home.

Thank goodness it was cool in the building. She was nervous enough without the additional irritant of pouring sweat. The elevator doors hissed shut, and Daphne drew in another deep breath.

What exactly would she say to Brady's superior, Special Agent in Charge Jerry Gallent? Brady had always called him "chief." Chief Gallent, head of the Boston office of the Secret Service. Daphne had spoken to him on the phone finally, after trying to reach him for several weeks, and they'd made this appointment.

What exactly *would* she say? She closed her wide blue eyes and sighed. Would she tell him that her fiancé, Brady Leighton, had told her in strict confidence, totally against security regulations, that he'd discovered there was a traitor in the Boston Secret Service office? Should she tell him everything—that Brady had been collecting proof that one of the agents in his office had given top-secret information to the Russians, vital information that would compromise the Service, the U.S. government and world peace?

She knew plenty; Brady had trusted her with his secrets. She knew all about his office, the foibles and eccentricities of his co-workers, the leads in his latest case, everything.

Except the name of the traitor. He'd told her he couldn't reveal *that* until he'd exposed the whole plot to his superiors in Washington.

"That's one piece of information that's just too hot to handle, Daffy," he'd said, smiling, his beloved, familiar face close to hers, his hand on her shoulder.

So now she had to face Special Agent in Charge Gallent with all the pieces of the puzzle but one, the most important one, the piece that revealed the face of the traitor. For all she knew, it could be the chief himself, or anyone else in the office.

And Brady couldn't divulge the identity of that person. Brady couldn't help her. Not anymore.

Brady was dead.

The elevator light showed 5, and the doors whispered open. An entrance across from her was labeled U.S. Secret Service in small, neat, stenciled letters.

The pleasant-faced receptionist issued Daphne a badge with her name typed on it. "Security," the woman explained, smiling apologetically. Daphne was led past desks and windowed office doors, aware that everyone there was watching her. They must have known that she'd been Brady's fiancée, and wondered what she was doing in the office. She felt curious gazes crawl up her back like insects' feet walking on her.

"Miss Farway," announced the receptionist.

Jerry Gallent rose from his chair and moved out from behind his desk, his hand stretched forward. He was below average height, although still half a foot taller than Daphne, and quite stocky. His face, which was supported by a bull-like neck, was square and fatherly but attractive. He had a certain sex appeal, that of a man who was comfortable with himself, who'd settled for what he was and decided he liked it. His brown eyes, deep-set under shaggy dark brows, were warm and expressive.

"Miss Farway," he said in a deep, gravelly, reassuring voice. "A pleasure."

She shook his hand; it was cool and strong. "Please call me Daphne," she said. "And I want to thank you for the flowers and that nice letter you sent."

"The least I could do," he said, his brows drawing together in a frown. "An awful thing, Daphne. A young, smart fella like Brady. We were all so shocked. I'll tell you, someone ought to do something about the crime in this city these days."

He pulled up a comfortable chair for her and seated himself behind his desk. Sitting down, he appeared broad and powerful; one would have expected him to be tall.

"I'm glad to have the opportunity of offering my condolences in person, at least," Gallent said kindly.

Daphne felt the familiar wave of emptiness, the black, engulfing void sweep her. She fought it. Brady was gone and she had a job to do. "Thank you," she said softly.

The chief was watching her carefully. Did he expect her to cry or break down or something? Or was he merely wondering why she wanted to see him?

"You've driven quite a ways," he offered. "A couple of hours from the ferry, isn't it?"

"An hour and a half from Woods Hole. I'm used to it."

"I guess you are, living on an island like that. Brady used to tell me about Martha's Vineyard. To hear him talk it was heaven on earth."

"It is lovely," she agreed, "but I didn't come into Boston to waste your time, Chief Gallent." She felt her cheeks grow hot with discomfort. This was the hard part. How much to say? She shifted in her chair and pushed back her short blond curls in a nervous gesture.

"You realize, don't you, that Brady's death was not an accident," she began.

Jerry Gallent leaned forward and stared at her. "Not an accident? What do you mean?"

"I mean, I don't believe that he was killed by a burglar who was trying to rob his apartment."

"I think, Daphne, you'll have to explain that a bit more."

"I think Brady was deliberately murdered."

"But why?" asked Gallent, agitated.

She couldn't tell him precisely why. If he were the guilty one, the traitor whom Brady had confronted, he knew why already. Not that she really believed Jerry Gallent was the one. Why, he had a very high security clearance, didn't he? And why would a nice, responsible family man like Gallent be involved in espionage? Brady had respected his boss's professionalism and skill. But still, she needed to feel him out before she could tell him the whole truth.

"I'm not sure," she insisted staunchly, "but I don't believe anyone could have gotten into his apartment and surprised him like that."

"So who do you think shot him, then?" asked Gallent carefully, as if humoring a child.

"I don't know. Maybe someone from that counterfeiting case he was on," she suggested.

Gallent's eyes flicked to hers instantly. "You knew about that?"

Lowering her gaze modestly, Daphne murmured, "Well, you know, he told me a few things. Not much. Nothing that was important. A man has to talk..."

Relaxing in his chair, the chief picked up a pencil and began playing with it, turning it end over end. "I think there've been more coups given away, more battles lost, more security breaches that way than any other. Pillow talk," he said disdainfully.

"Really, it was only gossip. Nothing important, like I said," Daphne hastened to explain. "Brady took his job very seriously."

"I know," relented Gallent. He fixed her with an implacable gaze. "Have you spoken to the police about your suspicions?"

"I've been in touch with them several times in the past couple of weeks. They're very kind and helpful, but they have no leads on the so-called burglar's identity."

"It's a shame," said Gallent, "but too often this sort of case goes unsolved."

"The problem is," Daphne continued, "nothing was found to be missing in his place."

"Nothing?"

"No. At least, nothing of any value. Brady didn't exactly have much worth taking, but still..."

"I see. And so that's why you're wondering if it was a burglar, at all?"

"It's more than that. You see, Brady was on to something—" Suddenly Daphne stopped herself, not daring to continue. Perhaps she'd already said too much.

"On to something?" His thick eyebrows rose.

"Well, I mean, the counterfeiting case and all," she inserted hastily.

"Umm." Jerry Gallent studied her for a moment. "And you're sure that's all you're basing your suspicions on?"

"I ... Yes. I'm sure."

"Look," he said then. "I can understand your concern, all the frustrations, but it's very difficult to believe that Brady was killed in the line of duty. I hate to say it—" he paused "—but I'm afraid Brady interrupted a burglar and the man panicked. It happens every day."

"But there's no proof of that," began Daphne.

"Listen, if there's anything I can do to help...*anything*, I certainly will."

"Maybe you could talk to the police yourself. I don't know. It just seems that someone should be doing more. I mean, there's no motive and there're no suspects."

She was dying to tell him everything, but she wasn't sure yet. Gallent, ridiculous as it still seemed, could be the man who'd killed Brady. "If you could just talk to the police," she repeated, "nudge them a little."

"I can do that." He nodded. "I have a few friends on the force. I'm sure if I speak to them ... Who knows, maybe there *is* something they overlooked. It can't hurt. Although," he added, "I have to tell you that I never thought Brady's death was anything but an accident." He smiled patronizingly.

"Any help you can give would be appreciated," she said.

He was humoring her; he'd probably do nothing at all about it. He thought she was crazy, paranoid, someone who needed to pin the blame on a specific person. Accidental death was so senseless, so futile.

She rose, feeling frustration swamp her, still longing to say more to this man yet afraid to tell him she knew Brady's death was no accident, no coincidence.

Brady had left her that day a month ago to return to Boston and confront the traitor. He'd kissed her goodbye on the dock at the Vineyard Haven ferry terminal, smiled gaily, boarded and waved to her from the fat-sided *Island Queen*. It had been hot and humid on the island of Martha's Vineyard that day. Beach weather. Tourist weather.

"Be careful!" she'd shouted to him through cupped hands as the boat had pulled away. But just then the ferry's foghorn had blown and he hadn't heard her. He'd been nodding and grinning and waving to her, and she'd lifted her hand to wave back when a sudden chill had seized her. She'd wished, at the time, that he'd heard her warning. Later, she felt that perhaps it could have made all the difference if he had heeded her words.

She'd remained there a long time, watching the ferry churn away from the island, watching the sea gulls hang motionless above the curling wake, begging for scraps of food from the tourists.

That had been the last time she'd seen Brady. He'd been shot to death that night in his apartment on Commonwealth Avenue.

"I just want to repeat," Jerry Gallent was saying, "how very sorry I am. I know you and Brady were going to be married soon. I understand your concern."

"Thank you," she mumbled again. It was useless. She couldn't confide in him, and he wouldn't believe her if she didn't. Impasse. She'd hoped to accomplish more by coming here, but obviously Brady's chief was satisfied to call it accidental death.

The badge pinned onto her thin yellow blouse pulled at the fabric, dragging it down embarrassingly. It wouldn't matter if she were flat-chested, she thought, trying to adjust it as she walked back down the hallway toward the receptionist's desk. She was glad to unpin the awkward thing and hand it back to the woman.

"I want you to know," began the receptionist timidly, "how sorry we all are."

"Thank you." It was becoming a stock phrase. A month of uncomfortable people telling her how dreadful, how awful it was, how sorry they were. Sometimes grieving seemed to be a game with rules that had been written by a sadist. All Daphne had wanted to do was suffer quietly, alone, like a dumb animal. Then, when the worst had been over and she'd come to grips with her loss, she'd emerged into a world where everyone became hushed and unnatural around her, issuing platitudes and pity and clichés that didn't help her a bit.

At times Daphne wanted to cry out at the injustice of treating her like a leper. But mostly she just smiled and thanked them and tried to forget it. It would pass.

Waiting in the cool corridor for the elevator, Daphne tried to think. What should she do next? Go to the police with her story? They'd laugh in her face. She had no proof—except for Brady's murder, which to them wasn't a murder at all but a perfectly normal, straightforward burglary.

Would everyone in the office talk about her now? Would they chuckle over Gallent's story about her ridiculous suspicions? The elevator swished and clanked, approaching. Footsteps rang on the hard floor behind her. She turned—out of vague, automatic curiosity—to see a strange man walking toward her. She had an impression of height and athletic carriage, a blur of sandy hair, strong features, a tie loosened at a muscular neck. And a Secret Service badge pinned to the pocket of his neat white shirt.

"Miss Farway?" he asked.

"Yes?" She had to tip her head up to look into his face. A nice manly face with a lovely cleft chin.

"I'm Weston Leroux. Wes. You may have heard . . ."

"You were Brady's partner in the counterfeiting case," she said, abruptly remembering. "He spoke of you." She held her hand out. He hesitated for a split second, then grasped it. "I'm glad to meet you."

"Likewise," he said. "I want you to know how sorry I am about Brady."

"Thank you." She felt like a windup doll. She hoped he wouldn't go on about it. Pity was so detestable.

"Look, I meant to call you a dozen times but I'm not very good at things like that. I liked Brady a lot. We got to be pretty close."

"He told me." At least this Weston was admitting his discomfort. That was refreshing.

The elevator arrived, thumping. Its doors hissed open. Weston Leroux looked at them as if considering something. "I wonder if you'd like to have lunch with me? That is, if you're not in a hurry."

She cocked her head. "Is this invitation to soothe your conscience?" she offered gently.

He grinned. "Guess I'm pretty transparent."

"Well, in that case, I'd love to. I'd hate to think of leaving you in emotional limbo."

"Great. Let me get my jacket."

The elevator doors slid shut; the mechanism swished, groaning, to another floor, leaving her standing there.

Wes Leroux. Of course. Daphne felt as if a weight had been lifted from her shoulders. How many times had Brady discussed his new partner? Everything Brady told her came flooding back into her mind. Wes had had a rough upbringing. South Boston, divorced parents, a mother who was totally incapable of handling him. Trouble with the law, foster homes. The military had straightened him out—the hard way, according to Brady. That and an older brother who apparently cared a lot about him.

Brady had liked his new partner. But more than that, he'd trusted him. He'd said a dozen times that Wes could be counted on—absolutely.

In fact, Brady had been going to tell Wes of the plot he'd uncovered as soon as he'd obtained a bit more proof....

"All set" came Weston's voice. He stood before her, his tie in place, a lightweight khaki jacket over his short-sleeved shirt. Everything about him was neat, military, perfect. Short sandy hair combed to the side. Smooth shaven. A brisk after-shave. Clear green eyes under straight brows. A bumpy nose, strong jaw, well-formed sensitive mouth.

They had to wait for the elevator. "Where to?" asked Wes easily.

"Someplace old and historic," said Daphne. "I'm a chump for the corny old stuff."

"Not fast food?" he asked drolly.

She chuckled. "Try again."

"The Union Oyster House," he stated firmly.

"Perfect."

They walked. Downtown Boston was really a very small place, rather cozy and intimate and bursting with historic buildings, each one duly noted by a bronze plaque or a quaint wooden sign. The scent of sea air drifted by on the occasional hot breeze, and narrow shaded alleyways beckoned.

It was nice to be walking with a good-looking man again. She couldn't resist studying him out of the corner of her eye. He wasn't really so tall, but the graceful way he carried himself made him appear so. His body was spare and neat and strong under the suit. Daphne was a little embarrassed, knowing more about Weston Leroux, she was sure, than he would have liked. He certainly didn't appear to be the juvenile delinquent type anymore. She was suddenly curious about the path he'd traveled from his troubled younger years.

He turned then and smiled at her, a boyish smile that changed his expression totally—from a sober aloofness to charming interest. She'd bet he didn't smile that way nearly as often as he should. She also bet he wouldn't smile when she told him about Brady's murder and the plot....

Ye Olde Union Oyster House, Est. 1826, read the sign. It was a very old brick building with awnings, small many-paned windows and dormers on the roof. Inside, Weston practically had to duck to avoid a good bump on the head from the low ceiling beams.

They were seated at a window table upstairs. The place was full of typical Bostonians: casually dressed New England businessmen, ladies from the suburbs on shopping trips, tweedy college professors, students.

A congenial lunchtime din filled the building, and Daphne felt able to relax over a white wine. Weston, as he was returning to work, had iced tea. They made small talk, and she decided to let it go on that way until the right moment to bring up Brady's "accident."

There was something magnetic about Weston, she decided. It was, perhaps, in the way he held himself, in his demeanor: totally at ease, self-assured, friendly. He was a darn good-looking man, although not picture perfect. He dressed nicely and with good taste for a bachelor. His hair was cut carefully, with no razor edges showing. She noticed that he hadn't a single gray hair on his head and that his complexion was very fair. She noticed, too, that his green eyes were fringed with uncommonly long lashes for a man, and she couldn't help but wonder if he had a girl-friend.

Wes ordered oyster stew. Daphne chose a salad. A basket of hot, freshly baked corn bread arrived—the house specialty. Butter melted on it invitingly.

"Look, Miss Farway..." Wes began. Then he smiled ruefully. "I can't call you Miss Farway. Brady always called you Daphne."

"Or Daffy," she suggested.

"Well, sometimes. But I think Daphne is more appropriate. Do you mind?"

She shook her head, licking corn bread crumbs off her fingers daintily. "And you're Wes, right?"

"Right. What I was going to say was this: if it bothers you to talk about Brady, tell me and I won't. I'm not sure how to handle this whole thing."

Daphne leaned her elbows on the table. "You know, I always thought it would be hard to talk about someone who died. You could never mention him or you'd cry. But it's not like that. I loved Brady. I still do. It's as if he were out of the room, or on a job somewhere. He's gone but he's not dead. Oh, I'm not making sense. But he's *there*, and it doesn't hurt to talk about him. I *want* to remember."

Wes was looking at her closely, as if trying to figure her out. But she was so uncomplicated really. And Brady must have talked to Wes about her. Surely he had. If Brady Leighton had a failing, it was his love of talking to others about those close to him. She narrowed her eyes and wondered, suddenly, exactly how much Brady had told Wes about her. It gave her a distinctly odd feeling to imagine what this stranger had heard.

More to the point was what Daphne knew about Wes Leroux. She dredged up all the morsels Brady had told her about him.

Trustworthy. That was the salient point. Brady had said the traitor was in his office. It could be any of them, Daphne supposed, but it was surely not this man, Brady's partner, whom he'd said he trusted with his life. She'd bank on that.

She sipped her wine, noting that the one thing Brady had neglected to mention about Wes was how stunningly attractive he was.

"I understand you live on Martha's Vineyard," Wes was saying. "I've never been there, although I almost feel I know your place. Brady talked about it so much." He leaned back, and Daphne noticed the outline of a gun under his jacket. Brady had never worn one when he'd been with her, but then, she hadn't visited him much during working hours.

A gun. She shivered mentally. The Secret Service, Daphne knew, had two main functions: to protect the president and his family and visiting dignitaries, and to protect the country from counterfeiters or violations against the nation's monetary security. It was a division of the Department of Treasury, a largely unknown fact, and its agents generally did investigative work—office work. Only rarely did a man actually face physical danger. But the gun wasn't needed to remind her that sometimes they were, indeed, put in jeopardy. Like Brady...

Nervously, she took another sip from her glass and looked out the small-paned window onto the narrow, picturesque Boston street. She'd have to tell him. Someone had to help her. There was no one else she could trust.

She took a deep breath, straining the buttons on her yellow blouse in the process, and pushed her curly bangs back. "Wes? I've got to tell you something. It's about Brady..." She'd started all wrong. "I mean, it's about something Brady told me."

He looked puzzled. "I'm not sure..."

She leaned forward across the table. "That's why I came into Boston today. But your Chief Gallent... Well, he wasn't any help."

"What is it, Daphne? Was Brady in some kind of trouble?"

"No. Well." She stopped and looked up to the ceiling, her eyes closed, trying to organize her thoughts. "You know that Gorvieski is stopping in Boston on his American tour."

It was no secret. Everyone in the country was familiar with the name Viktor Gorvieski, the general secretary of the Soviet Union's Communist party. A powerful man, a young and forward-looking leader who had been warming to the West. A man of a new generation who might bring peace between the superpowers, someone who would certainly bring moderation and reason to the bargaining table.

"Yes, sure." There was a frown on Weston's face, making him seem older than the thirty-three Daphne knew him to be.

"Brady found out something before he...died. He told me, Wes." She looked at him, trying desperately to be convincing. If *he* didn't believe her... "He noticed, first, that Gorvieski's itinerary, the one your office has been working on, was missing over a weekend. Gorvieski's Boston itinerary, with all its security precautions. It worried him, so he kept an eye out. He saw someone put it back and he decided to follow this person." She took another breath. Did he believe her? His face was intent, but she couldn't tell what he was thinking.

"This person met a Soviet military attaché in Boston Common and gave him some papers. That was when Brady decided he had to confront this ... this traitor. He discussed it with me. You can imagine how upset he was. Someone in his own office. And this trip by Gorvieski was so important. I mean, it would be disastrous if anything happened."

Wes spoke finally. "Are you trying to tell me that someone provided this Russian with our security arrangements? What for, Daphne?" His tone was slow and deliberate, heavy with question and doubt.

"So Gorvieski could be assassinated." The words fell from her lips breathlessly. "Brady was almost positive. He went over and over it, and there was no other possible explanation."

Weston sat perfectly still in his chair; his gaze was resting on her with great intensity, his green eyes never blinking.

"Brady checked out the Russian attaché that the traitor had been seeing, and the Russian was one of the old guard who wants to keep the Cold War going. The old guard hates Gorvieski and his new ideas and is jealous of his power and popularity. Brady explained it all to me." Her voice was pleading. Wes had to believe her.

Weston finally leaned forward over the small table. "What did Gallent say to all this?"

Daphne looked down at her hands. "I...I didn't tell him everything. Only that I thought Brady's death wasn't an accident."

"Why not?"

She looked up at him, meeting his gaze openly. "I don't know who the traitor in your office is. I was afraid—"

He interrupted her almost angrily. "You mean Brady told you everything but who it was?"

"Yes," she whispered. "I only know it was an agent in your office. He was afraid to tell me who, though, until it was out in the open. He said it was to protect me. Just in case."

Wes let out a deep breath and leaned back in his seat, concentrating hard. The seconds ticked by endlessly. Daphne was sure she didn't breathe once.

At last he spoke; his voice was hard. "Why *did* you go to see Gallent?"

"I didn't know what else to do. I'd called him a few times but he was busy or out of town and I had to do *something*. I thought if I felt him out, I thought if he believed me..."

"Believed you about what?"

"Brady's death." She fixed her wide blue eyes on him. "It wasn't an accident, you know. Brady was murdered. I knew it right away. He confronted the traitor and the man shot him."

"What...?" Weston began, shocked. He caught himself and shook his head slowly. "Hold on there. This is pretty heavy."

"I know. I've had a month to think about it. I'm sorry to drop this on you like a bomb, but what else can I do? You believe me, don't you?"

"Believe you? Daphne, this is a goddamn blockbuster. Give me a minute." He put a hand up to the back of his neck and rubbed it as if to relieve a knot of tension. Then he stopped short and stared at her. "Why tell *me*? Maybe *I'm* the one."

She shook her head emphatically. "No, Brady trusted you."

"Then why in hell didn't you get to me earlier?"

Twisting her hands in agitation, Daphne said, "I don't know. I was so upset. I couldn't sleep. I was sort of out of my head for a while. I . . . I guess I just didn't think. And then it had been a month and your chief never returned my calls and I knew I had to do something."

"I'm sorry," replied Weston, "you've been through it."

"No, no, it's okay. I should have called you first. To tell the truth, when you didn't come to the funeral, I forgot all about you." She smiled weakly. "I had a lot of things on my mind."

Wes was silent, massaging his eyes with a thumb and forefinger. Her heart thudded with apprehension. He hadn't said he believed her yet.

He stopped. "Let me get this straight. Brady saw this person from our office give Gorvieski's itinerary to a known Russian hawk. He assumed this was done for the purpose of breaching our security to assassinate Gorvieski. Brady went to confront this person and was shot, allegedly by a burglar. Am I right?"

"Yes." Daphne felt her eyes fill with tears, an uncontrollable reaction she had whenever she thought of Brady facing that man alone, seeing the gun, feeling the bullet smash into him. Horrible, horrible . . .

A shadow crossed Weston's face and he put a hand out as if to touch her arm, then withdrew it. But his voice was soft when he spoke. "Hey, are you okay? I'm sorry, I didn't mean to be so callous about it. I'm just trying to get this all straight in my mind."

She dabbed her eyes with a crumpled napkin. "I'm fine. I just can't help it sometimes." She paused, then asked again. "You believe me, don't you?"

He was slow in answering. When he spoke, it was half to himself. "Brady was real preoccupied for a time there. I thought it was because of Gorvieski's trip and all the overtime. But it could have been . . ." His eyes came up to meet hers. "The police. What do they think?"

"That it was a burglar. They haven't got any other explanation, and I knew that if I told them the whole story they'd think I was insane. I have no real proof."

"I'll have to check their reports, but yes, it all fits. It could be."

"It's true, I tell you! Brady wouldn't make this up!"

His gaze held hers intently. "No," Wes said slowly, "he wouldn't."

"Thank God you believe me," Daphne breathed.

He was still watching her, fixing her with grave regard. "Did you say anything else to the chief?"

She shook her head but then suddenly remembered. "I did tell him one thing."

"What was that?"

"Well, that Brady confided things to me."

"I see. And what did Gallent say?"

"He said something about 'pillow talk' and implied that information—security stuff—often got leaked that way."

"So the chief pretty much knew that Brady told you things he shouldn't have?"

"I guess he assumed that." A small knot of apprehension was coiling in Daphne's stomach.

"Do you have any idea what I'm driving at, Daphne?"

"I hope I'm wrong," she said quietly.

"You might as well have told the chief that you know everything."

"No! I mean," she hastened to say, "it *can't* be Chief Gallent!"

"Say it isn't," came Weston's low-pitched voice. "Say it's any one of a number of people in our office. The chief doesn't realize there's a traitor and believe me, he'll have every agent there in his office this afternoon lecturing them about breaches of security. And they'll know the reason for the lecture, too."

"Because of my visit," she said slowly, in a voice filled with dread.

"Exactly. Every one of them will know Brady talked to you."

"So I've let the traitor know that Brady confided in me."

His silence was all the answer she needed.

Daphne bit her lower lip. "I've really done it now, haven't I? Let the cat out of the bag."

"There's a chance of it."

"This is just . . . just great." She met Weston's solemn gaze; the deep concern she saw there didn't reassure her any, not a bit. "I'm in danger, aren't I?"

"I wish to God it were otherwise."

She wanted to ask him just how much danger she was in, but somehow the words stuck like glue in her throat. Instead she merely looked at him, fear squeezing her chest.

"Have you told anyone else about this?" His question shot at her like a dart.

She felt her face drain of blood. She nodded slowly. "My mother," she whispered.

His hard green eyes held her.

"Oh, no," murmured Daphne brokenly.

Silence hung between them, taut and threatening. The clatter of dishes and chatter of conversation surrounded Daphne, yet the noise seemed distant, muted, unreal. The only reality was Weston, across from her, his face troubled.

"Go home, Daphne," he said softly. "Right now. Don't talk to anyone, don't answer any questions. I'll be in touch, okay?"

She nodded, scared, her face drained of its usual high color.

"Nothing's going to happen right away. Whoever it is has to make sure…" He reached across the table and took her hand. "Everything's going to be fine. Don't worry. You did right by telling me."

CHAPTER TWO

THE TEMPERATURE READ EIGHTY-SIX on the digital display at a corner bank as Weston Leroux walked down Atlantic Avenue to his office building.

He had to admit to himself that Daphne Farway's story had shaken him badly. He'd tried not to let her see how disturbed he'd been. She had enough trouble. But now he felt chilled all over.

This was big, really big. His mind churned, examining information, discarding, conjuring up possibilities. Deep in his gut he had a void, an alien lonely feeling, because he knew there wasn't a soul in the office he could trust with his earthshattering story.

The circumstances surrounding Brady Leighton's death, Wes realized, had been subconsciously gnawing at him for the past month. The police theory that Brady had interrupted a burglar had never felt quite right to Weston. Now, of course, he knew why.

There was a lot he had to do. Gorvieski would arrive in Boston in three weeks, right after the president's Labor Day vacation, and someone had the knowledge to bypass the elaborate security measures set up by the Secret Service to protect the man. An assassination plot. And Wes was the only man on earth who could make sure it never came off.

Weston entered the fourteen-story cement building that housed the Secret Service office. Again he felt that unfamiliar chilling hand pressing on him, hurrying him toward an unknown destiny. As he pushed open the door and entered the office area, Wes realized with a sick feeling that he was having trouble looking his co-workers in the eye.

"Hey, Wes!" Agent Michael Toth strode out of his cubicle and walked over to Weston. "How's Brady's girl? What's her name?"

"Farway, Daphne Farway."

"Yeah. How's she doing, anyway?" Toth followed Wes around a secretary's desk and into Weston's own small office.

"She's fine. Under the circumstances," he added, avoiding Mike Toth's curious glance.

"Of course. I didn't know you knew her."

"I don't, really."

"Lunch, though," suggested Mike inquisitively.

Weston's back went stiff; he fought irritation. "Hey, you know me, Mikey. I just thought she might need a friend. What's it to you?"

"Nothing, Wes. Just curious."

Wes tossed his jacket over the back of his chair and loosened his tie. "Sorry. I guess it was the way you said 'lunch.'"

"Just being nosy." Mike sat down comfortably as if to settle in for a chat. "She's a nice-looking lady."

"Umm," replied Weston absently as he shuffled through a few papers. Then he looked up at Mike Toth, one of the only agents in the Boston branch of the Secret Service with top-security clearance. Mike had a very slight accent and manly good looks. He was middle European, a Hungarian by birth, actually. His head was shaved, Kojak style, so that his age could be anywhere from thirty-five to fifty.

They were friends. But today Wes didn't feel particularly friendly. He looked into those clear innocent blue eyes and wondered: *is it Toth?*

"You okay?" asked Mike.

Weston shrugged. "Fine. I was just thinking..."

"About a case?"

"Yeah," lied Weston, "it's this counterfeiting ring in Maine again. The situation has me baffled."

"Yes, well, I'd be glad to help, but the FBI has been bugging us to cooperate on a case of interstate hijacking. One of the suspects turned up with some phony fifty-dollar bills on him and a forged Treasury check."

Wes nodded. It went through his mind that Mike Toth had been with the Service for ten, maybe eleven, years. Wes himself had been there for six years and, of course, didn't know half the ins and outs that Mike did. Could Mike have ties in the old country, ties to the hawkish old guard? Or could someone in his homeland be blackmailing him through some family member still over there? What of Mike's talk about Hungary someday throwing off the shackles that tied it to Mother Russia? Was it a bunch of deliberately misleading baloney?

"So is Miss Farway in Boston for long?" asked Mike.

"Don't know. I guess I forgot to ask."

"She's from where? Cape Cod?"

"Martha's Vineyard," said Wes without thinking. "Or maybe it *is* the Cape," he added offhandedly. "She didn't say."

"She came to see the chief, didn't she?"

Weston glanced up idly. "You know she did."

"Just visiting?"

"I guess so."

"She sure seemed uptight when she left his office. Was it about Brady?"

Wes shrugged. "Hey, the lady didn't use me as father confessor. Now, dammit, Toth, I have work to do."

"You *both* have work to do" came a voice at the door. It was the chief. "And if you have all those cases on your desks cleared up, I'm sure I can find you something else."

Mike grinned and rose from his seat. "That's okay, Chief, we get the hint."

When Toth was gone, the chief paused for another moment. His fingers, Weston noted, were tapping the wooden doorframe. "Did Miss Farway say anything...unusual at lunch?"

Weston steepled his fingers and met his boss's gaze. "Like what?"

Gallent stepped into the office and closed the door. "She was hinting around this morning, something about Brady's death. I couldn't get her to say exactly what was troubling her, though. I thought, because you were close to Brady, that she might have confided in you."

"Nothing. Just small talk."

"So she never mentioned Brady's death as possibly not being an accident?"

"Not being an accident?"

"You know, his accidentally interrupting a burglar. She thinks it might have been something else."

"No, not a thing."

The chief pulled the door back open. "Well, I hope she can find some peace of mind, because it's been a month and the police don't have any more to go on now than they did then."

"I know," said Wes. "It makes me sick to think about it."

Gallent shook his balding head. "We're all sick about it. Brady was a fine agent...."

Weston sat for a long time, unable to get Brady out of his head. And Daphne was in his thoughts, as well. Too much so. Of course, that was Brady's fault for talking about her incessantly. How wonderful she was, how competent, how beautiful—although Wes would have described her as cute. Bouncy and curvy. In his mind's eye he could see her short blond curls stirring in the hot Boston breeze and the blue of her eyes reflecting the sunlight. She had worn hardly any makeup and her skin had the dewy, fresh look of a pink rose petal. She wore no earrings, no necklace, no rings. A down-to-earth girl. She had an irresistible smile, a bright, friendly smile, one that told a person she was utterly sincere. Lucky Brady.

Obviously, Weston thought, she was enterprising, too, having written several cookbooks, cleverly using the lore of Martha's Vineyard as background. Naturally, Brady had pointed them out in bookstores, even talked Wes into purchasing one as a birthday present for his sister-in-law last year.

Daphne was cute, all right, twenty-six years old and full of life. But she hadn't been so outgoing and relaxed at lunch. And somehow that bothered Wes—it didn't seem fair.

He felt he almost knew her, thanks to Brady; he even knew all about her mother, Audrey, and the old, ramshackle house they lived in on the far side of Martha's Vineyard. Weston knew plenty. He knew the date Brady and Daphne had set for their autumn wedding; he knew that Daphne was planning to move into Boston with Brady and had been apartment hunting. He knew that she and Brady had been sweethearts since their early teenage years. He even knew from a night on the town with Brady that Daphne wore a C-cup bra.

As Weston sat there staring off into the middle distance, he realized that he knew far too much about Miss Daphne Farway. It made him decidedly ill at ease. Wes didn't like to know anyone that well; he was more comfortable keeping an amiable yet definite distance—especially with women. But Daphne had been Brady's girl, and it had been okay to listen to his buddy's constant bragging. Daphne Farway had been merely a name—then. But now she had come to him, bereft, alone, anxious, needing help.

Help, he thought. She had dumped a time bomb right into his lap! And there wasn't a soul he dared trust. Not even his own boss, Jerry Gallent.

He went over the plot in his mind once more. It was diabolical and foolproof. If Gorvieski were to be assassinated on U.S. soil, the deed would destroy the fragile hope of peace between the superpowers. The upcoming summit would be canceled, and there would be no hope of arms control talks for years. Back to the Cold War—or worse.

So how to stop the plan? Sure, the itinerary Gorvieski was to follow could be changed, but what was to keep the traitor among them from leaking the new itinerary to the Russian who wanted Gorvieski dead? What Weston had to do, in only three weeks, was to find the traitor.

His mind churned. Who was it? Mentally, he went over every agent in the relatively small office. Some of the secretaries had access, by necessity, to top security documents, too. But then he remembered that Gorvieski's itinerary had been typed up by Brady himself. Even Wes hadn't had a chance to review it yet. But Jerry Gallent had. And Mike Toth had worked on it. So had Walter Greenburg, an agent who had transferred in from the San Francisco office a year ago.

No one else had actually had their hands on it yet. Nor would they, until the day of Gorvieski's arrival. It was locked up tight in the top-security file, and only five men had access to it: the chief, Toth, Greenburg, Wes and Tommy Taylor, the chief's assistant.

Taylor could be ruled out, Wes knew, because he'd just returned from a six-month computer course in Washington. That left three men and three lousy weeks...

Just as Wes had predicted, Jerry Gallent summoned all the agents and several secretaries into his office sometime around three that afternoon.

Wes, knowing what was coming, cringed when Gallent spoke.

"I've called you into my office," began Gallent, "to discuss security. I would never take anything away from Brady Leighton, but as you're no doubt aware, I was visited this morning by his fiancée, and it was clear to me that Miss Farway knew a few things she shouldn't have."

Mike Toth cleared his throat.

Walt Greenburg's eyes shifted nervously around the small office.

Wes tried to look noncommittal and watched everyone's reactions. Carefully.

"Needless to say," continued Gallent, slowly and deliberately, "each one of you is aware of the stiff penalty for breaching security. This pillow talk *will*—" he looked them all in the eye separately "—stop. Is that clear?"

"Aye, aye, Chief," said Toth.

"Yes, sir," came Greenburg's thin voice.

"I never say anything to anyone," said a secretary with security credentials.

Others nodded obediently.

Wes said, "Yes, sir," perfunctorily, realizing that Daphne was in more danger than ever. Now the guilty man *knew* Brady had talked to her.

At five-thirty, Weston left the office, fired up his old Volvo and fought the heavy evening traffic on Storrow Drive, heading toward the suburb of Brookline where his brother Jim lived. The familiar route was picturesque, winding along the Charles River, past the famous open-air shell of the Boston Pops Orchestra, past MIT on the far side of the river. Summer school students were strolling along the green-shaded riverbank watching rowing shells skimming the water like narrow, many-legged water bugs.

Jim Leroux had chosen a nice neighborhood in which to raise his family. All solid brick, English ivy and trees. Nancy Leroux, Weston's sister-in-law, epitomized Boston suburban life. Shetland sweaters, flowered skirts, colorful matching pumps. Nancy, at thirty-eight, was still very youthful and attractive. She wore her shiny dark brown hair shoulder length and blunt cut; her makeup was never smudged. Wes liked her a lot. She had a keen sense of humor and not once, in her fifteen years of marriage to Weston's brother, had she tried to fix Wes up on a date.

It was seven-year-old Elizabeth who raced to Weston's car when he pulled into the shrubbery-lined driveway.

"Uncle Wes!"

He stepped out and tousled her dark hair. "Where's your dad, Elizabeth?"

"Out back. Can I have a piggyback ride?"

One ride turned into three, since five-year-old Tanya and two-year-old Jimmy had to have one each, also.

"Will you leave your uncle alone!" demanded Jim Leroux finally. "Sorry, Wes. These kids have no blasted manners whatsoever these days."

Wes popped the top on a beer can, shrugged off his jacket, loosened his tie and settled into a hammock under the sprawling branches of an old elm tree. "I like the kids. They're great. Of course, I can always turn them back over to you and Nancy—" Weston grinned devilishly "—and return to my stark bachelor abode."

"You'll get yours someday," said Jim, his standard remark.

Wes and Jim Leroux were obviously brothers. They both had the same coloring—thick sandy hair and light eyes—but whereas Jim's were grayish blue, Weston's were a clear, light green. They both had strong features, but Jim's were blunter; he had a pleasant, homely face. His younger brother's features were more clearly defined except for the bumpy nose, a legacy of a teenage fight.

Jim was thirty-nine, six years older than Wes, and beginning to show a banker's bulge around the middle. Wes often commented on it, too: "Ever try working out there, Jim?" His brother invariably laughed it off.

"So to what do we owe this visit?" asked Jim while he shook charcoal from a bag onto an outdoor grill.

"I need to ask you something."

"Phone wouldn't do?"

Weston shook his head, sipping on the beer in his reclining position. "Nope. But I'm afraid I can't say why. Not just yet, anyway."

"Okay, so ask away."

"Does the computer at your bank have access to other Boston bank computers?"

"Some." Jim turned to look at his brother questioningly.

"But not all of them?"

"Most. This *is* the 1980s."

"So say I wanted to find out what an individual's bank account looked like, could I access it through your bank's computer?"

"A balance, yes. But as far as all the monthly activity in an account..."

"That's not possible?"

"Well..." Jim hesitated, then shrugged. "There are certain access codes we can use."

"Is it illegal to use them?"

"Designated officers can do it. But actually it's considered shady banking, Wes."

"But it *can* be done, right?"

"Possibly." He paused. "What are you up to, anyway?"

"It's a special...assignment. Top secret, Jim. I can't tell you."

"But I gather you may want to ask me to get you some information. Right?"

Wes tossed his beer can toward a trash barrel. It missed. "Possibly."

"Okay, Mr. Top Secret. What if I said no? Not without a subpoena?"

"I can't get a subpoena."

Jim studied Wes for a minute, then squirted some charcoal starter onto the coals. "Are you working outside the Service, then?"

Wes nodded. "So far. But I promise you one thing—it's big. And it's important or you know I'd never ask."

"There you two are." Nancy Leroux came around to the back of the house from the garage, lugging two grocery bags. Wes took them from her. "You look good," she said, kissing his cheek, a curtain of brown hair slipping and hiding half of her face.

"Well, I don't feel so great," he replied as he stepped into the house carrying the groceries.

Nancy followed. "Problems?"

"Afraid so."

"Can we help?"

"Not really. I'm on my own."

"Oh, my." Nancy pursed her lips. "A spy out in the cold. My handsome young brother-in-law."

"I'm not out in the cold, Nancy, and I'm *not* a spy."

"Well, I tell everyone you are."

"Great."

They put the groceries away and then joined Jim and the kids outside.

"Don't forget," said Elizabeth to her uncle Wes, "my birthday is..." Elizabeth put up three fingers.

"In three days," supplied her uncle.

"You haven't asked me what I want," she pouted.

"Maybe I'll forget," teased Wes.

"Oh, no, you won't! And I want a Cabbage Patch doll, Uncle Wes."

"I wouldn't buy one of those ugly things for my worst enemy," said Wes, his green eyes alight with laughter.

"They're not ugly!" protested the seven-year-old.

Weston kept up the game over hamburgers and salad, but all the while he felt his thoughts straying to that day three weeks hence—the day that Gorvieski would step off a plane in Boston and climb into a limousine.

Jim walked him to his car after the kids had been put to bed. "Look," Jim said, "if I can help... Even the computer..."

"You don't even know what it is."

"And I doubt you'll tell me. But I've never seen you look so preoccupied."

"Shows that bad?"

"Yes." Jim leaned over and spoke through the car's window. "Are you in danger, Wes?"

"Not me, not specifically. Not yet, anyway," he said distractedly, unaware of Jim's serious expression.

He drove through the warm dark evening to his apartment in Somerville. It might not be a picturesque or classy area, but it was cheap and convenient and clean. Practical for a single man with no pretensions to impressing the ladies.

His flat was on the bottom floor of one of the large, three-story wooden buildings that covered the hills of the Boston metropolitan area. He had rented it furnished, moved in his clothes and toilet articles and there it was— home.

He'd never really had a home. Perhaps Hubert's house was the closest he'd ever had. But still, it hadn't been *his*, not quite. It had been a foster home.

Brady had been about to have a home, he thought, flicking on the kitchen light and rummaging around for something to drink. But Brady was dead and would never have a home or share a laugh with Daphne again. The waste struck him once more.

Even as he hung his suit neatly in the closet and tucked his white shirt into the laundry bag, he could see Daphne Farway in his mind's eye. He pictured her as she'd been that afternoon: worried, leaning toward him across the table, her round young chest pressing against the table, her small hands playing nervously with a napkin, her voice soft and begging him for help. No one had ever asked Wes for help before; he'd never allowed anyone close enough for that.

Wes was at the Secret Service office by seven-thirty the following morning. He used his own key to let himself in past the security system and headed straight to the desk of

Gallent's secretary. In the bottom drawer was a small black book containing certain codes that would allow him access to particular data files kept in the computers.

He memorized the access numbers and closed the drawer.

The computers were in a locked room down the hall. He knew where the key was, however, as all the agents with top-security clearance were permitted to use certain memory banks. What Weston wished to avoid was anyone discovering that he was delving into personnel records. No one must realize that he was suspicious of anything or anyone.

He was relatively inept with computers, but he was literate enough with the office system to pull up the information he needed. By seven forty-five, Wes was committing to memory pertinent data on Mike Toth, Walt Greenburg and Jerry Gallent: their home towns, colleges, military service, wives, ex-wives, children, club affiliations, political preferences, friendships.

Then, with a few spare minutes and out of sheer curiosity, he pulled up his own file. "Weston John Leroux. Born January 2, 1953, Boston, Massachusetts. High school dropout. Military service: U.S. Marine Corps. Night school: Boston College. Five foot eleven, 170 pounds, light brown hair, green eyes. Single. No children. Entered Secret Service from Boston police force on recommendation of agent Hubert Samuels."

Then came the interesting part: "meticulous, diligent, loyal. A loner. Occasionally bucked the system. Promoted to Agent Leroux 1983. Top-security clearance."

The file read on, but there wasn't much there that Wes didn't already know about himself. He admitted, however, that he was mildly surprised at the depth of the security check done on him. For instance, they had his police record from his teenage years when he'd gotten into all sorts of trouble: car theft, joyriding, underage drinking. Weston was not proud of those years. But then Hubert Samuels and his wife had taken Wes in as a foster child and things had gotten much better. He'd finished high school and joined the Marines and straightened out. As for his real family, Weston saw only his brother. Their father was dead now and their mother, long since remarried, sent Christmas cards—maybe.

Wes shut off the computer and locked the door behind him, replacing the key. He heard the main door being unlocked and then saw Gallent's secretary enter the office, a bag of doughnuts in one hand, a Styrofoam coffee cup in the other.

"Good morning," said Weston briskly.

She jumped. "My God, you scared me, Wes! What on earth are you doing in so early?"

"Just checking on some new info on that counterfeiting case up in Maine."

She raised the white bakery bag. "Doughnut?"

By TEN IN THE MORNING, Wes had mapped out a plan in his mind. There were three immediate tasks he must see to. One: he needed to get help. That would be Hubert, who was semiretired from the Service and could assist Weston. Two: Wes knew that he had to spend all his time trying to expose the traitor, and that meant somehow getting a leave of absence. And three: at all costs, he had to protect Daphne and, to be doubly cautious, her mother. They could not be left alone on that island, as the traitor had undoubtedly surmised that Daphne knew something, thanks to the chief's lecture. Wes would not risk anything—not Daphne's safety or that of her mother.

He dialed Hubert's number. "Can you spare a week, maybe three, for an old friend?" asked Wes.

"What's up, boyo?"

"I can't say over this phone. I'll call you back in an hour. All I can say is that it will be sort of a vacation. Maybe paid, maybe not. I won't know that for a while." Wes knew that since Hubert's wife had passed away three years ago, Hubert had been at a loss. A vacation away from Boston and the August heat would do him good.

"Sounds fine to me, Wes. I'll wait for your call."

Weston knocked at the chief's door.

"Come on in."

"You're not going to like this," began Weston, "but I've got to ask for a short leave..."

"A *what*!" exploded Gallent.

"Personal problems, sir." Wes felt as if he were back in the Marine Corps, standing at attention. He hated to do this to the chief, but there was no other way.

From his Somerville apartment, Wes called Hubert and explained simply that he wanted him to pack a bag and head down to Woods Hole, Massachusetts, on Cape Cod, where he would catch the ferry to Martha's Vineyard. He gave him Daphne's address on the island.

"It's bodyguard work," Weston said.

"That's fine," replied Hubert, "but I'll have to make the drive in the morning. My car's at the repair shop."

Wes thought a minute. "Okay. I'll drive down there myself tonight. As soon as you get there tomorrow, I can take off."

"Can you say where you're going?"

"I figure on covering about six thousand miles in a couple of days."

"Driving, boyo?" taunted Hubert.

"No. Thought I'd fly it. See you tomorrow. And thanks."

"No problem."

Wes threw a couple of things into a nylon zip bag, including his spare handgun. He started the hour and a half drive south from Boston, leaving the city behind quickly. The Southeast Expressway was, as always, heavy with traffic—summer vacationers were flocking to and from Cape Cod.

As he drove, Wes had lots of time to think. He wondered if he should have called Daphne first, but then he remembered that he *had* told her that he'd be in touch.

The road followed the interior, hilly countryside south of Boston for a time, then curved out toward the sandy coastal land and the Sagamore Bridge that crossed the Cape Cod Canal. Then he turned south to Woods Hole and the ferry landing. The air was cooler there than in the city, fresher, salty. He took off his jacket and tie and tossed them into the back seat. It would be pleasant, Wes thought, to be driving down to the seaboard for a vacation, maybe doing some deep-sea fishing. As it was . . .

Daphne entered his mind's eye unbidden. He could see her face clearly, could see the soft light in her blue eyes, the fresh, suntanned skin, the small, feminine hands. He could almost smell the warm, delicate scent of her blond, curly hair.

"No point putting off having kids," Brady had once said. "There's never a good time for it, anyway."

"What about Daphne?" Wes had asked out of politeness.

"Oh, she wants children, too. You know the way she's built, she could probably pop out a dozen and then try out a new recipe!" Good old Brady—happy-go-lucky, open, a bit crude.

Yes, Weston thought, Brady sure had had a bright future. It was a sin, his death. But Wes couldn't help comparing his own life to Brady's, and somehow Wes kept coming up short. Sure, he had a congenial way with people, but that was all on the surface: Weston had made the decision long ago not to marry or have children. He quite frankly did not wish to repeat the same unattractive process his parents had initiated. Why let himself in for trouble? On the other hand, he thought with a twinge of self-pity, who would shed a tear if he, Wes, were killed? No one like Daphne.

Weston could see the hilly coastline and the outskirts of Woods Hole beyond that. Just forty-five minutes across the water lay the island of Martha's Vineyard, Daphne's home. A strange curiosity gripped him to see the Farways' old house, which Brady had so often spoken about. And, yes, he admitted, he wouldn't mind seeing Daphne again, to reassure her, naturally, to let her know he was on the job. He owed that much, at least, to Brady.

Above, in the late afternoon sky, sea gulls swooped and screeched. On the water, fishing boats bobbed gently like corks, their masts swinging lazily across the heat-hazed summer sky. It was serene and lovely, and Wes found it hard to imagine anything touching this idyllic setting, hard to believe that in this world someone could kill and plot assassinations and sell out his country and threaten world peace. He felt a sudden impatience to be with Daphne, to protect her from the ugliness, to make things right for her. His foot pressed a little harder on the gas pedal.

CHAPTER THREE

THE VIEW FROM THE WINDOW of Daphne's workroom usually went unnoticed, but today it drew her and disturbed her concentration. She paused over her writing and, resting her chin on her hand, stared out across the sand dune toward the lazy summer ocean.

Should she tell more about Bartholomew Gosnold and his daughter, Martha, after whom the island was named? Would it interest or bore her readers, specifically women who were looking for an easy, different, inexpensive recipe? She decided not to. The fact that the island, in 1602 as now, was covered with wild grapevines and that Bartholomew loved his daughter, Martha—that would suffice for this book.

The Farway house stood on high ground on the windward side of the island of Martha's Vineyard, looking straight south over the Atlantic Ocean. Below the big, rambling Victorian, a sand dune dropped away to the beach. A long dirt road wound out to the highway, South Road, that led either west to the Gay Head cliffs or east to the towns of Edgartown, Oak Bluffs and Vineyard Haven. Daphne's mother had attempted to grow grass in the sandy soil for years, but had finally given up; the big weathered house with its white trim and gables, gingerbread porches and turrets now stood in lonely glory amid scrub oak, sea grass and a tangle of bayberry, sumac, beach plums and the inevitable wild grapevines.

Daphne chewed on her pen—she always wrote with a thirty-nine-cent ball-point—and stared out the window like a recalcitrant schoolgirl. The day had the contours of summer: white sea gulls soaring, young brown gulls darting on the beach, sparkling water washing the ancient round pebbles, wild roses, pines on the hills. A soft sea breeze fanned in through the open window. There was a confusion of sky and sea over the ocean and a line of clouds that looked like islands floating on the water. The whispering quiet was suddenly punctuated by the raucous call of a gull that died as quickly as it had come.

Brady had loved this spot so. His family, city folk, had lived in Edgartown in a lovely old colonial house, but he'd adored Daphne's "up island" home. They'd planned to live in Boston but were going to spend every spare weekend on the island. He'd often spoken of building a second home on the Vineyard, although the huge Victorian monstrosity that Daphne's widowed mother refused to give up had more than enough room for all of them—and children, too.

Darn it! Her eyes filled with tears. She hated to be out of control, especially in public. Her mother kept telling her it was all right but still she detested other people seeing her suffering. The pain was unavoidable but it should have been a private thing.

But she'd get over it. She knew she would. It was just this awful interval of emptiness, of no direction.

A three-masted sailboat, a big one, scudded across the smooth water gracefully, heeled over, its canvas bellying out in the breeze. Daphne's gaze followed it until it rounded the western tip of the island at Gay Head and was lost to sight.

She sighed. Work was wonderful therapy when you lost someone, but today... today she would love to be on that boat going somewhere, flying across the water to an exciting, fascinating destination. Pipe dreams.

Her thoughts were brought up short. How could she be thinking about sailing off into the sunset? It had only been yesterday that she'd dumped her whole story into Weston Leroux's lap and he'd told her to be careful.

And here she was, alone, miles from anyone except a few hikers and old man Tilton in the next house a mile down the beach. Martha's Vineyard was only twenty miles long and ten miles wide, but there were very deserted spots on it nevertheless—like the Farway house. Somehow though, Weston's words, which had seemed so menacing in Boston, had lost their intensity here. She couldn't imagine anyone creeping up to this big old house.

And Wes had said he'd be in touch. She wondered what he was doing about the plot Brady had unearthed. Something, she was sure. Telling him had been so simple, really, that she should have done it before. But Brady's partner had been the last thing on her mind. As a matter of fact, she'd forgotten his surname until yesterday. Weston Leroux. She wondered if she would have had the same reaction to Wes if she hadn't heard his whole background, interspersed with Brady's jokes and comments and mock-Freudian interpretations. She closed her eyes and saw Wes as he'd sat across the table from her. Pleasant, intelligent, easy to talk to. That was what one saw on the surface. Was there more underneath? Of course. She'd seen a real concern, and, naturally, he'd cared about Brady. But then everybody had loved Brady.

She knew Wes must feel some sort of residual bitterness or confusion or insecurity from his rough childhood. He certainly seemed to have adjusted well, though.

And he had no right to be so darn attractive. There was something about his looks that appealed to her. An interesting face. Imperfect but with beautiful, strong lines and an odd mixture of smoothness and vulnerability.

The front door slammed. "Yoo hoo, I'm home!" came her mother's voice. "Daphne-e-e!"

No use working at all. Maybe she could get back to it later. Daphne shuffled her papers together, carefully put the plastic cap on her pen, and went down to see her mother.

Audrey Farway was putting her tennis racket away in the hall closet, and her trim rear end, covered by ruffled tennis panties, stuck up into the air. She straightened up and said, "Oh, *there* you are. Working?"

"Trying to. How was the game?"

"Great! I played with Simon Thompson and we beat the pants off Edie and Tom. Six zip, six zip."

Audrey was fifty-five, although she would have had to be put on the rack to admit it. She had the same curly blond hair as her daughter and the same big blue eyes. She was petite, perfectly turned out at all times and quite content with her tennis and her friends and her firm social position on the island. She knew everyone, and if she met someone new, Audrey had his genealogy, grade average in school and bank balance within ten minutes. Her acid tongue, however, sometimes got her in trouble and scared men away in droves.

Daphne acknowledged her mother's fearlessness and toughness and laughed at her social pretensions.

"Do you want lunch?" asked Daphne.

"No. I ate at the club. Naturally, Tom bought," Audrey added, smirking.

The phone in the living room rang. Daphne went to answer it, a bit apprehensively. The telephone hadn't exactly been the bearer of good tidings lately. If it were another condolence call, she'd scream. She gritted her teeth and lifted the receiver. "Hello?"

"May I speak to Daphne Farway, please." A man's voice, vaguely familiar.

"That's me. Who is this?"

"Wes Leroux."

"Oh, hello." Her heart gave a little jump; was he going to tell her to be careful again?

"You're going to think I'm a jerk, but I'm stuck here in Woods Hole."

Surprise snatched at her. "What on earth are you doing there?"

"I told you I'd be in touch."

"I thought you meant a phone call or something."

His voice sounded a bit impatient. "Daphne, I didn't like leaving you alone last night, but I had some checking to do. I certainly wasn't going to let it go any longer."

Renewed apprehension ran through her, silent and sharp as electricity. She wished he hadn't reminded her. "You mean you're coming to *guard* us?"

"Right now I'm not going anywhere," he said wryly. "I got this far and found I needed reservations weeks ago to get my car on the blasted ferry."

Daphne started to laugh. He sounded so aggravated, so off-islandish, so put out. "Of course. You should have asked me."

"Don't rub it in. I thought I'd better get some directions from you for a taxi. You do have cabs on that island of yours?"

"Oh, yes, we have them. But I'll pick you up."

"I wasn't hinting around."

"I'm sure you weren't," Daphne replied, chuckling, "but I'm still going to pick you up."

"It's really not necessary."

"Of course it is. I'll be there. Just name the time and place."

"I'll give in gracefully. It's the two-thirty ferry from Woods Hole."

"Is there anything... I mean, are you here because something's happening?" Daphne asked tentatively.

"No, nothing to worry about. I'll tell you everything as soon as I see you."

"Okay. Bye." She hung up thoughtfully. It seemed as if he'd cut her off, as if he hadn't wanted her to say anything more. Was he afraid her phone was bugged or something? She picked up the receiver again and listened. It sounded normal, just a dial tone. How did a bugged phone sound, anyway?

What did Wes Leroux want? Had he found out something important already? Or were she and Audrey really in danger, as he'd intimated? She paced the living room floor, hugging herself. Should she tell Audrey about Wes, about the possible danger? No, not until there was something definite. Not that her mother would be the least bit alarmed. Somehow Audrey took these things awfully lightly.

She pulled up to the pier at Vineyard Haven just as the big white ferry was disgorging its hundreds of passengers. The town was nestled on a hill, and the dock area, near the old whaling harbor, was crowded with restaurants and bicycle rental shops. Cars were inching their way off the ferry and another long line was parked, waiting their turn to board.

It was high season on the Vineyard. The tour buses stood ready in lines to receive the afternoon's curious for the island tours, the bicycle shops readied their wares for the hundreds who would choose to cycle leisurely along the many miles of bike trails, and the Colonial restaurants girded their loins for the onslaught of dinner guests. The tourists exclaimed over the quaint shops and exquisite old early American houses, fanned out to choke the narrow old streets lined with huge, spreading trees. Daphne had seen it all so many times that she didn't even notice. She stood on tiptoe to gain some height and searched the crowd for Weston.

She located him finally, near the gangplank, an incongruous figure among the perspiring, camera-laden tourists. Erect and relaxed in slacks and a madras plaid sport coat, he seemed a little ominous and official looking, and very alone; his expression was serious amid the gaiety of the vacationers. He might as well have worn his Secret Service badge, she thought fleetingly, even while her heartbeat quickened in spite of herself. She'd almost forgotten those long-lashed bedroom eyes of his.

She caught herself. What a time to be noticing something like that! She began threading her way through the crowd toward him. He saw her right away and raised a hand.

"You made it," she said, breaking into a welcoming smile.

He grinned back. "Barely." The smile changed his whole aspect. Daphne felt herself wanting him to smile like that often.

"This is quite a place," he said, looking around.

"You should see the whole island. Edgartown is the oldest. And Oak Bluffs is funky Victorian. Then there's a farmhouse in Chilmark that was built in sixteen something."

"Do you give guided tours?" he asked, smiling.

"Sure—" she shrugged "—we all learn it in school."

"I'm afraid," he began, "I'm not going to have time to see all those things."

"Oh." She felt a small spurt of fear again as she led him over to where her sky-blue Volkswagen convertible was illegally parked in the shade beneath a graceful old maple tree. He threw his bag into the back seat.

"There's something going on," she hazarded.

"Not really. There's a lot to discuss, though." He wasn't looking at her.

Daphne got in the driver's side and started her car. She had to wait for a crowd of tourists to cross the street before she could pull out. She bit her lip in anxiety.

"Don't worry. I've got it all under control. I called a friend of mine. He'll be here tomorrow."

"But aren't you . . . ?"

"I'm going to be away for a few days," he said quietly. "Say, I hope this isn't putting you out. I suppose I could have made hotel reservations, but I'd feel better about your safety if I stayed at your place. That is, if you have room . . ."

"*Room?* Heaven help us, do you know how many *rooms* there are in the old place? Twenty, at last count."

He whistled. "I didn't realize."

She drove past the bank and hardware store, both disguised as weathered fishermen's cottages. "Didn't Brady tell you? I'll bet he did. I know how he talked."

"Maybe I should have listened better," Wes replied carefully. "How far is your house, by the way?"

"About eleven miles. Up island, we call it. Through West Tisbury, then we can take either South Road, which is closer to the shore, or Middle Road, which goes through the farm country around Chilmark."

He was looking out the window, watching with mild interest the unique, enchanting countryside of the Vineyard. Daphne always felt a spurt of pride when showing off her island. People expected a flat, sandy landscape, but the island evoked surprise with its rolling farmland, huge trees, wilderness seascapes, tiny Colonial villages and unusual blend of scents and sounds and sights.

"This doesn't look much like an island," said Wes as Daphne steered around an oak-shaded curve, past a stone wall.

"Those stones," she indicated, nodding, "came off an English ship in the late 1600s. They were used as ballast for the crossing to America."

"Amazing."

"Yes, it is. There's a lot about the island that's romantic."

"Romantic?"

"You know—the whalers and Indians and the early colonists."

"Oh." He gave her a sidelong glance.

"Anyway," said Daphne, "this is the protected side. Where I live looks more like an island. Romantic—" she smiled "—but different." Then she cast him a quick look. "Tell me about this friend of yours who's coming."

"His name is Hubert Samuels. A real old friend. In fact, I used to live with him. He's more or less retired from the Service but absolutely trustworthy. Brady knew him."

"A bodyguard," Daphne said to herself.

"A *safeguard*," Wes stated evenly, and continued, "Look, I'm really sorry to arrive on your doorstep like this, but Hubert couldn't get here until tomorrow and I hated to leave you alone until then, like I said."

"*You* shouldn't apologize. I asked for it. I'll bet this is a real pain in the neck for you."

"It transcends pain," he joked.

"So do you know who it is?" she ventured.

"No," he said, a shadow crossing his face. "But I've got it narrowed down to three men. The only ones with the security to get their hands on the itinerary. Now I have to do a little digging . . .''

"But you said you were going to be out of town." Deftly, she avoided a family on bicycles. The road passed beneath a huge old maple tree; dappled sunlight dashed across their faces.

"I am. I'm going to get my information firsthand."

"Where? Who?"

"Curious, aren't you?"

"You're darn right."

"Okay, I'm going to St. George, Utah, first."

"Where?"

"A small town in southern Utah, not that far from Las Vegas. Jerry Gallent's hometown."

She gave him a quick sidelong glance. "You think it's him?"

"He's one suspect. Another is a fellow from San Francisco, Walt Greenburg. So I'll go there, too. The third is a hometown boy from Boston, Mike Toth."

"What do you expect to find out?"

"You never know." Wes shrugged. "Habits, personalities, friends, hobbies. Somewhere there's a clue. And I'll find it. The trouble is, there's so little time. Investigations like these can take months, even years."

"And we've got three weeks."

"We?" He looked at her, surprised.

"Sure. I started this, didn't I?"

"Brady started it," he reminded her grimly.

"Well," she said with false cheer, *"we're* just going to have to finish it for him."

Daphne felt a lightening of the spirit for the first time in weeks. She was *doing* something. It was scary and dangerous and exciting. And it would be Brady Leighton's legacy to his country. It was as if Brady had sent her this stranger, who really didn't seem to be a stranger, to finish the job for him.

She took her eyes from the road for a second. Wes was staring out across the Chilmark hills. His profile was perfect—except for that bumpy nose. His collar was open, his tie loosened, his neck was strong and sinewy. His thick sandy hair blew around in the moist wind. Suddenly, Daphne wanted to feel the texture of his skin, to touch the bump on his nose, to breathe in his scent. She felt suddenly weak and giddy, tingly and ashamed of herself.

Dragging her eyes back to the road, Daphne drove along silently for a time. As if aware of her discomfort, Wes kept his head turned away, too, watching the island slide by.

"Our own bodyguard!" chortled Audrey upon being introduced to Weston.

"Very nice to meet you, Mrs. Farway," said Wes.

"Call me Audrey—everyone does. Even Daphne. I can't bear Mommy. It's just not me."

Daphne was aware of Weston's eyes flickering to hers. She smiled to herself. Everyone reacted that way to her mother.

"Audrey," said Daphne firmly, "he's staying here tonight. Then he's sent for a friend of his to stay here because he's leaving on a trip—an investigation."

"Who's your friend?" Audrey turned to Wes, all the while testing the strings on her new graphite tennis racket.

"His name is Hubert Samuels. An old friend . . ."

"How *old* is he?" asked Audrey.

Wes looked bewildered. "About sixty-one or two."

"Aha, someone of an interesting age," Audrey said shamelessly.

"Let Wes catch his breath," admonished Daphne, "for goodness' sake."

"Do I get to tail someone?" pressed Audrey.

Wes laughed. "Hey, you never know."

"Good. About time something more exciting than John Belushi's funeral happened on this island." She turned to Daphne. "Put him into Felicity's room. You'll have to excuse me, Wes. I've got a hot singles match against the club pro. See you." And she was gone.

"Now, look, I don't want to put anyone out of her room," Wes offered.

"Oh, Felicity's not around anymore," explained Daphne, grinning.

"I see." He didn't see at all. That was obvious.

"Felicity is a ghost. The room is thought to be haunted."

"Oh."

"It's a long story. If Felicity bothers you, you can have another room..." She was daring him.

"Oh, no, I think Felicity and I will get along just fine."

Daphne was proofreading a chapter on the back porch an hour later when Weston found her.

"Busy?" he asked.

"Not very," she said idly, putting her papers down. She'd changed into shorts and a pale blue low-necked T-shirt, and her feet were bare. She was sitting on a cushioned bamboo chair with her legs drawn up under her, Indian-fashion.

Wes had discarded his jacket and tie and wore only a short-sleeved white shirt. His arms were muscular and beautifully formed, and she couldn't take her eyes off him.

He sat down across from her. "Can we talk?"

She snapped her eyes up to his face. "Sure," she said confidently.

"I'll be leaving tomorrow, as soon as Hubert comes. I assume he can stay here."

"Of course."

"He'll know what to do. Will your mother listen to him?"

Daphne grimaced. "I don't know."

"Do your best. Keep things locked. Your car, for instance. No standing against lighted windows at night."

"You mean . . ."

"These are just standard precautions, Daphne. Routine."

She nodded, her eyes wide.

"I'm going to look into our three men's backgrounds. I'm hoping to find a motive." He paused. "I'm a bit worried about the traitor getting on to me, but I don't have time for anything elaborate. I'll take my chances. If anyone calls here asking about me, you know nothing, right?"

"Wrong."

He looked at her quizzically. A gull called harshly down the beach, and a breeze ruffled Daphne's papers.

"I won't be here, Wes. I'm going with you," she blurted in a rush.

His green eyes fixed her with displeasure. "Don't be ridiculous."

"You just said it yourself. If the guilty man finds out that you've been asking questions, he'll know you're on to him."

He was silent, studying her. "I said I'd have to take my chances. I've got cover stories."

"But anyone could describe you, and if it gets back to our man he'd identify you instantly. Don't you see? Then your whole investigation's blown."

He leaned back and crossed his legs, resting his ankle on the other knee. "What can *you* do to remedy that?"

"Ask the questions for you. Nobody in your office is likely to recognize me. I'll use a different name. You just tell me what to ask."

"I won't allow it," he said mildly, positively.

"You know it's the only way," insisted Daphne, rising. She padded silently across the porch, then stopped at the door. "I've got to start dinner now. Want to help?"

He looked at her, bemused and a little angry. "I wouldn't be much help, I'm afraid."

"You can cut up onions or something. I'm still not through convincing you I have to go along, am I?"

"No, you're not. This is a job for a professional, Daphne. It's no joke."

She stiffened then, as if an electric current had run through her. She narrowed her eyes and stared at him. It was very quiet on the porch except for the swish of the waves and the breeze rustling the sea oats. "A joke?" she finally said. "I'm the last person in the world who would consider this a joke. Brady got killed because of this."

Her words hung in the silence.

"I'm sorry," he finally replied. He rose and approached her; up close she knew he could see the blotches of red on her cheeks and the angry tears in her eyes. "That was cruel. Daphne, I'm trying to protect you. That's what Brady would have wanted. I can't let you go traipsing around the country asking dangerous questions."

"He told me," she whispered fiercely. "He trusted me. Why can't you?"

He frowned. "You're twisting things around. Look, this is dangerous."

"More dangerous for you than me."

"Maybe. I don't know. You'd be safer here with Hubert."

"I would not and you know it."

He turned away, as if to avoid the truth he saw standing clearly in front of him.

"Don't patronize me. I'm a big girl. I can help. You *need* me. Admit it, Wes." Her voice was uncharacteristically hard.

"Let me think about it," he said then, very carefully.

"Come on, cut up some onions for me," she replied, as if it were all settled.

The kitchen was big and homey. It had been redone twenty years before, Daphne told Wes. "The house was built in 1848, the period of the big whaling fortunes. My dad inherited it, but he wasn't really from an old family here. It's Audrey who's the true native."

"It must be quite a job to keep the place up," Wes said, looking at the water stains on the ceiling.

"Oh, that," said Daphne, following his gaze. "That was from the hurricane of '38. The big one. Audrey left it there as a memento."

"I see. And I suppose you recall the big blow?"

"In 1938? Oh…!" She looked down, blushing. "You're kidding."

"What're you making?" he asked.

"Something from my first book. Fish chowder. It's easy. Here, cut this up." She handed him an onion and a knife and pointed to a cutting board.

Audrey arrived at six-thirty, just in time to exchange tennis shorts for a skirt. They ate, very casually, at the old maple table in the kitchen. But Daphne's fish chowder was delectable: cream and onions and potatoes and carrots and flaky white haddock. She'd also reproduced, almost exactly, the Union Oyster House's famed corn bread.

Audrey was in top form, delivering anecdotes and gossip and her opinions with equal fervor. She turned to her daughter over the blueberry cobbler. "You did tell him about Thomas and Experience and company?"

"Well, I'm not sure he's into that sort of thing, Audrey."

"Of course he is. Everybody is. It's his heritage, too." She pounced on Wes. "My family is directly descended from Thomas Mayhew, the island's first settler...1642."

"Most commendable," said Wes, "but who's this Experience fellow?"

"One of Thomas's descendants. Great name, isn't it? I was going to name my son Experience, but I never had one."

"Never had one what, Audrey—an experience?" teased Daphne.

"And what would you have called him for short?" asked Wes. "Ex?"

Audrey shot them both a hard glance. "He would have been called Philip after his father, of course." She shook her head, as if in disgust at youngsters' shenanigans. "Now look here, young man, I want to know about this Samuel Hubert. After all, he's going to be staying in my house. Is he to be trusted? I mean, he won't steal the silver, will he?"

"Hubert, Mrs. Farway, Hubert Samuels."

"That's what I said."

It was obvious Weston was having trouble keeping a straight face. "Your honor and the honor of your gracious home are safe with Hubert, I promise you."

"I guess I'll have to take your word for it." Audrey subsided ungraciously. "How long will he be here?"

"I don't know. However long it takes me to find the right man."

"No more than three weeks," put in Daphne.

"Three weeks!" exclaimed her mother. "Is he going to be in your way, Daphne? After all, *I'm* gone most of the time at the club, but you have to work."

"He won't—" began Weston.

Daphne calmly interrupted. "I won't be here, Audrey. I'm going with Wes, to help him." She felt his eyes swivel and fasten on her.

"You are? Well, I'm thrilled to find out. Nobody tells me anything." Audrey peered from one to the other. "So I'm to be here with good old Sam, am I? Things get more and more interesting."

"*Hubert*, Mrs. Farway."

"Right."

But Daphne was holding Weston's gaze, questioning him silently. He needed her and she needed desperately to do something, to prove to herself and the world that Brady's death was not futile.

He returned her scrutiny, his straight brows drawn together, his finely sculpted lips forming a thin line. There was doubt in his look and discomfort and a large measure of anxiety. She wondered if she'd have to fight him for the right to go along; it would be unpleasant, but she'd do it if she had to.

"Well?" she asked softly.

His face relaxed into a faint, almost sardonic, smile of capitulation. "All right, you win," he said. "We travel light, understand?"

"Perfectly," Daphne breathed.

"What's this, some kind of secret code or something?" asked Audrey querulously.

"No," said Daphne, "it's a beginning."

Daphne decided to finish proofreading her chapter that night, because she was leaving the next day and it had to be completed. She did it in bed, propped up by two pillows, with her clock radio on. An old dog-eared dictionary made an indentation on her blue flowered quilt. She was trying very hard to concentrate, but several things distracted her.

First, there was this sudden trip she was going on with Weston. He'd phoned the airlines and reserved a ticket for her, giving a credit card number to the ticket agent.

"I'll pay you back," Daphne had said as soon as he'd hung up.

"No need. That was my company card. By the time the vouchers are reviewed by accounting, either we'll have succeeded or there'll be such a flap they won't notice," he said dryly.

What would it be like to travel with Wes? It made her a little nervous. Would he be irritable if she took too long dressing in the morning? Did he need a cup of coffee before he was human? Did he eat a big hearty breakfast or did he turn green at the sight of food in the morning? There were so many things she didn't know about this Weston Leroux, despite Brady's talking about him. Maybe the opportunity would present itself to ask him. A compelling curiosity seized Daphne. What went on under his smooth, easygoing surface? Were there cracks in his polish? Brady had said there were.

Wes was an enigma, really. She thought he liked her but he presented such a mellow facade that it was impossible to know what he truly felt. She wanted to pin him down and ask him.

She read another sentence: "The aroma of bread baking is irresistable." Oh, boy, she'd almost missed it. She corrected the word neatly to "irresistible."

Then there was the worry over her own danger and possibly Audrey's. She'd made sure the doors were locked and pulled her curtains tightly. She felt hairs prickle on the back of her neck as she thought about a man waiting out there behind a sand dune. A man with a gun in his hand, the same gun that had shot Brady. She shivered.

She tried to finish the page before her, but her mind refused to stay tied down to the words. Leaning back against the pillows, she closed her eyes. Tiredness washed over her, but it was mixed with anticipation that sent spasmodic thrills of adrenaline bursting through her body.

She stiffened suddenly. A thump had come from downstairs, a muffled, small sound, like someone bumping into furniture. Audrey? No, Audrey would turn all the lights on. Besides, her mother had been asleep for an hour.

She heard it again and fearful images flew into her head like a flock of bats, fluttering and squeaking and rustling. The man with the gun, the faceless murderer, Brady's killer, the traitor. He'd found her and somehow gotten into the house.

Weston! She could slip down the hall and ask him to look. That was his job, wasn't it? But the thought of knocking on his door at night... And it was probably nothing. A mouse...

She found herself rising, almost as if she had no will of her own. She threw a light bathrobe over her shoulders, crept to her door and listened. From downstairs, she heard the distant creak of an old floorboard. She opened her door silently and slipped down the hall on bare feet. Her heartbeat thumped crazily in her ears; fear tightened in her chest.

The bottom of the stairs. Hugging the wall, she slid along it and peered into the living room. There was a small tick, as if someone were brushing against knickknacks. Her heart flew into her throat. The big house was bathed in shadows. She remembered only too well the endless games of hide-and-seek she'd played in it as a child, and the gut-wrenching horror of waiting in a hidden place to be found....

A shadow detached itself from a blot of darkness. Silently it crossed the room to a window. Daphne drew her breath in sharply and tried to shrink back around the corner. But the figure must have heard her, for it stopped dead in the act of pulling aside a drape and turned toward her. A spear of moonlight touched the face of the figure, freezing it in ghostly silver.

Daphne gasped. It was Wes.

She reached out and flipped on the nearest light switch. Her limbs trembled in reaction and a cold sweat had broken out on her forehead. "Wes! You nearly scared me to death!" she breathed.

He stood there, frozen in the sudden light. "Sorry. I was just checking doors and windows."

Daphne tottered to a chair and collapsed limply into it. She stared up at him, feeling drained. "Why didn't you turn on a light?"

"I was afraid I'd wake you up."

He stood there, a touch uncertain for the first time. He had no shirt on, and his lean torso gleamed in the single light. There was hardly any hair on his chest, Daphne noticed. She closed her eyes to blot out the picture, but it was there, on the inside of her eyelids, just the same. She wondered briefly, recklessly, how it would feel to be held against that smooth, muscular body.

Her eyes flew open and he stood above her, his gaze shadowed, a glint of light on the beautiful curve of his jawline. "Are you okay?" he asked.

She tried to laugh. "Sure, now I am."

He moved self-consciously and his gray shadow on the wall behind him moved, also. "I thought you were asleep."

She shook her head. "I . . . I think I'll go back to bed now." She rose and found that she was face-to-face with him, much too close, and that her legs were still liquid-weak. She took a step back and came up against the chair.

Wes reached out a hand to steady her. "You're not going to faint on me, are you?"

"No," she whispered, feeling his hand on her arm as if it were a brand burning her skin. They stood like that for a moment, linked by his touch, alone in the silent shadows of the room. Daphne's breath came quickly and her pulse hammered in her ears.

Wes broke the spell, dropping his arm. "I'll take you upstairs," he said softly.

Later, in bed, Daphne went over the episode in her mind. Over and over it. She saw his expression but could not decipher it; she saw his green eyes flicker over her and then retreat into coolness. She saw his shoulders, curved with lean muscles, his strong forearms, his flat stomach.

Over and over, into the long, dark night.

CHAPTER FOUR

"I'LL PICK SAM HUBERT UP," said Audrey flatly.

"You mean Hubert, and I think maybe..." began Wes.

"I wouldn't bother arguing." Daphne looked at Wes over the rim of her coffee mug. "My mother always gets her way."

"How exceedingly true," agreed Audrey, smiling smugly. "The eight o'clock ferry?" she asked.

Wes nodded.

"And what does this Sa...Hubert look like? I mean, I can't just go picking up *anybody*."

"He's around sixty, like I said, thin gray hair, a kind of Vandyke beard, about five-eight."

"Umm..." Audrey cleared the kitchen table, carefully stacking the morning dishes and finally disappearing upstairs to change out of her robe.

Weston turned his gaze onto Daphne. "Your mother is relatively amazing."

"I realize that's a backhanded compliment," replied Daphne . "It takes some time to get used to her. She's really a softy at heart, but she can be quite pushy."

"So I gather."

Daphne rose from the table and poured them each another cup of coffee. She felt Weston's eyes following her, weighing, judging, wondering if he'd made an error allowing her to go along on his trip.

He was very transparent at the moment, she decided, wearing his emotions unguarded on his face. He was stirring his coffee absently, his sandy brows drawn together, his eyes thoughtful, his mouth forming a thin line as a muscle jumped on one side of his jaw.

He'd already said she could accompany him. It was a good plan and he knew it. She'd be advised to keep quiet on the subject.

Audrey reappeared downstairs in her most revealing tennis dress and lacy panties; her makeup was flawless, a little too picture perfect for tennis. Daphne shook her head ruefully.

"I'm off to the ferry—" Audrey smiled, putting on her large, rose-tinted sunglasses "—to pick up *mon* bodyguard."

When she was driving down the sandy road, her small sassy red Saab kicking up dust, Weston turned to Daphne. "I think your mother ought to take this more seriously."

All Daphne could say was "So do I."

They walked back into the cool interior of the house. Daphne excused herself to finish tidying up in the kitchen, and Wes said he'd take a shower.

The old place creaked and rattled whenever people moved around in it, climbed the stairs or strode along the upstairs hallways. She could hear Weston above, on the second floor; she could follow his progress along the hall and into his room. Then the pipes gurgled and burped throughout the century-old Victorian, and she knew he was in the shower. It was distracting.

After she dried her hands, Daphne also climbed the steps and went into her workroom. She realized she had to pack, but nevertheless she couldn't ignore the latest draft of her book. A new publisher had shown interest—and offered more money. On the other hand, she was finding it difficult to get through even a single sentence. It was disconcerting and she knew exactly why: the water had stopped running and she was envisioning Weston down the long, dim hall, in the guest room, drying himself with the blue towel, pulling on his khaki trousers. Daphne told herself that it was natural to be conscious of a houseguest, that it was normal to be aware of his whereabouts. Yet she couldn't recall ever before picturing a guest with rivulets of water streaming down his naked back.

She was sitting, trying hard to think of a word, tapping her pen on her teeth when a creak in the floorboards behind her made her jump.

"Sorry," said Wes, "I didn't mean to scare you."

"Oh, I...I didn't hear you come in." She turned all the way around in her chair to see him. He was standing in the doorway, one shoulder leaning casually on the frame. His hair was damp, combed flat to his head. His face and the skin of his forearms looked a little pink from the recent shower.

"I've got something for you," he said.

She looked at the hand that was hanging at his side.

"It's not much of a weapon, Daphne, just a small .22 handgun."

"A . . . gun?" The hair bristled at the back of her neck.

"Just in case."

"But I'm going to be with you," Daphne protested. "Why would I need the gun?"

He smiled suddenly, his green eyes going all soft and warm, the long lashes falling over his eyes like miniature fans. "You won't be taking it on the flight," he said. "Airport security."

"Oh, of course."

"It's to keep here, for when you get back. I won't be around all the time."

"But Hubert . . ."

"Hubert can't be every place at once, Daphne. The gun is extra security. Put it in a safe place and don't worry about it."

Daphne placed the gun in the bottom drawer of her nightstand beneath the dried up bottles of nail polish, Kleenex and all those magazines she was going to read someday. Then she packed an overnight bag and changed into a white summer dress and white sandals. Daphne almost never wore jewelry, but today she put on colorful round earrings and makeup and was just finishing using a curling iron on her bangs when she heard Audrey's car race up to the circle in front of the house.

Wes met Hubert and Audrey at the door and Daphne came down the stairs just in time to catch the end of Hubert Samuels's complaint.

"If you don't mind," he was saying to Audrey, "I'll take a cab next time. If there *is* a next time, that is."

"Old men," ground out Audrey in disgust as she swished past them, her tidy bottom beneath the tennis dress swaying with just the right amount of disdain.

Daphne put her hand to her forehead.

"She drives like a goldarn maniac!" said Hubert loudly to Audrey's retreating form. "I darn well better be paid for this," he finished hotly.

After Daphne had met Hubert properly, the three of them sat on the porch on the bamboo furniture that had seen better days. Audrey, the perfect hostess, served them coffee, as if nothing unsettling at all had passed between herself and Hubert.

Wes quickly explained to Hubert the story of Gorvieski's visit and Brady's discovery of a plot.

"Great Scott, me boyo," Hubert gasped, "you said bodyguard work! This is amazing!"

It was some time before Hubert stopped asking questions and the reality of Weston's story sank in.

"I'm certain it's one of three people," Wes went on. "It's either Greenburg, Mike Toth or the chief."

"The chief?" Hubert toyed with his handsomely cropped beard.

Wes confirmed his conclusion. "Other than myself, they're the only ones in the office with access to the itinerary. Tommy Taylor's been away for six months."

"I see. And me, of course, but seeing how I haven't been on active duty since April..."

"Exactly." Weston then told Hubert about Daphne's suggestion that she go along to help ferret out information on the three subjects.

Hubert shook his head, obviously as against the idea as Wes had been.

"You understand," Daphne was quick to interject, "that if the traitor finds out Wes was asking questions, he'll know we're on to him. Why push his hand?"

"But it could be dangerous," said Hubert, looking grimly at Weston.

Daphne gritted her teeth. "I'm in danger here, too. Maybe more so than I would be moving around. And besides, Wes will be right with me."

"I don't know..."

"And also," she said, "no one knows what I look like, so if the guilty man gets word that someone was asking questions about him, he'll never be able to put one and one together. I'll use a phony name, of course."

"My daughter's pretty shrewd, Sam," piped up Audrey from the doorway, "like her mother."

Hubert shot Audrey a hard look. "So why am I here to guard Daphne if she's going with Wes?"

"Because," said Audrey pertly, "even if I didn't know anything, our man has got to assume that I do. Anyone close to Daphne is in danger. That includes you two gentlemen, as well, doesn't it?"

Weston's face hardened, Daphne's eyes grew round as saucers, and Hubert pulled on his beard. Audrey shrugged, saying simply, "I *do* read and watch TV, you see. I know what goes on in the real world."

"The real world," muttered Hubert, looking down the sandy beach. "Martha's Vineyard."

Audrey rolled her eyes and daintily sipped her coffee. "Oh, Sam," she said sweetly, "you wouldn't happen to play tennis, would you?"

Daphne and Wes drove the VW to the ferry landing at Vineyard Haven. From the other side, they would use his car. While they waited for the tourists to disembark, they looked out over the water. Wes explained something that Hubert had told him earlier.

"Last night Hubert got a call from Jerry Gallent," he said. "The chief wanted him to come back to active duty until the Gorvieski visit is over. I guess Hubert had to tell him that he was sick or something. It was pretty lame, anyway, but Hubert didn't have time to make up a better excuse."

"I don't see . . ."

"It's like this. I suddenly ask for a leave of absence and then Hubert gets called in to replace me and he says he's sick. Everyone in that office knows that Hubert has never in his life taken a sick day and they also know how close Hubert and I are."

Daphne turned from the rail and leaned her back against the rough wood of the pier. "So you're thinking that the suspect might put it together. First I show up and open my big mouth and then you take a leave and then Hubert . . ."

"Maybe. In any case, I'm a little concerned."

"If only I hadn't . . ." began Daphne.

"Hey, it's not your fault." He moved in front of her and put his hands in his pockets as if he didn't know what to do with them. "If I'd have contacted you after the funeral, done something . . ."

"Well, it's certainly not *your* fault." She tried to smile brightly, but her attempt failed as she saw a shadow of doubt pass over Weston's face.

"There's something that's been eating at me," he began, and Daphne felt the uncertainty within him. Usually he seemed uncomplicated, easygoing and mellow. But just then she sensed a vulnerability, a part of himself he kept hidden most of the time. "It's about Brady," he was saying, and Daphne felt him putting a barrier up between them. Abruptly the pleasant companionship was gone. Uncomfortable, she played with her purse strap.

He glanced at her as if for approval, for permission to go on. She wanted suddenly to suggest that they not talk about Brady, but she said nothing. Why, when she was with Wes and he spoke of Brady, did she feel these twinges of guilt?

"Daphne, I really copped out royally the day of Brady's funeral," confessed Wes. "I *was* going to go to it. But then something happened inside me and I couldn't face seeing him. I couldn't stand to watch him being lowered into the . . . I'm sorry. That's morbid. But I just wanted to apologize for not being there."

"It's okay. I know. I couldn't stand it, either."

"But you went."

"I didn't have a choice, Wes."

"Yeah, well, maybe if I hadn't been such a coward, you would have thought to talk to me before going in to see the chief . . ."

Daphne shifted her weight uneasily, wanting to drop the subject of Brady. "You want to cry over spilled milk?" she asked.

"That's not my style."

"So let's forget it. For now I'm Agent Farway and we're both going to do our best. For Brady's sake. Okay?"

He didn't speak for a long time. Finally he said, "Okay. Sorry I got so personal there. I should have remembered what Brady used to tell me about you."

"And what was that?"

"You're smart and down-to-earth and do a good job taking care of yourself."

"Oh? And tell me what else he used to say."

Abruptly a taunting smile appeared on Weston's face, softening it, making him seem very charming and very boyish. "There're some things not fit to be repeated in mixed company."

THE FLIGHT LEFT Boston's Logan Airport at noon. Las Vegas, Daphne thought, the airport closest to Jerry Gallent's hometown in southern Utah. Who would have guessed her very first trip to the city of lights and glitter would be on a mission involving espionage and assassination? And yet to have been left behind on the Vineyard, wondering, worrying. That would have been hell.

Weston, who was seated next to the window, tapped her on the shoulder, pointing. "Ever seen the Grand Canyon?"

Daphne stretched over, being careful not to press too closely against him. "It's magnificent," she breathed. Below were the jagged, shadowed gorges of the canyon, their striated walls massive and ancient, like giant open wounds on the earth's crust.

"It's quite a sight, isn't it?" remarked Wes, his warm breath touching her cheeks.

Daphne leaned back into her own seat. "It's so... big. I never imagined."

"Brady told me once that he was going to take you out West. Roam the deserts and do some white-water rafting."

"Oh, we talked some about a trip," she said, trying to sound offhand. But there was that blasted pang again, deep in her heart. The plans, the trips, the dreams...

"I don't know why I do that," Wes said quietly. "I keep bringing him up. God knows I don't mean to."

"It's because he's our link, Wes. It's as if we've known each other for a long time but Brady forgot to actually introduce us."

"Maybe."

The plane touched down in Las Vegas in midafternoon, three hours earlier than it was in Boston. It was hot—the dry desert kind of hot: the temperature could reach 115 degrees but amazingly feel more like eighty-five back East.

"It's the lack of humidity," Wes said in response to Daphne's exclamations about the heat. He turned on the air conditioning in the rented Mustang.

"Still," said Daphne, fanning her face with the rental car agreement, "I feel as if I can't breathe."

The desert and Las Vegas were a revelation to Daphne. Glitz on a flat brown desert under a merciless, baking sun. Wes drove her down the famed Strip. Even during the day when one needed sunglasses just to look out the car window, the trillions of neon lights lining the Strip were turned on.

Daphne was enthralled by the sights. Casino after casino. Circus Circus, The Desert Inn, Stardust, The MGM, Caesar's Palace. On and on.

She asked the usual question: "Do people actually *live* here? I mean, do kids go to school?"

Wes laughed, his head tilted back. "Sure do. There are some who have never even been inside a casino."

"No."

"Yes. Honest. There are actually people who like the desert climate and the easy access to the West Coast and all."

"You've been here before, then," remarked Daphne.

"Oh, once or twice."

She wondered: with whom?

The streets were jammed with cars and taxis and tourists on foot. Women, strolling from casino to casino, were dressed to the nines, their diamonds competing with the strong hot sun for brilliance. It could have been day or night for all they cared.

Daphne was actually itching to stop and see the inside of a casino, but it was a hundred-mile drive across the desert and up into the hills to St. George, Utah. Before she could blink, the lines of casinos suddenly ended and they were on a dual highway, surrounded by cactus-spangled desert.

The cool breeze from the air conditioner caressed her face. It was hard to believe, as she looked out over the desolate expanse, that it was so terribly hot outside. There were mountains, she saw, off in the distance, massive, gray rock formations devoid of vegetation, unreal looking in the heat haze, like shimmering, rough-edged pyramids from another world.

Daphne exclaimed over the scenery, refusing to act the part of the sophisticated traveler. "Oh, look at that giant cactus. Just like in the movies." She was aware of Weston's amused glances at her. "Don't laugh at me," she said pertly. "I'm enjoying this. And, yes, I've been a few places. New York, Florida. And, oh, yes, Philadelphia. And I went to school in Boston. I'm not so provincial.''

"I'm not laughing," he replied. "I'm enjoying your enthusiasm. Women try to act so blasé usually.''

"Is that why you haven't found one you like yet?" asked Daphne unabashedly.

He thought for a minute. "Maybe it is. I hate anything artificial. I can't stand women—or men—who posture. That's why I liked Brady.''

A sudden silence fell between them.

"Sorry, there I go again," Wes said.

"It's okay," said Daphne quietly. "You don't have to apologize every time his name comes up. After all, he's the reason we're here and we can't very well ignore that, can we?" She was looking straight ahead through the windshield as she spoke but she was aware of Weston's gaze on her. She didn't turn to meet it.

How did Wes view her? Did he think her disloyal to Brady because she was not weeping and wailing and trailing black veils around? His expression gave nothing away. It was always smooth and polite and pleasant.

"What did Brady tell you about me?" she asked boldly. "I mean, besides the things you can't mention?''

He shrugged. "Oh, you know how Brady talked." He took his eyes from the road and glanced at her. "He thought you were pretty special, you know." Then he frowned. "He really didn't say anything that private. I hope you weren't offended by that.''

"Oh, no. I have nothing to hide," she said airily. "Did you feel sort of like you knew me when we met?''

He was silent for a time, and then he turned to her. "Funny you should say that . . .''

"Embarrassing, isn't it?" Daphne remarked. "And all Brady's fault. He had a big mouth, Brady did.''

Wes said nothing. Had she unsettled him? Well, she'd tried to, hadn't she? Honestly, sometimes she was just as bad as Audrey! Putting Wes on the spot like that. She looked at him again. He was concentrating on the road, a slight frown lining his forehead.

The highway began to rise up from the parched desert floor. Brush and myriad cacti were more prominent now as they twisted up into the hills and entered Utah.

"St. George is close," said Wes after a stretch of silence.

Daphne wished she were more comfortable in his company. Her eyes strayed often to him. Too often. He'd taken off his suit jacket and rolled up his sleeves. The sun coming in from the west gilded his forearms, lighting the long tapered muscles and competent hands as he drove. He wore sunglasses, and she couldn't see his eyes or tell if he were aware of her watching him from time to time.

When the silence became uncomfortable, she asked him exactly what he hoped to accomplish in St. George.

He told her. According to computer records, the chief had been born and raised on a ranch near St. George and had attended school there. They would check out his distant past, the things little known about a man once he reached adult level, the off-the-record information that could possibly provide a clue as to what made him tick.

"I don't see what a few old high school teachers can tell us," Daphne said.

"Maybe nothing. Then again, there're still records, and you'd be amazed what can turn up—the patterns begun in a person's teenage years. Gallent was home just last year for a class reunion. His thirty-fifth, I think. They'll remember him, all right—small-town boy made good."

"Still," Daphne began, "this could all be a very expensive wild-goose chase."

"It's standard procedure—don't worry. Anyone in intelligence, military or civilian, would follow the same routine. Go as far back as you can if you're checking someone out." He looked over at Daphne. "And as far as the expense, that's standard, also."

"Amazing," she said, "the way our tax dollars are spent." And he laughed good-naturedly, looking young and carefree and awfully attractive.

"I understand why we're going to St. George to look into Gallent's background. Why not look into Greenburg's childhood, then?" she finally asked. "Or Toth's?"

"Toth's childhood was in Hungary. And as for Walt, well, his father was an engineer and they moved a dozen times. I don't have time to chase around to every place he's lived. The longest he stayed anywhere was in San Francisco, so it's our best bet."

"Oh," said Daphne. She guessed Wes really had done his homework.

"St. George," he finally announced and she turned to look out the window.

It wasn't much. Motels lined the highway, which rose steadily on into the Utah mountains. The pair turned off and headed into the small town. It was an inviting little place, Daphne decided, with tree-lined streets and even a tidy, if miniature, downtown mall. Weston finally pulled up in front of Jerry Gallent's high school and stepped out, stretching his lean frame. Daphne did the same and was instantly struck by the difference in air temperature between Las Vegas and St. George. It was far cooler here, refreshingly so, with pure, mountainlike air that she breathed in deeply.

"Listen," Wes said, "I can do this if you want."

"No. What if, for some reason, whoever I speak to gets suspicious and calls your chief? At least Jerry Gallent would be unlikely to know it was me. Now you, on the other hand..."

"All right. Still—" Wes leaned toward her a little "—I don't like it. It's not your thing, Daphne. You're no actress."

"I was Dorothy once in *The Wizard of Oz*. Seventh grade." She was ready to set out when his hand caught hers.

"Daphne," he said, "make it convincing. And please...be careful." His long-lashed green eyes held her motionless for a moment. Then his hand released hers and he cupped her chin gently. "Okay?"

"I will, Wes, really." She moved away and stepped out of the car, but she could feel him watching her, could sense his concern even as she pushed through the doors and walked into Jerry Gallent's past.

It was Mrs. Dunn who would remember Jerry Gallent best, Daphne was told, but she was at home, of course. Obligingly, the secretary phoned Mrs. Dunn with Daphne's cover story, gave explicit directions and soon Daphne stood at the door of Mrs. Dunn's neat brick house and practiced smiling as she knocked. A thin, gray-haired lady answered, her face as severe as her navy blue dress.

"Excuse me," began Daphne, "but the secretary at the high school just called..."

Mrs. Dunn removed her glasses and looked at Daphne, from the curling blond hair, down her face, along her white dress, right to her open-toed sandals. "Yes?" she said coolly, and Daphne felt as if she were about to hand in an overdue history paper, overdue and worth maybe a D.

"I'm Darlene Fulton," said Daphne in a shaking voice, "from the *Boston Globe*, in Boston," she added helplessly.

The glass of wine Wes bought Daphne an hour later did little to calm her. "I swear," Daphne said in the hushed bar and lounge, "I thought I was about to flunk. What an old tyrant."

"I'm sorry she gave you such a hard time." Weston leaned back against the cool red vinyl of the booth.

"She did. But actually I got a lot out of her," Daphne replied proudly. "She was very exact, choosing her words carefully, as if I were asking her about the president or something."

"So what're the high points?"

"The chief's considered to be very honest. He was class president twice—Mrs. Dunn looked it up in the yearbooks for me—and he was most likely to succeed and co-captain of the football team in his senior year. She said he was very well liked by both teachers and students. I think she really liked him because he was what she called a 'once-in-a-lifetime student of history.'"

"That's it?" remarked Wes, and Daphne felt a little as if she had failed.

She looked up at Weston; his face was inscrutable, but that muscle was ticking away in his jaw. "Mrs. Dunn also said that the chief did love his poker games with the boys. She even told me that during their reunion last year the boys—and I quote—'played a few hands.'"

"Interesting."

"Maybe he's a compulsive gambler," suggested Daphne.

"Could be."

"And he needs lots of money."

"Greed can be a motive."

"It certainly can," finished Daphne with conviction.

From the motel lobby she phoned some of the names Mrs. Dunn had given her—old school chums of Jerry

Gallent who still lived in St. George. The first was out of town but the next, an insurance man, spoke to her at length.

"I heard Jerry played poker with his commanding officer in Korea," said the man, in response to Daphne's question. "He was over there awhile, you know. Got out early on a medical discharge. Hernia, I think. Say, you don't have to write *that* down, do you?"

The next name on the list was a man who obviously disliked Gallent. They'd been co-captains of the high school football team. He reiterated the town's opinion of Jerry with grudging respect. Nothing there.

By the third phone conversation, Daphne felt as if she were listening to a tape recorder.

After making the phone calls, they grabbed a bite at the "best" restaurant in St. George.

"What an odd place to find ourselves," commented Daphne.

"You mean St. George, Utah?"

"Yes. I mean, here we are traveling together, eating together and we hardly know each other and . . ." She'd said the wrong thing. Weston's face turned blank, carefully blank. Had she embarrassed him?

He was silent too long.

"Did I say something wrong?" she finally asked, pushing away her half-eaten plate of food. She didn't quite know how to act with Wes. She had to pussyfoot around, to be careful. She was so used to Brady. She used to be able to say anything to him. They'd had wonderful fights, too. Yelling, angry, loud arguments that always ended in laughter and kisses. Somehow she couldn't imagine Wes yelling. There was so much bottled up inside him that one yell would destroy his cool facade and all sorts of emotions would come spewing out—like Pandora's box.

She suddenly felt she had to do something to make amends. "Hey, I'm sorry," she forced herself to say lightly. "It's only my big mouth. I take after my mother sometimes."

"Daphne..." he began.

She paused questioningly.

Wes shook his head, as if angry with himself. "Nothing. Are you done?"

"Yes," she answered, puzzled.

It was sunset by the time they got on the road again to drive out of the red Utah hills down to the baking desert floor.

"Do you think I found out anything useful?" Daphne finally asked, feeling the need for approval.

"Hard to say," said Weston, staring straight ahead at the road.

"Well, what *did* you expect to find out?"

He turned for a minute to look at her, then returned his eyes to the road. "I'm not sure. I won't know until I...we've...investigated the other two."

Daphne felt the urge to snap at him. What had he expected to find out in that remote little town in Utah, anyway? That Jerry Gallent was a member of the Communist party?

Was Weston pleased with her or not? He hadn't said a word about whether she'd done well. He hadn't said anything like thanks or job well done.

"I did my best," she said in a subdued voice, disheartened.

He didn't answer. She admitted to herself that she was a bit miffed. Was Wes disappointed with her, sorry he'd brought her along?

There was an odd tension in the car, something new between them. Was it due to the long day or the urgency of their task? Daphne wanted desperately to recapture the previous easiness of their relationship but it seemed to have been left behind somewhere in St. George, Utah.

She crossed her arms stiffly below her heavy breasts and sat silently looking out the window at the red glow beneath the horizon, where the setting sun glared like a plane that had crashed and burned.

Las Vegas could finally be seen in the distance, its bright lights forming a glowing dome of orange above the desert. By the time they were driving down the Strip, it was ten o'clock. Their flight to San Francisco was at midnight. It struck Daphne then that she was tired, that she wished it were Brady driving the car, sitting beside her, that they could check into a hotel and sleep—really sleep, for neither Brady nor Daphne had felt the necessity of making love every minute. Those days had passed just after college.

Oh, Brady, she thought, *I miss you.* And then tears of loneliness and frustration burned hotly behind her eyelids. *Damn,* she breathed silently, it wasn't fair. She was nearly three thousand miles from home, in a fast-lane town, tired as she could be, stuck with a stranger. And one who wasn't being particularly companionable at the present.

She was wallowing in self-pity when Wes pulled off the glittering Strip into a parking lot. She shook herself awake and looked up: Circus Circus read the garish neon sign above them.

"How about an hour for some sights?" said Wes.

Daphne cleared her throat. "You mean go into a casino?"

"Sure." He smiled warmly then and her belly tingled with sudden pleasure.

"I'd love to."

Suddenly her fatigue was gone. The loneliness, however, was lurking there still, deep in a corner, hidden but ready to pounce again. And then Wes took her elbow very gently as they walked through the immense parking lot, and the fear and loneliness crouched yet a little lower.

Circus Circus lived up to its name. Above the hundreds upon hundreds of slot machines and green felt gambling tables, above the dim lights and ever present dull roar in the immense amphitheater, there was a circus act being performed. High wire, no less. Dazzling girls in scanty, shining costumes swung on perches or walked tightropes or did somersaults above a webbed net. It was enthralling to Daphne. In her ears bells and sirens rang—jackpots on slot machines. Coins clanked heavily into trays, and people shouldered past them, bleary-eyed, carrying drinks in plastic glasses. About half of the throng milled around; the other half was gambling.

"Ever tried a slot machine?" asked Weston.

Daphne turned to look up into his face. He was smiling at her. "No," she said, "never have. Gambling is illegal in Massachusetts."

He dug into his trouser pocket and produced three quarters. "It's on me. Pick your poison."

"My..."

"Machine. They're the worst odds you can get but it's fun, anyway."

"My Lord, what if I get hooked?"

"Aren't too many machines on Martha's Vineyard, are there?"

She found a vacant one-armed bandit and inserted one of his quarters in the slot. She looked at Weston devilishly and pulled the large handle. Bright cherries and lemons and oranges spun in a circle. Then with a thump, thump,

thump they stopped. Two quarters clanged into the tray and Daphne let out a small screech. "I won!"

"The big one." Wes shook his head humorously.

She shot him a so-what look and put another quarter into the greedy machine. Nothing. She tried again. Three lemons. The machine spit out dozens of coins—five dollars worth, anyway—and Daphne laughed in delight. The old woman at the machine next to her glanced over in disgust and resumed methodically pulling the handles on the three machines that she guarded with her life.

"This is great! It's *easy*!" said Daphne as she scooped the coins into a paper cup provided by the generous management. "Don't you want to try, Wes?"

"No, thanks." He crooked a brow, the smile still on his mouth. "I've lost enough in these things."

Daphne shrugged. "Well, we've got a few minutes and I'm having fun. Mind if I go on?"

"Have at it."

"Remember," she said as she pulled the handle once more, "I'm from a fog-bound little island."

"I'll try to remember," he said dryly.

She pulled and pulled the handle. Sometimes a few coins would clang into the tray, usually not. Finally she was down to her last quarter. She pulled the handle. Nothing.

"Too bad," said Wes, grinning from ear to ear.

"Blast it. That was fun, though." Then she cast him an imploring look. "I'm out of quarters. Totally. Do you think I could borrow one more? I have a hunch. Then I'll owe you a dollar even."

He searched his pockets again. One last quarter lay lurking with his keys. "Here." He handed it to her. "But don't go crying your eyes out if you lose again."

"I won't." She put it in the slot and pulled. The cherries whirled, and the bright oranges and lemons. Around and around. In the far reaches of the casino sirens sounded, and bells were ringing; overhead the glittering girls swung and applause filled the heavy, smoke-filled air. Cherries and oranges and lemons. Thump. One orange. Thump. Two oranges. *Thump*.

The bell rang before Daphne realized she'd won. A twenty-five dollar jackpot!

Wes was grinning at her. She let out a little squeak of astonishment. The constant drone of noise in the dimly lit, smoky casino enfolded her, the spotlights danced before her eyes and then she was in Weston's arms, exulting in her good fortunes, thrilled and laughing.

She clung to him for a moment and she could feel his hands on her back, pulling her closer. For a split second they were pressed together as if by the very clamor and hot, heavy air that surrounded them. His thighs burned against hers while his hands lingered, clasping her.

Then suddenly they were apart. She realized it was Wes who had put her at arm's length, who had all but torn her hands away. Shame, deep and degrading, consumed her instantly and she couldn't look at him. She couldn't even move, so oppressive was the weight of the guilt. Finally she forced herself to turn and collect her winnings—a profit that seemed tarnished and ugly to her now. And then they were walking out of the casino. Apart. Neither looked at the other.

Daphne's mind reeled; he was thinking that she was cold and callous, that she had already forgotten Brady, that beneath her proper exterior lay just another lonely woman lonely and too willing.

They got into the rented car in icy silence. As he was pulling away from the parking lot and out onto the Strip Daphne turned her head and looked at his stern profile. Suddenly she wanted to scream at him, to tell him that

Brady was dead and buried and she was alive! And somewhere deep inside her a dislike was growing; she wanted to believe it was for Wes but she knew that it was more for herself.

How could she have truly loved Brady and yet, a month after his death, be throwing herself at a man?

And not just any man. Oh, no, Daphne had to reach for the forbidden fruit—Brady's partner.

CHAPTER FIVE

THE PLANE WAS FULL of San Franciscans, returning home after a blitz of the fleshpots and money pots of Las Vegas. Everyone was slightly bleary-eyed. A few hard-core partiers ordered drinks from the flight attendants and continued the game to its bitter end.

Daphne glanced out the plane's window. They were circling now, on approach to San Francisco International. Their route took them out over the dark silent Pacific coastline, but she could see the lights to the north, the lights of San Francisco. A cool, elegant, handsome port, a city of romance and fog and steep hills.

Daphne glanced at Weston. He was immersed in an airline magazine, in a quiet place of his own. She would have loved to share those minutes with someone special—with Brady, naturally, but then that was impossible.

Wes was an experienced traveler. He whisked them out of the airport and into a limousine that deposited them at a modest hotel on Columbus Avenue near Washington Square. Daphne almost froze to death. Her white summer dress proved totally inadequate to deal with the moist chill of a San Francisco night.

It was nearly two in the morning when Daphne stumbled into the hotel lobby. Her eyes felt scratchy, her dress was wrinkled and her head ached with weariness.

"Two adjoining rooms," she heard Weston telling the night clerk. She was surprised he hadn't requested different floors.

"Leave the connecting door unlocked," Wes said, as he opened her door and flicked on the lights.

"Sure." Daphne yawned uncontrollably, trying to cover her mouth with a hand.

"You'll be okay?" he asked, standing in the dim hallway, watching her through tired eyes.

"Sure," she repeated dully.

He closed the door on her, and soon she could hear faint sounds in the room next door. She pulled off her sandals, unzipped her dress and stepped out of it. It was five in the morning, Boston time. Ugh. She unlocked the connecting door as he'd told her.

Why? In case he had to save her from Brady's murderer? She almost laughed, but she was too exhausted.

After pulling on her favorite long pink T-shirt that said Martha's Vineyard across the front, she brushed her teeth and collapsed onto the bed.

Oblivion eluded her. She was overtired, too exhausted to sleep. Her mind flipped and flopped, recreated conversations, rehearsed scenes for the next day, chided itself, scolded and made excuses.

It did everything but sleep. She'd lain awake far too often this past month, since Brady's death. It was a horrible feeling. Her mind would spin, fastening on disconnected images and snatches of conversations; her heart would begin to pound.

She saw Brady in her mind's eye, but there was a new emotion associated with him now. Not love or sadness or loss. No, instead she felt herself shrinking with guilt. Daphne had always been unable to lie to herself and she couldn't now. She would always love Brady, but she'd never felt for him the undeniable desire she'd felt for Weston in the casino.

Was she being disloyal to Brady's memory? Or was she merely being human? She'd never forget Brady, but he was gone. And Daphne was still alive. Alone, scared and confused.

She tried turning the television on softly. She dozed off, then jerked awake and the mental acrobatics began anew. Outside her window she could hear the night noises of the small, elegant city on the bay: a siren in the distance, a car horn, the squeal of tires.

Eventually she sat up, flicked on the light and dialed for room service. "A glass of brandy, please. Room 501. Thank you." That would put her to sleep, surely.

Time passed, oddly disjointed. Minutes seemed like hours, yet the quarter of an hour it took room service to arrive seemed to flash by.

There was a knock on the door, terribly loud to Daphne's sensitive ears. Even expecting it, she felt her heart jump at the sound. Going to open the door, she felt foolish. Ordering brandy in the wee hours of the morning. What would the waiter think?

"Room 501. One brandy," said the waiter. Why did he speak so loudly?

"Let me pay for it now," whispered Daphne, suddenly realizing it would go on the bill and Wes would see it. She rummaged in her big straw purse.

"First visit to San Francisco?" asked the young waiter, trying to earn a generous tip.

Daphne wanted to shush him. She smiled nervously and nodded, pulling out some bills.

"I hope you have a nice time." His cheerful voice seemed to fill her room, reverberating against the walls.

She was handing some crumpled bills to him when a noise caught her attention. Her head swiveled toward it; the waiter's did, too. And then, shockingly, the connecting door swung inward and Wes stood there in a half crouch, his shirt unbuttoned, his feet bare, his hair tousled.

There was a gun in his hand.

The waiter gasped something unintelligible. Daphne was paralyzed, unable to make her brain function. "What?" she managed finally.

"Hey, lady, no tip's worth *this*," the waiter was muttering as he backed toward the door. "I seen jealous guys before, but this..."

Weston's gun sagged, its barrel pointing to the floor. His tense crouch transformed into an ordinary stance. He scrubbed a hand across his face. "Sorry," he rasped.

Hurriedly, Daphne shoved the bills at the waiter and, muttering apologies the whole time, closed the door behind him.

Then she turned to face Wes. "What's going on?" she demanded.

He shook his head wearily. "Nothing. I'm sorry, I was asleep and I heard voices from your room."

"But what...why?"

He leaned a shoulder against the doorframe. "I'm supposed to protect you, remember?"

"Against a waiter?"

"I didn't know it was a waiter, Daphne. I was asleep." Then he looked at her more closely. "What are you doing up—" he glanced at his watch "—at four in the morning? And why the waiter?"

She looked at the floor. "I couldn't sleep. I figured a drink would help. I'm really sorry. I never thought it would wake you up."

"I've learned to sleep pretty lightly," he said dryly.

She was suddenly aware of the two of them facing each other in the dim hush of the night—alone in a strange city. She wore only the long pink T-shirt and he wore his slacks, unbelted. His shirt hung open, revealing his smooth, muscular chest. Turning away, she felt herself blushing. How awkward.

"Daphne." His voice was soft and infinitely patient. "Come on in my room and tell me what's the matter."

"I'll keep you up. I couldn't."

"I'm already up. Bring along your brandy."

It didn't take much urging. Her loneliness pushed her into his room as if it were a hand at her back.

"You're sure you don't mind?" she tried once before giving up. Maybe he didn't think as badly of her as she'd thought.

He did something with the gun—the safety, she guessed—laid it on the dresser and sank down into the one comfortable chair in the room. Daphne sat gingerly on the unslept-in side of the king-size bed. Automatically, she hunched her shoulders, an old habit she'd developed to try to disguise her big bosom.

"Now, why can't you sleep?" Wes asked finally.

Daphne looked down and wiggled her bare toes. "I've been having trouble sleeping since Brady died."

"Drink your brandy," he said gently. He sounded as tired as she felt.

She sipped it. It burned all the way down, making her elbows and knees feel disjointed. Holding the glass cradled between her two hands, she stared into the amber fluid and then found the courage to look straight at Wes. "I wanted to apologize for the way I acted tonight. In Circus Circus, I mean. I know you didn't like it. I'm sorry—it won't happen again."

"You were excited," he replied.

"Are you making excuses for me?"

"No, no. Look, it's been a long day for both of us..."

"I really did love Brady, you know."

Wes nodded, his face shadowed. Daphne took another swallow of her drink. "I've been so alone without him, so adrift, like a boat without a rudder. It's scary."

"I'm sure it is."

"And I embarrassed you tonight."

"No, not at all." He made vague gestures with his hand, as if warding off the thought.

"You think I'm disloyal." She shrugged. "It's true, in a way. Maybe because my father died when I was so young. Audrey... well, Audrey's great but not a fountain gushing security. I guess Brady was sort of a father to me."

"You don't have to tell me this," said Wes uncomfortably.

She hung her head and wiggled her toes again. "I don't want you to think I'm some sort of... floozie."

Wes turned his head away. "I don't," he said carefully.

Daphne glanced up at him. "I'm trying to explain about myself. I'm not doing very well, am I?" She tilted her head back recklessly and swallowed the rest of the brandy.

Wes leaned forward, his elbows on his knees. "Look, Daphne, you don't owe any explanations to me. You hardly know me."

Wrong, she thought. *I know you. Brady told me all about you.*

But he was continuing. "I'm a loner, Daphne. Nobody's very close to me. Brady a little. And Hubert maybe. Even my brother doesn't really know me. I'm not sure you want me to hear your confessions."

"I'm sorry. I've put you on the spot."

"Yeah, sure, a little. You're a bit disconcerting, you know?"

She leaned back against the headboard, feeling her eyelids grow heavy. Even if he didn't want to hear, it did her good to tell him. Her feet were stretched out in front of her, so far away. She wiggled her toes again, just to see if they were really attached.

"Want another drink?" he asked.

"Sure. I really have to get some sleep."

Wes called. They waited while the time ticked away. Daphne felt as if she should be tense, alone with a stranger—an attractive man, whose diffidence drew her like a magnet.

A knock on the door. Weston got up and opened it. She heard the waiter saying, "This is really Joe's station but he wouldn't deliver here 'cause some nut with a gun threatened him."

It was kind of funny, but she was too relaxed to laugh.

"Daphne." His voice woke her from an instant's doze. "Your drink."

"Oh. Thanks." She smiled up at him somewhat blearily.

He drank his neat, with a practiced flip of the wrist. Then he set the empty glass down.

"I'm keeping you up," she said.

He shrugged.

"Talk to me. Tell me something interesting about yourself."

"Not much to tell."

"Sure there is. Hubert, for instance."

Wes looked up as if searching for words in the air. "Hubert and his wife, Janice, were my fifth set of foster parents."

"You were a bad boy."

He gave a short harsh laugh. "I was impossible. I hated everybody and wanted to hurt the world. But I learned."

"What did you learn?"

"I learned that if I behaved decently I would be treated the same way. Hubert taught me that. He's a good man. Of course, he'd raised his own family, too. Janice was a saint. She died three years ago." He paused. "You know, I cried when Hubert told me about her. I hadn't cried in years."

"Go on."

"I was in the Marines after Hubert. The usual tour of duty. Funny. I didn't feel bitter like most of the others in Vietnam did. But then I was an MP—that's military police—and I didn't see much front-line action. After that, I joined the police force in Boston as a regular street cop. Then Hubert put it in my head to apply to the Secret Service."

"And here we are."

He stood restlessly, went to the window and pulled the heavy green drapes apart. She studied his back, the shirt falling loosely from his shoulders, and his narrow hips. There was a tension to him, like electricity.

"Wes."

He turned slowly.

"I just want things straight between us. And it's hard because Brady, well, he made us know each other before we'd ever met."

"It's kind of a crazy situation," Wes said, smiling a lopsided smile.

She grinned at him in return. They were friends again. She felt ever so relieved. "You know, Wes, you're really a nice guy. You're easy to like. It's just that I can't figure out how much I'd like you if I really got to know you. Maybe I'd find out I didn't like you as much or, then again, maybe I'd like you a *lot* more.'' She waved a hand airily. ''It doesn't matter. I'm just talking too much.'' Her eyes felt so heavy. She looked at the second brandy glass; it was empty. No wonder. ''What a mouth I've got,'' she murmured, half to herself.

''It's a lovely mouth,'' Wes said softly in reply.

She murmured something, and then tried to form her words carefully. ''I think I'm a little loaded. So you can say no, if you want to...''

''No?''

''To coming over here and just holding me. Do you mind?''

''Daphne,'' he began, ''I...'' But he did come over and sat on the edge of the huge bed. She reached over and put her warm hand in his and squeezed it gently.

''Thanks,'' she said, knowing she slurred the word but not caring. Amazing how bold alcohol could make a person. She edged toward him and even though she felt his reluctance, he put an arm around her shoulder.

She felt dizzy, as if Weston's presence were merely a dream. She lifted her face to his, her lips parting expectantly. ''Would you kiss me?'' she whispered. His head bent and she could feel his mouth on hers, feather light, hesitant. His arm tightened around her shoulders a little and when his lips began moving against hers, her thoughts began to spin along with the room. Then she felt his hand moving over her breast, lightly cupping its heaviness.

She moaned, meeting his long-lashed gaze, and for a heartbeat of time she wondered if the naked desire she saw in his eyes was only wishful thinking. But the sensations were so wonderful, so full of utter pleasure, that she closed her eyes and let herself float on a cloud of indulgence. His lips, the male smell of his skin, the feel of his hand on her breast. A lovely ache curled in her belly. Her breath came shorter, in little gasps, and she could taste the brandy on his breath.

She wanted to let herself go; her body craved a man's closeness and her heart needed succor. She had been so lonely, so lost this past month. A human being, a man, a *nice* man like Wes . . .

"DAPHNE." A hand on her arm was shaking her gently. "Daphne."

She opened her eyes. It was light in the room, and Wes was leaning over the bed. She sat up quickly. "Is it late? I'm sorry. I must have overslept."

"Yes, it's late. But we both needed the sleep." He was smiling faintly.

She remembered, vaguely, as if it were a dream, talking last night—this morning, actually. And the waiter and the gun . . .

"Oh, my Lord," she gasped, "I'm in your bed!" Hot embarrassment flared in her. She hopped out of the bed as if it were made of burning coals. "I'm sorry. Oh, how awful of me." It all rushed into her head then: his hand in hers, his mouth, the room spinning, then the darkness and the wild dreams.

"You fell asleep and I hated to wake you up to make you move," Wes said.

"But then where . . . where did *you* sleep?"

"I slept, don't worry," he replied, and paused. "Nothing happened, Daphne."

She could barely meet his eye; instead she retreated swiftly to her own room. "I'll be ready in twenty minutes," she said shakily over her shoulder.

"Okay, don't worry. And there's coffee on its way up. I noticed you had a cup yesterday morning, so I ordered us some."

"Oh, that'll be great. Thanks."

In the shower she had time to recall everything. She squeezed her eyes shut in a grimace and whispered, "Oh, no, oh, dammit!" to herself a few times as the water pounded, painfully hot, onto her head.

Where *had* he slept? In *her* bed? Of course the bed-clothes were all mussed there, anyway. Or next to her? That bed had been tangled as well but of course he'd already been asleep in it before she had usurped it. He'd said nothing had happened.

But what had she said to him last night? Something awful about maybe she'd like him better if she got to know him? Had she really said that and then kissed him? *Oh, my Lord...* she thought.

She shampooed her hair briskly and then stood, letting the foam and water wash over her. Oh, boy, she'd done it. And what had *he* said? She couldn't recall his words but she'd gotten the impression that he was alone, that he allowed no one near him.

Was Wes remembering what he'd told her? Was he embarrassed or cursing her for being a prying female?

Or did he need someone to confide in? Had he wanted to kiss her like that?

She dried her curly hair, letting it fluff up however it wanted. She put on makeup—eye shadow and a little mascara for her pale lashes—a wrinkled denim skirt from her bag and a bright cornflower blue camp shirt. Then her sandals. She even pulled a cardigan out of her bag, recalling the previous cool evening. She'd always thought of California as hot but not San Francisco, she guessed. Live and learn.

Wes was waiting for her with a cup of coffee. "Sugar?" he asked politely, as if last night had never happened. Obviously he was better at concealing his feelings than she was. Or maybe he simply had no particular feelings about their early morning fiasco.

"Yes, lots." She smiled. Then, sipping her coffee, she asked, "Have I held you up terribly?"

"No, I slept in, too. No problem. We can always take another day if we have to."

She couldn't keep her eyes from straying pointedly to his bed. He'd pulled the spread up as if to negate its existence.

"I'd like to call Hubert. It's late morning there now. Suppose they'll be home?" he asked.

"Well, Audrey usually plays tennis in the morning and stays at the club for lunch. Try paging them at the club. I know the number."

He dialed and then had to wait for a few minutes. "Hubert? How's it going?" He paused and listened for a time.

"I can imagine," he said wryly. "No, nothing here. Yes, a bit. Oh, she's fine. Tell Audrey to take it easy on you old guys. Yes, tonight, if we make it back in time."

"Everything's fine," he said to Daphne after hanging up. "Audrey's giving Hubert a rough time."

"Oh, dear."

"He loves it. It's the most female attention he's had in three years."

Daphne rolled her eyes. "Audrey's attention can be lethal."

Wes laughed. "Hubert's tough."

"He'll have to be."

At the front desk Wes asked directions and was told that the address he wanted was within walking distance.

"Let's walk," he suggested. "It'll get the cobwebs out of my head."

"I've never been in San Francisco," Daphne confessed.

"Well, then, we'll walk and I'll show you all the points of interest."

"You've been here before?"

"Several times. With the Marines and once on a Secret Service job." He paused briefly. "The first time I hitchhiked here. I was seventeen. It wasn't a real pleasant visit that time."

"What happened?"

"I hung around awhile, got good and hungry and called my brother. He sent me a bus ticket. It was a real hungry ride back to Boston, too."

"Why did you come out here in the first place?"

"Trying to get away from things. Myself mostly."

They emerged from the hotel into a cool, moist morning. Daphne shivered and pulled on her sweater.

"This is the other California," said Wes. "Chilly and foggy. Not exactly a surfing climate. And if you put your toe in the water here, even in the summer, it'd probably freeze off."

They walked over the steep hills of the city and along the trolley tracks. Wes pointed out Telegraph Hill and Nob Hill, even the quaint cable car barn.

It was a beautiful and wonderful place. Once he stopped her and pointed between some buildings to the bay, sparkling with a cold, cobalt brilliance. She could just make out the island of Alcatraz—"The Rock"—and the graceful Golden Gate Bridge that was wreathed eerily in fog.

But the view didn't affect her as much as it could have. She was much too aware of Weston's hand on her arm to appreciate the charm of the scene, much too aware of his closeness, of the scent of his after-shave, of his breath tickling her springing short curls as he stood behind her and pointed.

She moved away from him ever so slightly and took a deep breath. And she couldn't help wondering, did Wes feel the same heat stir in his veins?

Walter Greenburg had lived in an apartment on one of San Francisco's nearly perpendicular streets. It was a small studio in one of the old bay-windowed painted houses that abounded in the city. The house was violet colored with yellow trim. There were petunias in window boxes, lacy curtains, a wrought-iron fence and steep steps up to the front porch.

Wes briefed Daphne on the role she was to play and the questions she was to ask and then waited down the street with a newspaper.

Knocking at the door that was marked Manager, Daphne mentally rehearsed her lines. She was a stepsister of Walter's, desperately trying to locate him on a family matter. This was the last address anyone had for him.

A motherly-looking woman with wiry gray hair answered her knock. Daphne introduced herself as Kay Greenburg, praying the woman would not ask for identification.

"You're Walter's stepsister? So, come on in. I know he left a forwarding address. I'm Nora Tannenbaum. Nice to meet you."

Mrs. Tannenbaum's flat was filled with pictures, obviously of her children and grandchildren. The furniture was old-fashioned and dark; one entire round mahogany table was covered with tiny blown-glass animals.

"My menagerie," Nora Tannenbaum said fondly as she noticed Daphne's glance. "Why, Walter gave me that one for my birthday just last year. Now sit down while I get his address for you. You came from where? My goodness, but you don't look like you live in Las Vegas!''

"Well, some of us actually live there and never even see the inside of a casino,'' lied Daphne smugly.

"Oh, yes, here it is. I'll copy it down for you. Boston.'' Mrs. Tannenbaum sighed. ''I hated to see him leave but it was better, poor boy.''

"Why do you say that?'' asked Daphne, pouncing on the opening.

"He didn't tell you? Oh, I suppose not. It was his lady friend. Who's to say? I'm not Victorian and I knew what was going on between them. That's all right; they were both old enough to know what they were doing. It was because she was Russian. If he'd picked a nice American girl, he'd still be here. Poor Walter.''

"Russian?'' urged Daphne.

"A lovely-looking lady. Maybe one, two years older than Walter. She spoke beautiful English. But then she'd lived here for a while. She was with a Russian trade delegation. Computers or something, I think.'' Mrs. Tannenbaum folded her plump hands and sighed. "Tragic. He wanted her to defect, he told me. He was sure she would. But in the end she didn't and their relationship went poof and Walter dragged himself around looking like his best friend had died. I tried to cheer him up. He was like my own son. Chicken soup—homemade, you know.'' She sighed lugubriously again.

"You say Walter is in Boston now,'' prompted Daphne.

"Yes, he transferred. That office he works for moved him. I never did quite understand what Walter did. Security. I hope he likes Boston. My, their winters must be cold.''

Daphne rose, holding Walter's address in her hand. "I do thank you, Mrs. Tannenbaum. Do you remember the lady's name, by the way? I might look her up."

"Oh, certainly. I'm not senile yet. Her name was Vera Sherinsky. She sent me a Hanukkah card."

Daphne impressed the name on her brain in red letters. "And where does she work?"

"I don't know. Downtown, I suppose, in one of those new earthquake-proof buildings."

"Well, goodbye, and thanks again."

"If you see Walter, tell him to write. Just a word—it wouldn't kill him."

Daphne smiled triumphantly as she hurried up to Wes. "Wait till you hear *this*!"

Her story finished, she waited impatiently for Wes to comment on it. "So? What do you think?" she burst out. "He transferred to Boston to look innocent and has been sending her information all along!"

"Could be," said Weston, staring unfocused into the distance. "Then again, he could have transferred to get away from her or because he suddenly realized he'd compromised his security clearance by even dating a Russian girl. Maybe he was afraid the agent in charge of the San Francisco office would find out."

"Do you want me to see this Vera?" asked Daphne.

"I'll do it. There's no way I can be traced through her. At least not in time. I'll give her a call, but first we've got to locate her."

"Oh."

"I'll give the local Secret Service office a ring. Russian trade delegations. They'll know."

After his call they walked until Daphne's feet ached, but Wes insisted on taking her to Fisherman's Wharf. A fitful sea breeze blew there, sweeping away the fog, and the sun began to spear through the mist. The aproned crab men stood outside with their vats of boiled crabs and bins of sourdough bread, just as in the postcards.

They ate an early lunch in one of the seafood houses on the Wharf. Fresh abalone salad and sourdough bread and aromatic hot tea.

"I should be scribbling down recipes," said Daphne, "but my mind just isn't on it."

Had last night ever happened? It was so different today. Two people at work—that was all.

Daphne sat over another cup of tea while Weston phoned Vera Sherinsky in the restaurant foyer. He came back to the table with a frown on his face.

"Well?"

"Very together lady. She couldn't really talk much. Of course, the Russians have all their employees' phones bugged. But she confirmed Mrs. Tannenbaum's story. She did say he'd left San Francisco to forget her, or so he said. And also that he'd been real worried about his boss finding out."

"Has she heard from him since he left?" asked Daphne eagerly.

"She says no, but who can tell?"

"She's lying," stated Daphne firmly.

"Oh? You're so sure?" asked Wes, his eyebrows raised tauntingly.

"Of course. If he really loved her so much he'd have kept in touch."

"I see. A romantic at heart."

"Absolutely," said Daphne staunchly.

They took a taxi back to the hotel to get their bags. Weston was silent on the ride, looking out his window. What a paradox he was—one moment warm and close, the next withdrawn. It was as if he liked Daphne but was

fighting it. A loner, he'd called himself. And he obviously
wanted to remain one. Daphne knew that she was the type
of person who didn't let a relationship just drift, even a
casual one. If she liked someone, she *liked* him. She threw
her whole self into associations, wanting to know everything about a person, wanting his allegiance, his loyalty,
his affection. She guessed there was some insecurity in her
that demanded so much of her friends. And Weston
couldn't handle her emotional demands.

"Stop here," he suddenly said to the taxi driver,
"please."

Daphne looked around, startled. They were in front of
a toy store. "It's my niece's birthday," he explained to her
sheepishly. "I almost forgot." He hesitated. "Do you
think... I mean, I'm not very good at little girls' pres-
ents..."

"You need some help."

"I would be everlastingly grateful."

Daphne chose the cutest Cabbage Patch doll: "Dorita
Dyann" her name tag said. "Take me home and love me."
There were adoption papers, too. Wes just stood by inef-
fectually.

"Would you like me to wrap this for your little girl?"
asked the clerk.

Daphne froze and blushed, then glanced sideways at
Wes. His face was expressionless. He looked at his watch
and said, "Sorry, we're in a hurry. Thanks, anyway."

Their flight to Boston left San Francisco International
in the early afternoon. It was actually three hours later in
Daphne's head, as she hadn't yet adjusted to the time
change and was exhausted.

When the landing gear thumped down on the plane's
approach to Logan Airport, Daphne woke with a start.
Her neck had a knot in it and her mouth felt dry. She was

staring down into a man's lap: neat summer khaki pants, a sinewy outline of thigh muscles under the fabric, a belt buckle. All her muscles snapped taut and she yanked her head up, realizing with alarm that she had fallen asleep with her head leaning on Weston's shoulder.

It took all her courage to turn and meet his gaze.

CHAPTER SIX

"THE LAST FERRY'S ALREADY GONE," observed Daphne.

Weston looked at his watch. "Guess so." Then he glanced at Daphne. She appeared so young and weary standing there in the airport crowd, with dark mascara smudges under her eyes and her short sun-streaked hair curling up around the circle of her face.

Did he dare suggest that they stay at his place? It sure would be convenient.

"So, where to?" she asked.

"Let me think a minute." His hesitation was due more to masking his own indecision than to any real need to ponder the choices. If they did stay at his flat, how would she react to his proximity? It was already too late for the brother-sister act. That particular farce had gone down the drain the night before in San Francisco. He wondered if Daphne had the faintest idea how she affected him. She was so open, so natural. All her feelings showed on her face and in her gestures. All those warm lovely emotions. It only took the merest whiff of her clean-smelling hair or the touch of her hand or her smile to drive a knife into Weston's guts.

His partner's girl. His *dead* partner's girl.

He shook himself mentally. There would be no love-making between them. He would not allow it; this woman was not one to be toyed with. If Wes had learned nothing else about Daphne Farway, he did know one thing: she was for keeps.

"You can take the bedroom," he said, hoisting their overnight bags, "I'll sleep on the couch."

"What?"

"I'll sleep on my couch," he repeated.

She cocked her head. "We're staying at your place?"

"I just said that, didn't I?" He saw her stare at him, bemused, and then two bright spots of color blotched her cheeks.

They pulled into Jim Leroux's driveway shortly after eight. There were brightly hued balloons tied to trees, fluttering from the front door knocker and wrapped around the tidy, early-American lamppost.

Daphne smiled. "I always swore that Brady and I were going to invite the whole school to our kids' birthdays."

Daphne and Brady, Wes thought, the dynamic duo, two people who had it all together, who viewed life with optimism and cheer. He couldn't help but wonder then if Daphne had ever known another man—in the physical sense. If she and Brady had met and dated as young teens, then probably not. How rare these days. One man and one woman, for always.

"Daphne Farway!" said Nancy Leroux as she crossed the living room. "*You're* the author of that cookbook Wes gave me for my birthday. How thrilling to meet you. That blueberry cobbler recipe is fantastic! And the Nantucket chowder."

"Oh, thank you," murmured Daphne, embarrassed, as always, at praise.

"Imagine meeting you in person. I'd love to ask you about that clam cake recipe. Mine just won't turn out."

Excited screams rose from the children. "Loud, aren't they?" Nancy remarked wryly. "It's a nightmare. And I have two more birthday parties before Christmas. They'll have to carry me out of here in a pine box.''

Weston and Jim stood among the children and watched the two women.

"She's very attractive," remarked Jim. "You been hiding her?"

Wes shook his head. "Hardly. Daphne was Brady's fiancée."

"Your partner? The one who was . . ."

"Right."

"So what are *you* doing with her, then?"

"She's helping me on this case. It's a long story, Jim, and I'd just as soon keep you in the dark, for your own sake."

"In the dark but nevertheless willing to let you use the bank's computer?"

Weston's brows drew together. "I was hoping I wouldn't have to ask, but I'm going to need some information. Any chance of getting into your branch tomorrow? Really early?"

Jim looked at him pensively for a moment. "All right. I'm trusting you completely on this. I'll meet you at the side entrance at seven-thirty."

"Thanks. I really appreciate . . ."

"Uncle Weston!" Elizabeth Leroux burst into the living room, her pretty patterned skirt swirling, her beribboned dark braids bouncing. "You missed the cake!"

"Hi, pumpkin." Wes took her in his arms and hugged her. "Happy birthday."

"And here's your uncle's present, dear" came Nancy's voice. She looked at Daphne and smiled. "It was sweet of you to remember."

"I LIKE YOUR FAMILY," said Daphne later as they drove across town. "Nancy is quite a woman. I mean a lady. So nice. I felt just like one of the family." Then she seemed to realize what she'd said and fell silent.

Wes was aware of her discomfort. It was too bad they had to be so careful with each other. He said, "They liked you, too," and then his voice trailed away from the uncomfortable subject.

Weston's apartment was small and tidy. Totally devoid of personal mementos. He knew, as he watched Daphne glance around, that she must be thinking him awfully aloof. A loner. It was true. But then, that was how he wanted it. Sentimentality got in the way of things and twisted a man's thoughts. He wondered if she had really listened when he'd told her that last night.

She stood in the middle of his living room, looking around. "Should I put my bag in your room?"

"Oh, yeah. Here, let me get it for you."

They walked into his bedroom together. It really was impersonal, he thought. The room had only a double bed, a wooden chair and a dresser with some pocket change and old Celtics game stubs scattered on top. Then he realized that this was the first time a woman had ever been to his flat. He'd always gone to their places.

"Bathroom's in here?" asked Daphne, nodding to a half-opened door.

"Oh, sure. Listen, I'll just leave you for a minute if you like." He backed out of the room, aware that both of them had avoided looking toward the double bed.

"Thank you," said Daphne. "I need to freshen up." When he was standing in his living room, uncertainly, she poked her head out of his bedroom for a moment. "Wes?"

"Yes...?"

"Look," she began, and he couldn't help but notice that her pink lipstick very nearly matched the fresh, summer glow of her cheeks, "I know this is awkward for you. Maybe I should have gotten a room somewhere."

"No. This'll be fine. Besides, I'd feel better not leaving you alone."

"Okay." She turned, then briefly paused. "I just wish you wouldn't stand there looking so...so *uncomfortable.*"

He felt like a fool. She was right. "Sorry...I just..."

"I know," she finished for him, and then vanished behind the closed bedroom door.

She'd changed into a raspberry-colored blouse when she returned. "How about dinner?"

Wes was leafing through his mail. He tossed it onto the coffee table. "There isn't much."

"I'll look. If you don't mind, that is?"

"No. No, go ahead. But I'm afraid even the author of those cookbooks is going to have trouble in this man's kitchen."

His refrigerator was pathetically empty. A six-pack of beer, some sour milk, which she poured down the drain, some cheese, a loaf of bread, a bottle of ketchup, a dried-up lemon.

She stood on tiptoe and scanned the contents of the cupboards. Campbell's soup, two cans. A jar of mayonnaise, a box of macaroni and cheese, a can of tuna.

She took down the can of tuna. "It's a wonder you're alive at all, Wes, eating like this."

"Well, I..."

"Usually eat out?"

"Yes."

He sat at the kitchen table and watched her go to work. She moved around his tiny place efficiently, totally ignoring him, obviously unaware of his eyes resting on her too frequently. He liked the feminine, capable way she moved, the way those C-cup breasts of hers strained the buttons on her shirt, the nice muscles in her upper arms, the firmly molded curves of her calves as she stood on her toes, reaching into the cupboard again. She had an okay bottom, too. A little larger and rounder than some, but it did stick out alluringly. He could even see the outline of her panties beneath her skirt.

He settled back against the wall, popped open a beer can and watched her concoct a tuna casserole with bread crumbs and shredded cheese on top. She slid it into the oven, which was smoking from spilled pizza cheese, wiped her hands on his old green sponge and turned to him.

"Ready in a few minutes."

"This is marvelous."

"Tuna casserole?" She made a face.

Wes laughed. "It's better than I usually have."

"Except when you go out." Then she sat down across from him and folded her bare arms on the top of the table. "Listen," she said, "I imagine you date someone. If I'm hanging you up tonight . . ."

"No, I didn't have any plans."

"Well, I mean, if you would have called somebody or something like that, feel free. I'm happy with a magazine and a good night's sleep. Honest."

"Hey. . ." He laughed uneasily. "Who do you think I am, Don Juan?"

"Well, you hear so much about the wild single life these days." Those wide blue eyes of hers fixed on the salt and pepper shakers.

"Don't believe everything you hear."

"Then you have someone special."

She was definitely fishing. But Brady had probably told her all about him anyway. He shrugged. "There's no one I'd call special."

Then she looked him directly in the eye. "You should have someone, Wes. I mean, you're a good person."

"Thanks," he said brusquely.

"No, I mean it."

"I'm sure you do, Daphne, but believe it or not, I'm happy as I am."

She stared at him dubiously and shrugged. "It's none of my business, anyway."

"No," he agreed lightly, "it isn't."

The dinner was fine. He helped her do the dishes, and by that time it was after ten. They went into the living room and Daphne sat down to leaf through the few old magazines on his table while Weston finished sorting through his junk mail.

"I'm really done in," she said finally, yawning. "Where're your sheets?"

"My sheets?"

"You know, sheets, blankets and stuff. I've got to make up the couch for you. It's the least I can do."

He did have a spare sheet and one extra blanket. He stood close, watching her tuck the sheet around the cushions carefully and smooth the blanket on top, turning it down, readying it for him. Then she went into the bedroom and came back with one of the pillows from his bed.

She tossed it to him. "Here. Now, if you can bear to lose my exciting company, I think I'll turn in."

Weston felt as if he should offer her a drink or something; it seemed terribly awkward standing there with a pillow dangling from his hand, ready to say good-night or sleep well or pleasant dreams.

Daphne, too, seemed a bit tentative and the color in her cheeks was higher than usual. He wondered how many nights they would be thrown together in this close, strained proximity. How many nights before they found themselves standing just a little too close, until one might reach out for the other?

He knew he was staring at her and the difficult silence had gone on too long. He finally cleared his throat. "Good night, Daphne," he said simply, still holding the stupid pillow. "Sleep well."

He sat down on the lumpy couch that she had so considerately made up for him and his thoughts drifted. He could hear the water running in the bathroom sink, then the toilet flushing and finally the bedsprings creaking as she turned in. He wondered, fantasizing, if she were sleeping in that oversize T-shirt of hers. Finally he kicked off his shoes and pulled off his shirt and trousers and stretched out in the warm darkness. But sleep didn't come, not immediately. Wes was far too aware of Daphne's presence in his tiny flat. Only a thin separating wall was keeping him from pulling her into his arms again and tasting the honey of those sweet pink lips.

It was the opening and closing of a cupboard door in the kitchen that dragged Wes out of sleep. Daphne, he registered. She must be making coffee or something.

He rolled over and looked at his watch. Six-thirty. Then he stretched. "Good morning," he called lazily.

She peered out of the kitchen archway. "Good morning," she said cheerfully. "Did you sleep well?"

Her hair was mussed and kind of cute, and she was still wearing that T-shirt of hers, the one, he recalled, that left very little to a man's imagination.

"I slept fine," he lied, recalling those musings that had kept him lying sleepless for too long.

"Rise and shine," she said, turning away. "Coffee'll be ready in a few minutes."

He rose, pulled on his trousers and then went into the bathroom and showered. When he appeared in the kitchen he was wearing a fresh pair of slacks and buttoning his shirt.

"Coffee?" Daphne held up the pot.

"Sure. Black, please." As she leaned over him and poured he could detect her natural scent, could see the firm outline of those breasts beneath the fabric. He looked away.

"So you said this morning we'll do some checking at a bank?"

He nodded. "Yes, but not *we*."

"Oh?" She sounded disappointed. "But I thought . . ."

"The checking I'm going to be doing is not really on the up-and-up."

"So how will you get access to the information?"

"I'd rather you didn't know."

"I see." She put two pieces of bread in his toaster. Weston watched her carefully, very aware of her shapely legs and tiny ankles and the outline of her bottom beneath the T-shirt. She turned to him. "Toast? That's about all there is."

"There's cereal."

"No milk. I threw it out." She wrinkled her nose.

"Toast, then."

"Wes?"

"Yes?" He looked up at her.

"Why can't I be in on this part of your investigation?"

"Because it involves someone close to me. I'm asking this person to do something a little shady."

Silence fell between them for a minute; only the sound of the toast popping up disturbed the quiet.

"There's no butter," said Daphne. "How about jam?"

"Sure, that's fine." He watched her lean over to get the jar out of the refrigerator door. Then she found two plates, carried them to the table and seated herself across from him.

"Wes," she began, "is this person you're going to get help from, this person close to you...I mean... Oh, never mind." She took a bite of toast and jam. "So what shall I do while you're gone?"

"It's unsafe for you to stay here alone."

"Well, there're no shops open at...what time did you say, seven-thirty?"

"No, there aren't. But maybe I could drop you off at a coffee shop. You could have a real breakfast and I'd meet you there at nine."

"I guess that would be all right."

He studied her for a moment, noting the position of her bowed head, the gentle curve of her neck, the delicacy of her hands cupping the coffee mug. "What were you going to ask me a minute ago, about this person I'm going to see this morning?"

Daphne's glance met his for a second and then moved away. "Nothing, really."

He knew he was treading on dangerous ground, but he couldn't help pressing. "Were you going to ask me if it was a woman?"

Color rose up her neck. She looked at him. "Maybe. I don't really know. There's a lot I don't know anymore." Her voice floated away.

He'd wanted to hear precisely that and now he wished he'd never asked. His discomfort, he knew, was suddenly a tangible thing, filling the small room, as if the walls were pressing in on both of them as they sat there. He should say something, make light of it. But somehow his heart was thudding too heavily against his ribs, and pithy words refused to form in his head.

The minutes stretched out in a line, lengthy and brittle. "Look," he said quietly, "Daphne, I..." But she was not there with him; he sensed she was with Brady somewhere, lonely and confused and aching. Even though Brady Leighton was dead and gone, in some obscure way he was still standing in the room with them.

Daphne finally stood and rinsed the cups and plates in the sink. Wes rose slowly and moved to the center of the kitchen, poised between grabbing her in his arms to force Brady's memory from her head and leaving the room.

She turned, as if sensing the pain and indecision in him. Their eyes met meaningfully.

He wanted to pull her to him, to feel her warmth, her curves. He wanted to grasp in his hands some of the clean, unfettered emotion that filled her. He despised his own reluctance but could not overcome it, for he despised his urges even more. He wished he could say to hell with Brady, but he couldn't. He'd already been too close to giving in.

Did she know what she did to him?

Her eyes fell. He hoped, prayed, that she had no idea what was going on in his head. She'd never speak to him again if she did, and he couldn't bear that. He wanted her near, and yet her nearness was achingly unbearable.

She looked up and seemed to be about to say something but she only stared at him, making his skin crawl with desire. Then she turned and left him there alone in the kitchen.

Daphne showered. He sat in the living room staring at the bathroom door, envisioning the shower stall, the hot water caressing her naked skin, running down the deep cleft between her breasts and down the plane of her stomach.

Why on earth had he ever asked her to stay in his place? Had it been some sort of perverse masochism? He knew what her nearness did to him. He should never have put them both in this awful situation. But of course he hadn't been able to resist. He'd wanted to suffer her proximity.

Could there ever be anything between them? Even if Brady wasn't always hovering near, there was Weston's own decision not ever to become entangled with a woman. And with Daphne it could never be just casual sex. She was a for-always lady.

She appeared at ten past seven dressed in her raspberry shirt and a fresh pair of white slacks.

"I'm ready," she said, smiling with constraint.

He stood up and put on his suit jacket, tightening his tie in a hasty movement. "Let's go" was all he said.

They drove through the light early morning traffic in silence. It was Daphne who finally spoke. "After you finish with this bit of digging," she said offhandedly, "where to then? Back to the Vineyard?"

"Not yet," he replied. "We're going to check on Mike."

"Mike?"

"Mike Toth. He lives in the area."

"Am I going to help, then?"

"Yes."

"Well, what exactly do I do?"

"Ask some questions like you did in San Francisco."

JIM LEROUX'S BANK was in the new, high-rise part of Boston. Wes parked and strode along the sidewalk that ran in front of the tall, white concrete and glass structure. Jim was waiting for him at a side door of the building.

It didn't take long. Jim Leroux was a whiz with the mainframe computer, quickly pulling up information on Jerry Gallent and Mike Toth, both of whom had accounts with branches of Jim's bank. He had trouble, however, locating Walter Greenburg's account, and it took tapping into seven competitor banks before he located Greenburg, Walter A. And then there was nothing of interest, anyway. Still, when Wes rose from his seat alongside his brother, he was pleased with their findings. Chief Gallent's account had shown a huge deposit, over eighty thousand dollars, back in early July and Mike Toth's account showed monthly checks written to an obscure Hungarian relief organization that Wes knew could be a cover for just about anything.

"Have I been of any help?" asked Jim at the door.

"I think so," said Wes. "At least this information has raised a few questions."

"I don't know if that's good or bad."

"Neither do I," said Wes ruefully.

After picking Daphne up, Wes telephoned Hubert from a nearby booth. "Everything all right there?" asked Weston.

"Sure, fine, boyo. But goldarn, this female is a handful! I'm telling you, Wes, she baits me at every step. And calls me Sam!"

Weston turned his shoulder away from Daphne, lowering his voice on the phone. "Just hang in there, Hubert. We're on our way to Toth's neighborhood in Dorchester and then we'll head back to the Vineyard."

"Find out anything interesting yet?"

"Maybe. I'll tell you everything when we get back."

"And I suppose I'll be stuck here longer?"

"'Fraid so, Hubert."

"Say," said Hubert then, "would you mind stopping by my place and picking up my tennis racket? Oh, and my court shoes? That's all this woman ever does, and if I gotta be with her..."

"Sure, no problem. Where are they?"

"The hall closet, or maybe check the garage. Okay?"

"Yep."

"Oh, and the key's still under the flowerpot."

"I never would have figured *that*, Hubert."

They drove to Dorchester, a blue-collar neighborhood south of Boston proper. Mike Toth's home ground.

"This must be awful for you," said Daphne softly. "I didn't realize before, but these are your co-workers, your buddies. Men you trusted."

"Yes," repeated Wes in a hard voice. "It's no picnic."

"Gosh, I'm sorry I dragged you into this, Wes. I hadn't thought..."

"Someone had to do it. Look, whether or not they're my friends means nothing at this point. I'm doing my job, that's all."

"Like Brady," whispered Daphne, half to herself.

Weston drove silently after that until they entered streets lined with houses that all appeared to have been built at the same time, maybe the twenties. The same steps up to front porches, the same lace-curtained bay windows, the same tidy small yards. Corner grocery stores and kids playing in the roadways. Dorchester.

Weston explained to Daphne that if she could question a couple of Mike's neighbors and feel out exactly how strong the ties were that Mike had for the old country, they might have a lead on his true sentiments.

"For all anybody knows," said Wes, "Mike could be a full-fledged member of the Communist party." Then he told her about the monthly checks Mike wrote to the so-called relief organization.

"Interesting," said Daphne. "Maybe he's our man, then. His motive could be plain old sentiment. After all," she reflected, "Hungary is a Soviet satellite. Maybe he's a Russian mole or something, a plant."

"Could be. But the chief can't be ruled out; he has a really questionable deposit made to his account. Recently. Greed is always a motive, too. And there's Walter's lady friend in San Francisco."

"How are we going to know? I mean, how do we pin it all down?"

Weston turned onto Toth's street. "I'm not certain just yet. We'll go back to the Vineyard and piece some things together with Hubert."

He watched Daphne walk down the neat, middle-class street, glancing at numbers on doors and finally climbing the steps of a row house next door to the Toth's. After her breakfast, he'd coached her as best he could, knowing that these Middle Europeans might be tight-lipped. Her cover was simple; she was to tell the neighbors that she was doing a thesis on Hungarians in America and Mike Toth, as a Secret Service agent, was of great interest to her research. Confronted with a face as innocent as Daphne's, they'd talk to her, wouldn't they?

EVERYONE HAD THE SAME THING to say: Mike was a good boy, a dutiful son, loved his beer with the boys on Friday night, was bitter about his ex-wife taking him to the cleaners and was a rabid Hungarian nationalist.

It didn't fit with the picture of a traitor, but one never knew...

Weston pulled up in front of Hubert's house around noon. "Hubert needs his tennis gear," said Wes. "Something about his hall closet or garage. We'll find the stuff."

"I've got an even better idea," said Daphne, stepping out onto the curb. "You go get us some sandwiches to go and I'll find his gear. I'm starved. Where's the key, anyway?"

"Under the flowerpot. Where else?"

Twenty minutes later, Wes pulled back up to the curb in front of Hubert's. He entered the house and called for Daphne. No answer. He called louder, a small bubble of alarm forming in his chest.

Finally he heard, "Out here!" coming from the garage. "Wes, hurry!"

He raced through the house, pulling his gun from its holster automatically, crouching as he burst through the kitchen door and into the garage.

She was alone. Her face was pinched and drained of color. In her hand she held several old envelopes and her knuckles were white from gripping them.

"Daphne," he asked cautiously, "what's going on?"

She shook her head, obviously distraught, and breathed, "Look at these."

"What are they?" He took the envelopes from her hand.

"*Look* at them, Wes!"

They were bank statements. What? And then he understood. Daphne had snooped into Hubert's private possessions. Surprise swept him. "You pried into Hubert's things!"

"Look at them," she implored, hugging her arms around herself in agitation.

Reluctantly, Weston tore his accusing gaze from Daphne and looked down at the envelopes.

"Please," Daphne was saying, over and over, "please hurry."

He opened one, scanned some bank statements and leafed through some canceled checks. Then he opened another.

"Those huge checks," Daphne said, "the ones made out every month on the first. They're for cash."

"So what?" he shot back at her.

"Five hundred dollars in cash!"

"So?"

"It's not a mortgage, Wes. For God's sake, you don't write checks for cash to pay your mortgage!"

"No, of course it isn't," he replied irritably.

"Then what?"

"What are you getting at, Daphne? What the devil's come over you?"

"Does Hubert gamble? Could he have a monthly game?"

"No way. He's frugal. Never even got into the weekly office pools on football."

"So he isn't using it for gambling then. Or anything like grocery money."

"Of course not." Wes narrowed his eyes impatiently. "Why don't you just come right out and say what's got you so upset."

"I think . . . What if it's a payoff or something?"

"What if it's pocket money?"

"Look around you! Does this place look as if it belongs to a man who carries around five hundred dollars in *pocket* money?"

Wes shook his head in disgust. "I still don't see what you're driving at."

"Listen," she said in an imploring voice, "I've been standing here trying with all my might to figure out what in heaven's name a man like Hubert would need so much cash for and . . .''

"I'd say it's none of your business."

"Please, Wes, *think*. What do people do with so much cash?"

He scrubbed a hand through his hair. "Pay bills—I don't know."

"His bills are paid by check. They're all here," Daphne said. "See? There *is* no good explanation."

"Look," he began.

"Please hear me out. Only one thing comes into my head, Wes. Blackmail."

"That's crazy," he shot back. "Your imagination is running wild."

"Not that wild."

"I still say you're leaping to conclusions. Let's just put these statements back and collect Hubert's gear."

Daphne squared her shoulders. "So you're going to just ignore this? Pretend it never happened?"

"Nothing *has* happened."

"Because you won't listen!"

Wes sighed. "Okay, I'll listen. But then we're going to put these statements back and get out of here."

"Okay. Say Hubert *is* paying someone blackmail. Then it would be so easy for someone to force him to do something else."

"Like what?"

"Like give them top-secret information."

"Come on," scoffed Wes. "That's too ludicrous to believe."

"I don't know. Maybe. But there's something fishy going on here and he's alone with my mother, Wes."

"That's ridiculous. I know Hubert."

"Do you, Wes? Do you really? I don't know what that money was for every month for years and years, but he's with my mother and *I* can't take the chance. Can you?"

Wes looked at her long and hard in the hot, stuffy garage. In spite of himself, he felt an anxious gnawing in his gut. "Let's get out of here," he said finally, replacing the statements in an old cardboard box and taking her arm too roughly.

CHAPTER SEVEN

"I SHOULDN'T HAVE LEFT HER alone with him," Daphne kept saying as they drove along the Southeast Expressway to the Cape.

"Your mother," Weston bit out, "is fine. Hubert isn't the man."

"Then why didn't she answer the phone?"

"How do I know? She was probably out somewhere. I tell you, Hubert isn't the traitor."

"Of course you would probably never believe he was." Her lips compressed into a tight, silent line when she saw a wounded look flash across Weston's face.

"Even if he were," said Wes under his breath, "he'd never harm your mother."

But what about Brady? thought Daphne, picturing Hubert and Audrey alone in the rambling old house, Hubert desperate, knowing that Wes and Daphne were hot on the trail of the traitor. *His* trail.

What would Hubert do? Would he be forced into a corner when confronted and like an animal lash out at them all? Would he even stop to think if he could get away with murdering again?

She saw all sorts of things in her head, whirling images of Hubert shooting them and setting the house on fire to cover his tracks. Or he could bury them in the soft sand or something. Maybe dump their bodies at sea! The mental picture of their three corpses, bloated with seawater and picked at by fish, filled Daphne's mind hideously.

"Will you stop worrying," ordered Weston irritably. "I tell you, it's *not* Hubert."

"I'm praying you're right, Wes. But do me a favor and drive up to the house with your gun loaded and ready."

"I'll handle it *my* way," he snapped.

At moments, Daphne realized, her fears could very well be irrational. All she'd found were some canceled checks made out for cash. Yet each time she searched her mind for possible uses of so much cash, she came around to the same conclusion: it had to be used as a payoff of some kind. And if Hubert Samuels were involved in blackmail, could it be with the Soviets?

The ferry crossing was a nightmare; the fat chugging boat seemed to move through the swells too slowly, like a crab trying to cross an ocean floor. And the boat was jammed. Tourists continuously elbowed Daphne and Wes at the rail, taking pictures and exclaiming over the dozens of noisy gulls that swooped down to feed from crumbs tossed in the air.

Finally Vineyard Haven materialized before them. When the ferry nudged gently against the pilings, they were able to shoulder through the crowd and get to Daphne's car before the traffic was blocked hopelessly. Daphne insisted on driving and did an excellent imitation of her mother behind the wheel.

"Slow down!" commanded Weston once as Daphne took a curve in Chilmark at forty miles an hour. "Good God, woman."

They approached the long, sandy drive leading up to the Farways' Victorian manor. Daphne spun her tires in the sand, almost struck a two-hundred-year-old maple, then stepped on the gas pedal even harder.

Wes swore under his breath.

"Never mind that," gasped Daphne, barreling up in front of the house. "Is your gun ready?"

He climbed out of the car, staring at her angrily. "Stop being so damned melodramatic."

She looked up at the house, her imagination going wild again, then glanced back at Wes. "What are you going to do?" she urged.

"First, I'm getting out of this blasted jacket." He stripped it off and tossed it into the back seat. There were sweat stains under the arms of his shirt, all the way down his back and dampening the waistband of his trousers. But Daphne barely noticed; her eyes were pinned to his shoulder holster and the butt of the gun protruding in its sheath.

Wes began walking toward the front door; Daphne dogged his footsteps. He swung open the door. "Hubert!" he called.

"Audrey!" Daphne piped up hopefully even as she caught the scathing glance that Wes threw her.

Neither her mother nor Hubert Samuels replied. Weston called out again, and once again. No reply.

They checked the back porch. Vacant. Then Daphne, frantic that it was too late, that Hubert had already gotten rid of her mother, ran shakily across the wide sand dune to scan the beach below.

Suddenly her heart lurched. There they were, below on the beach—fishing! Daphne spun around. "They're down there, Wes!"

Wes crossed the dune and stood beside Daphne, looking down to where Hubert and Audrey were seated on captain's chairs, fishing rods in spiked sand holders, beers beside them casually stuck in the sand.

"Stay here." Wes took her arm forcefully. "I mean it, Daphne. Don't interfere. I'll send Audrey up to you."

"All right," she agreed, looking down at her arm where he gripped it.

"I'll talk to Hubert," said Weston. Then he released her, and his eyes rested on the red blotches left on her flesh from his fingers.

"It's all right," Daphne said, following his gaze. "I know what you're going through."

"I doubt it," he said coldly.

She watched him make his way along the crest of the dune and down the sea-oat-lined path to the beach. Neither Hubert nor Audrey saw him approach, as he stayed directly behind their line of vision.

Hubert was the first to spin around in his chair. With her heart pumping furiously, Daphne watched the scene unfolding. Hubert stood, then Audrey. Wes said something to her and Audrey shrugged, picked up her fishing gear and began to make her way across the burning sand toward the path. Then Wes was alone with Hubert, and Daphne could see the tight set of Weston's shoulders and his slightly bowed head as he appeared to be speaking.

"What's going on?" puffed Audrey when she reached the top of the dune. "Wes looked like a devil was chasing him."

"Please be quiet, Mother."

"*Audrey.*"

"Okay, *Audrey*, just let me watch this."

"Watch what?"

"I'll explain later. Please."

"Well," grumbled Audrey. "I was about to win a bet from old Sam there. It really ticks me off." She started to head toward the house, her agitated voice receding. "And I would have won, too. A Hopkins lure is the only way to catch a bluefish, you know. Everyone but old Sam there knows that."

Down on the beach, Hubert seemed to be looking at Wes in amazement. Then he put his hands on his hips and kicked the sand, his neck and head beet red in the hot August sun. Wes shook his head. Hubert kicked the sand again and began pacing the beach in quick, angry strides. Then he stopped and confronted his accuser.

Their raised, angry voices reached Daphne on the warm sea breeze but she could only make out inflections. Weston was spreading his hands as if to say, What else are we to think? And then Hubert seemed to be arguing, no doubt telling Wes exactly where he could go.

It was an ugly scene, and yet profound relief washed over Daphne. Her mother was perfectly safe. If it was Hubert who had given the itinerary to the Russian hawks, at least Wes and Daphne had found out in time.

Could it have been Hubert, though, with his kind twinkling brown eyes and dapper Vandyke, who had killed Brady? Was that possible?

"Aren't they done down there yet?" came Audrey's voice in her ear.

"Look, Audrey," said Daphne, "this is dead serious. We think... It's possible Hubert is the one."

"Sam!" squawked Audrey. "Bull." Then she turned and stomped away, muttering.

When Daphne looked back down at the beach, Wes was alone. Her heart thumped heavily. What had happened? Where was...? But then she saw Hubert, striding quickly along the edge of the surf, his shoulders hunched, his hands jammed in the pockets of his madras shorts.

Her stare returned to Weston. He must have felt her eyes on him, for he looked up at her standing there and she saw pain written on his face. When he finally climbed back up the dune and stood stiffly in front of her, Daphne could barely meet his gaze.

"What ... what happened?" she managed.

"What do you *think* happened, Daphne?"

"You told him what I discovered at his house."

"Not exactly." Wes turned and put his hands in his pockets and gazed out to sea. A hot wind stirred his sandy hair, lifting it from his brow; his green eyes caught the fire of the sun and held it. "I told Hubert what *I* had found out."

"You! But why..."

"Because I didn't want you in any more danger than you're already in. Let Hubert vent his anger on me."

Daphne rubbed one of her arms as if she were cold. "That wasn't fair to you. I was the one who snooped."

Weston turned toward her brusquely. "Don't tell me you're worried about his feelings!"

"I ... I don't know what I think."

"I guess it doesn't matter. The issue is this: Hubert wasn't saying anything, just cussing me out about prying into his personal business."

"He said nothing?"

"He told me to ... stuff it."

"And he just walked away?" asked Daphne, bewildered.

"That's right."

"Well, where will he go? I mean..."

"I don't know. Back to Boston, probably. There's certainly nothing keeping him *here* now."

"What are we going to do?"

Wes shrugged. "For one thing it's not 'we,' it's me, Daphne. I suppose all I can do is follow him and get to the bottom of this."

"But do you really think it's Hubert?"

When he looked at her, Daphne was chilled by the chips of green ice she saw in his eyes. "Isn't that what you wanted me to believe all along? You should be happy."

"I think you know better than that." Her chin jutted out defiantly.

"Bad choice of words, then. Call it relieved. Whatever. All I know is that I don't want you staying here."

"But if it's Hubert and he's heading into Boston—"

"Look," interrupted Wes, "we don't know for sure, do we?"

She shook her head slowly.

"So please comply without an argument. I won't have you and Audrey staying here alone. Where can you go?"

"I guess to the club. The tennis club."

"Fine." He turned on his heel and strode toward the house. For a long time Daphne stood there uncertainly, shaken by the force of his pain, which buffeted her like the hot heavy wind kicking up along the head of the dune.

She ached to go to him and help him. But instinctively Daphne knew that he'd reject any attempt on her part to try to give him comfort.

The sand shot up around her again, stinging her eyes and causing them to water. She finally walked toward the house in Weston's footsteps, feeling him still there, a wraithlike presence in the air, wounded and in need.

WES WAITED IMPATIENTLY while the two women packed bags. Then he insisted on following them to Audrey's tennis club, where they would get a room for the night. He drove Daphne's little blue bug behind her mother's red Saab, following them at breakneck pace along the winding island roads.

He knew he appeared cold and angry to Daphne but it was his only defense right then, his only protection against his anxiety about Hubert, his bewilderment when faced with the possibility of wrongdoing by a man he'd loved like a father. If he couldn't trust Hubert, his world was fragmented, without base. He tortured himself with images of Hubert giving information to the Russians. But Hubert hadn't been in the office lately. Or had he? Had he been in when Wes was out on an investigation? No one would even have remarked on it—everyone would assume Hubert had been called in. As far as killing Brady was concerned, Weston's mind balked at the thought. It wasn't possible.

And the worst part of the whole affair was that Hubert had refused to explain anything, even to Wes.

After pulling up next to Audrey's car in the parking lot of her club, Wes got out and approached the women. He wondered if Daphne had divulged the whole story to her mother on the way over, and he felt himself cringing with shame for Hubert.

"I'm going to take off now. I'll leave your car on this side so I can get back if I need to. Don't go back to your house, Mrs. Farway, you understand?"

"Yes, sir!" Audrey saluted facetiously. "I *love* masterful men, don't you, Daphne?"

But Daphne only smiled wanly at her mother's humor instead of picking up on it. She looked terribly sad and tired and worried, and Wes wanted to hold her in his arms and soothe her frown away, to stroke her velvet-smooth skin until she relaxed and purred like a soft, blond kitten.

He couldn't, of course.

"You'll be careful?" Daphne asked him pleadingly.

His sympathy vanished. "Of Hubert?" he shot back.

"Of...whatever."

"Sure, I'll be careful, don't worry."

"I'll worry, anyway," she said softly. "Call me as soon as you find him or have any news, okay?"

"Yeah." He was short with her, hurt and unwilling to accept her concern. He knew his attitude was childish. He drove straight to Hubert's house, feeling like a shuttlecock that had been batted back and forth, back and forth.

Hubert's car wasn't there and the door was locked. The key was still under the flowerpot where Daphne had left it. Inside, there wasn't a sign that Hubert had returned. Maybe he'd beaten Hubert back.

It had occurred to him that if Hubert were truly guilty he'd run for cover. Leave town? He couldn't imagine Hubert leaving his hometown. Or his daughter, who lived just a few miles away in Lexington, with her children.

Dodie. Of course, he'd call Dodie, Hubert's daughter. They'd been practically raised together when Wes had lived with Hubert. Dodie was a couple of years younger than Wes, but they'd remained friends. Christmas card friends but, still, they'd shared a common family for those years.

He found her number in Hubert's desk. God, he hated snooping, but it was faster that way. She answered on the third ring. He could hear a baby screaming lustily in the background.

"Hello?" she said somewhat breathlessly.

"Dodie, it's Wes."

"Well, what do you know? Long-lost brother and all that."

"You seen your dad recently?" he asked carefully.

"He came up last weekend for dinner. Why?"

"Oh, I'm trying to locate him. They want him at the office."

"You know, he called a couple of days ago and said he was on some kind of a job. I don't know where, though. It's good for him to be busy, so I didn't ask much about it."

"Yeah, well, if he gets in touch, tell him to call me."

"Okay. Say, how's it going with you? Any prospects?"

"You mean female-wise or job-wise?"

"Female, of course," she said matter-of-factly.

"Maybe."

"About time, Wes. Gotta go now. The newest addition is about to turn purple here. See you."

He hung up slowly. Should he call Hubert's son, Al, in Fresno? He doubted very much if Hubert would have contacted Al, who was too far away to be of any help whatsoever. No, he'd wait to do that; he could always phone Al tomorrow.

He'd stay awhile, he decided. Hubert was a real homebody; he'd show up sooner or later and then they'd have it out. He turned on the radio and looked in Hubert's refrigerator. It was more inviting than his, at least. There was a package of ham and some pickles. Orange juice, plastic containers of leftovers. Hubert was fastidious about his person but sloppy at home. Clean but sloppy.

He ate a ham sandwich while listening to the CBS seven o'clock news, all the while keeping one ear cocked for Hubert's car in the driveway.

"Gorvieski, the General Secretary of the Central Committee," announced the suave voice on the radio, "will be visiting that venerable birthplace of liberty, Boston, Massachusetts, right after Labor Day. Security will be the tightest ever seen in this country, and the crowds along the as yet undisclosed route are expected to be covered by—" He clicked it off, chilled. Four days were gone, and he was no closer to uncovering the traitor's identity. And now this thing with Hubert—his instincts told him it couldn't be Hubert selling out his country. But he could be wrong.

He washed his one dish and glass and sponged off Hubert's counter. Where in hell was the man?

He considered calling Daphne. He was sorely tempted, in fact. Just to hear her voice, soft and breathless and caring. His hand went to the phone. Then he stopped and drew it back. He had nothing to tell her. No Hubert, no news. It would be ridiculous to call just to say hello. He could apologize for his coldness that day, but Daphne already knew why he'd been upset. She seemed to understand him awfully well—too well. And it didn't make her the least bit uncomfortable talking about him—or herself. All those messy emotions that he steered away from. To Daphne they were normal, even interesting. How wonderful to be so whole.

And suddenly, blindingly, he loathed Brady's complacency, his taking Daphne's love for granted, his casual acceptance of her. It didn't matter that Brady Leighton was dead; Wes despised him, anyway, and raged mentally at the man's crassness in not having appreciated the preciousness of Daphne's love.

Pacing Hubert's living room, he cursed his own stupid, criminal jealousy.

It was still light out; neighbors were barbecuing in their backyards and children rode tricycles on the sidewalk. Wes couldn't stay in Hubert's house another second, listening to the family life around him, remembering the acceptance and affection he'd found in that very house. He ran from it as if suffocating.

He headed toward Somerville and his own apartment. He'd keep calling Hubert's number, and if there was no answer by tomorrow, he'd try Al in Fresno and make the rounds of the neighbors to find out what places Hubert frequented these days.

He drove steadily through the warm summer night, window open, elbow resting on the windowframe. Automatically, he braked, turned, shifted. Traffic hummed around him, and the lights of oncoming cars flared in his face and then were gone. His mind spun.

Hubert, of all people. It was impossible. Then he thought of Daphne. When he got home he'd call her. He owed her that much. No sense being cruel, leaving her wondering if he'd found Hubert.

He recalled her telling him that she was insecure. It had been in the hotel in San Francisco that night. To Wes, she seemed the most secure, whole, in-control woman he'd ever known. With him it was like pulling teeth to dredge up his feelings, but she talked about herself so easily. She'd been so innocent that night, so unselfconscious in her oversize T-shirt, no makeup, bare feet. Her toes fascinated him—pink little things with bright toenail polish. He loved her toes and her small hands that were soft but capable. She wore no rings on her fingers, no necklace.

He pulled up to the curb in front of his building, thanking heaven that there was a parking place right in front. He was too tired and too defeated to search for one.

Carefully he locked his car, then crossed the lawn. It was dark and quiet. Not a particularly friendly neighborhood. No families out on their porches or children running around, as on Hubert's street. A private, transient neighborhood that suited him perfectly.

He'd call Daphne right away.

He unlocked his door, fumbling in the darkness. She'd been there that morning, sleeping in his bed. Would the sheets still smell of her perfume?

He stepped inside, reached out and snapped on the light, closing the door behind him. It was hot and stuffy in his place.

He had time to thrust his keys into his pocket and take a few steps into the room when there was the sound of glass breaking and a sudden pain, like a nail hammering into his head, a red-and-white explosion. His knees went soft and a wave of nausea clogged the back of his throat, receded then clogged again.

His face hit the floor hard and he had no idea how he'd gotten down there. A feeling of utter stupefaction and overwhelming fear filled him, before blackness opened up and swallowed him.

CHAPTER EIGHT

DAPHNE PLAYED A HALFHEARTED GAME of doubles with Audrey against a couple from Miami. She was an indifferent tennis player at best, but that afternoon she was worse than usual and Audrey was furious with her.

"You could have returned that long shot!" Audrey snapped. "I let it go for you. It was perfect for a passing shot!"

"My mind wasn't on it," Daphne responded. "Sorry."

"Sorry! Sorry doesn't win games!"

"I'm worried about Wes—and Hubert."

"They're big boys. They can take care of themselves. They've both managed without you for years."

"I know." But still she worried and wondered and regretted the fact that she wasn't sitting by the phone in their room in case Wes tried to call her.

She felt horribly responsible that she had been the one to uncover Hubert's guilt. And Audrey had been perfectly fine when she and Wes had returned, so perhaps it wasn't Hubert, after all. She prayed it wasn't—for Weston's sake, if nothing else. There was no way to apologize to either of them if she was wrong. She should have minded her own business and kept her mouth shut. Regret swamped her, murky and clinging.

Wes hadn't called by five, so she tried his apartment. There was no answer. He probably hadn't had enough time to get there, anyway.

She tried Hubert's number, just in case either of them was there. No answer there, either.

"We're going out with the MacKenzies," Audrey announced as she sashayed into the room. "I suggested the Shiretown Inn."

"I'd rather stay here in case Wes calls."

"Nonsense. If he calls, the desk will take the message. We have to eat. And the MacKenzies are such nice people. Did you know they have a son at Harvard Law School?" Audrey's voice softened. "Come on. It's about time you got out and saw some people. It'll cheer you up."

She consented. At least it was something to do, something to take her mind off the painful state of affairs she'd created. Images tormented her: Hubert lying in wait for Wes with the same gun that had killed Brady. It couldn't be, could it? Wes trusted Hubert—that should have been enough for her. But everyone had something to hide, and obviously Hubert had his own secrets. It tortured her that she'd been the cause of sending Wes into danger. Or if Hubert were indeed innocent, she'd ruined their trust for each other and they'd both despise her.

Listlessly Daphne put on the one dress she'd brought, a brightly flowered sundress in shades of blue. Audrey chattered away as she applied her makeup and fluffed her curls, which, she often pointed out, didn't have a touch of gray in them. Then she slipped into a stunning designer dress.

"Put on some rouge," she directed. "You're pale. And some eye shadow. Here, I've got some blue that'll be perfect."

"Audrey, please, I'm not going to be presented to the Queen."

"Always look your best. You never know," cautioned her mother.

"Never know what?" muttered Daphne rebelliously.

Audrey picked Dan and Meredith MacKenzie up at their hotel. Polite smiles and remarks about the hot weather abounded.

"We're taking you to the Shiretown Inn. It's a lovely place," explained Audrey, looking over her shoulder at the couple from Miami in the back seat. "Authentic island Early American. Good food, too."

She sped along the coast road toward Edgartown, telling the MacKenzies about Thomas Mayhew, her revered ancestor. Daphne had heard it so many times that she could have finished her mother's sentences. She looked out at the sea dancing and sparkling in the evening light. Off to the right, the *Island Queen* was chugging toward Vineyard Haven. The ferry caught the late sun, reflecting it in a blinding white glare. It would dock, then return to Woods Hole at seven-fifteen, its last trip for the day. Entering the harbor, the *Queen* gave its customary earshattering blast. The sound drifted compellingly on the onshore breeze, buffeting Daphne's ears, as if it were some sort of signal.

"Audrey," she said firmly, as soon as the sound had dispersed on the hot evening air, "drop me off at Vineyard Haven. I'm going to Boston."

Audrey looked at her as if she were insane. "But I made reservations for *four*."

"I'm going to Boston. Wes left my car in Vineyard Haven and I've got extra keys, so I'll be able to get home. I'll be back tomorrow."

The MacKenzies were uncomfortably silent in the back seat.

Audrey was still gaping at her; Daphne grabbed the steering wheel as the car drifted toward a very old, very solid stone wall. She turned to their guests. "I'm sorry, but this is sort of an emergency and I've got to catch the last ferry. Please excuse me and have a wonderful dinner. The bluefish at the Shiretown is excellent."

She just made the ferry, but there was no way she could get her car on. The boat was full and even going directly to the captain and pleading an emergency did no good. It occurred to her then that this was an ill-fated voyage and that she should turn around, get a taxi, go to the Shiretown Inn and forget the whole thing. But she was too island-bred stubborn. She'd get to Boston if she had to hitchhike!

Too nervous to sit and enjoy the forty-five minute trip, Daphne paced around the lower deck. Around and around. What she would do when she got to Weston's she had no idea. She wouldn't even think about it. She just knew she had to be there; she had to somehow try to rectify the mess she'd made of things.

She'd told Audrey, out of the MacKenzies' hearing, not to return to their house for any reason whatsoever. "Please, Audrey, we don't need any more problems."

"But I left my blow dryer there."

"Never mind. Buy a new one. Don't go back."'

She wondered, as she made her way impatiently between children and shopping bags and fishing rod cases, if Audrey would obey her warning. You never knew with Audrey Mayhew Farway.

An idea struck her and she paused in her pacing and made her way to the bridge, where the captain stood steering the boat in his jaunty nautical cap.

He was young and very blond and quite handsome.

"I really am sorry we couldn't fit your car on," he began, seeing Daphne approach. "I do try to give the islanders a break, but tonight was impossible."

"I've still got to get to Boston." Daphne tried to sound calm. "I wonder if you could make a request over your loudspeaker that I need a ride. Most of these people are heading to Boston, anyway."

He looked at her for a moment. "Well, it's against regulations."

"Please, this is very important. I've lived on Martha's Vineyard all my life and never asked for a favor before." She smiled charmingly at the young captain.

"I guess it's all right," he said doubtfully.

The loudspeakers boomed all over the boat: "A passenger needs a ride to Boston. Please contact the captain before disembarking if you can give this passenger a ride. Thank you."

Would it work? Or would she have to go around to the car owners, soliciting a ride herself? She would if she had to. Daphne waited breathlessly near the bridge as the shore of Cape Cod materialized out of the bank of evening fog. She shifted her weight from foot to foot and played nervously with the wooden toggle of her straw purse.

The *Queen*'s horn had gone off on its approach to Woods Hole before anyone answered the captain's announcement. A tiny elderly lady walked briskly up to the captain and said, very loudly, "I'm Abby Howell and I'll take that passenger to Boston. Who is it?"

Daphne saw the blond captain bending down to the woman and pointing to her. Quickly Daphne made her way over to them. "Can you give me a ride?" she blurted out. "I'd be so grateful. I can pay..."

But the tiny lady cocked her head up, peered at Daphne over her bifocals and said, "I can afford the gas, dear, but I'm in a hurry, so let's not dawdle. You ready?"

"I'm ready," replied Daphne, "and I'm in a hurry, too." She turned to the captain and gave him a brief, wide smile. "Thanks. I promise it won't happen again."

It took an hour and a half flat for Abby to get Daphne to Weston's apartment in Somerville. The lady drove her big twenty-year-old Oldsmobile right down the center of the expressway, oblivious to any other drivers on the road. A thick cushion under Abby raised her almost as high as the top of her steering wheel, and she blithely disregarded such niceties as stop signs and traffic lights. Daphne cringed and slid down in her seat, afraid to look, her right foot automatically pressing a nonexistent brake pedal.

When Abby left her off in front of Weston's building, Daphne heaved a sigh of relief. "Thanks again, Mrs. Howell. I really appreciate the ride. I hope I didn't take you too far out of your way."

"Not a bit. Don't worry, dear. I love to drive. Only got my license ten years ago when my husband died, so it's still new to me. It's a lark." Abby Howell pulled away from the curb, her tires yelping, and zoomed off down the street, leaving a choking cloud of black exhaust behind her.

Weston's car was parked in front of his apartment, and there was a light on in his window. He was home, then. She felt her heart give a big thump of nervousness. Wes would be furious at her arrival. Hadn't he told her expressly to stay out of it?

Daphne stood there in her blue flowered sundress looking at Weston's door. This was typical of her, she knew. She couldn't leave people alone. She had to be in there demanding, pushing.

And where would she stay? Would she have to take Weston's bed again? How thoughtless of her. She knew he wouldn't let her stay at a motel alone. Lord, she'd done it again. Well, there was nothing to do but face the music.

She walked toward his door, her feet dragging, practicing a cheerful smile and a hasty apology. The streetlight reflected sparks off something under Weston's window. Broken glass. Stepping off the walk, Daphne looked closer. Yes, glass. She glanced up. His window was broken, empty but for a few shards left in the frame. How odd. Were there gangs in this neighborhood that did things like that? Or had he forgotten his key?

She tapped at his door. The soft humid night surrounded her like cotton, caressing her bare shoulders and neck and arms. She stood on one foot and rubbed her other one against her calf uneasily. He must be home—his car was there. She knocked again, louder. Maybe he'd gone for a walk.

Timidly, Daphne reached for his doorknob. It turned: the door was unlocked. How curious. She knew Wes always locked doors. So had Brady. She pushed it open and stepped inside, calling his name. She'd wait for him, she decided.

There was broken glass on the floor inside, too. Why hadn't he cleaned it up? Wes was so neat . . . She took another step in. This was a terrible thing to do, barging into someone's home uninvited, unexpected. And it was late, too—nearly ten.

She stopped short in utter shock, her heart flying into her throat. She was frozen there for an unutterably long moment, an eternity, until her muscles moved again.

Wes was lying on the floor in the middle of the room, facedown. Her voice came to her first. "Wes!" she croaked hoarsely. Then her legs responded. She ran, stumbling, and threw herself down beside him on her knees, her heart pounding all the time in agonized cadence: *he's dead, he's dead*.

She was too terrified to roll him over at first. She'd learned in first aid that you never move a person unless you know what's wrong with him. She felt his skin. Thank God, he was warm. His chest moved faintly. He was breathing. Then she saw the blood. She drew in a harsh breath and felt for a wound. It was on his head—a small gouge, a furrow in his scalp. The blood dripped from it to the floor in slow crimson globules. She rolled him over, panting with the effort. His face was pale and streaked with blood, but he was breathing. He was alive!

"It's all right," she heard herself saying, "you'll be all right." She ran to the sink, wet a cloth and then wiped his forehead so that she could see if there was more damage. No.

She looked up then in desperate panic. Whoever had done this could still be there! She ran to the door, panting, slammed it shut and locked it. Then she pulled the curtains over the broken window. My God, what if they were trapped in there!

Hubert had done this! He'd lain in wait for Wes, just as he had for Brady, and shot him. But this time his aim had been off. He must have thought Wes was dead or perhaps someone had come along accidentally to scare him off.

She raced into the bedroom for a pillow and put it under Weston's head, realizing vaguely that she'd lost a shoe somehow.

He groaned. "Wes! Wes!" she half sobbed. "Can you hear me?" She pressed the bloody cloth to his forehead. "Please, please." The hospital. Emergency service. Could she get him into his car? An ambulance? But she was afraid to leave his side, afraid to go to the phone. She eyed it longingly from across the room. He groaned again.

"Wes, please, can you hear me?" *My God, he's dying…*

His eyes opened and blinked. They were unfocused and blank. She bent over him. Blood spotted her skirt. She whispered brokenly to him, having no idea at all what she said. Tears dropped on his upturned face; they were hers, she realized stupidly.

He moved a hand. His eyes cleared, and he blinked a few times. His lips moved faintly. Daphne felt a wild surge of elation. He wasn't dying! "I'm going to call for an ambulance now," she breathed. "Wes, can you hear me?"

A frown clouded his face. His lips formed a word. "No."

"You've been hurt. You need to go to a hospital, Wes," she said slowly, as if to a child.

"No," he said more strongly. "No hospital." He closed his eyes in pain. "No police."

"You have to..."

"No...not safe."

She thought frantically: what was he trying to tell her? *Not safe*. Of course, she realized then, the hospital would have to report a gunshot wound to the police. Then the killer would know Wes was still alive and would try again.

If that were true, the whole responsibility for taking care of Wes, for keeping him safe, for keeping him *alive*, fell on her.

Sinking back on her heels, Daphne put her face in her hands. She was trembling all over as if she had a chill. No help. There was no one to help.

What if he died? She took a deep quavering breath and tried to still her shaking. She'd have to calm herself, to think, to be clever.

They had to get out of Weston's flat. The killer might come back to check. Weston's car was outside. If she could get him to it...

Her first instinct was to run home to the island, but the ferry didn't leave till morning. Still, she'd have to get him out of there right away.

Jim! His brother! She dragged the phone as near to Wes as it would reach, and fumbled through the phone book. Leroux, James. Daphne dialed the number, did it incorrectly and had to dial again. A baby-sitter answered. No, she didn't know when Jim and Nancy would be back. Late, they'd said.

Daphne lunged to the sink and wet a dish towel. She pressed it to his head, where the blood still welled up slowly, endlessly. Pain shivered across his features.

"I'm sorry," she sobbed. "I'm sorry. Please, Wes."

His eyes opened again. "Daphne."

"Yes," she cried, "it's me, Wes."

"Someone shot..." His voice trailed off.

She stroked his cheek, smiling through her tears. He was waking up!

"Get gun..." he mumbled.

Where was it? She looked around wildly.

"In my car."

"Later," she said. "We have to get out of here first, Wes. Can you walk?"

His eyes closed. "Soon," he said. "Help me sit up."

She slid her arm under his back and braced herself. He was heavy. Even helping as much as he could, he was heavy. She got him so that his back was resting against a chair. Sweat stood out in oily droplets on his face. He was putty color. He tried a smile but it appeared as a wan twist of his lips.

"Do you know who did this?" she breathed finally.

"No." He started to shake his head, and then winced.

"You need a doctor!" Daphne wailed.

"No doctor, promise me," he demanded harshly.

"But you're hurt."

"I'll live." He stared at her for a moment, the dried blood on his face giving him a lopsided appearance. "What in hell are you doing here?"

"Wes, I...I got the last ferry. I couldn't stand..."

He groaned. "Hubert, damn."

Her face hardened. Didn't Wes realize who had done this?

"I was going to call," he said. "Hubert never came home."

No, of course not. He was waiting here, to shoot Wes. She stayed silent.

"You have your car?" he asked faintly.

"No, but yours is out front."

"Keys in my pocket." He gestured weakly.

She dug her hand in his pocket, averting her face. His keys were there.

"Damn, I feel like jelly."

"I can help you."

He eyed her silently.

"I'm pretty strong."

His lids fell over his eyes; his head sagged. Crimson drops spattered on his lap.

"Wes, wake up!" she cried, scared.

His head jerked. "Gotta try."

He pushed himself up slowly, holding on to the chair. Daphne pulled off her remaining sandal, found the other on the floor and jammed both into her purse. Wes was leaning on the chair, panting with effort. She got her arm around him and lifted. He was so heavy! Staggering, she tried to support him.

He sagged, dead weight against her. His feet shuffled like those of an old man. Slowly, slowly. The door seemed so far away. And then when they got to it she had to unlock and open it. Would bullets smash into them both? Was the killer waiting for them? The slow, dragging steps across the threshold were pure terror for Daphne. Now! Now he'd shoot. They were sitting ducks and she couldn't leave Wes...

Nothing broke the silence of the warm night. They lurched together down the walk. She could hear Weston breathing hoarsely; his back was damp and sticky with sweat where her arm supported him.

His car was locked. Desperately, she tried keys in the stubborn lock until it opened. He sank onto the seat and his head fell back as if he'd passed out again.

Dashing around to the driver's side, she slid in and then leaned over to see how he was. "Wes," she whispered, "are you all right?"

He mumbled something.

Get out of here, her mind screamed at her. She started the car and found the seat was back much too far for her; she could barely reach the pedals. But there was no time to adjust it. Pulling away from the curb, Daphne watched the road in front and behind. She also scanned the dark buildings, and only turned the headlights on when she got to the corner.

She breathed a sigh of relief when she reached a big thoroughfare with lights and traffic and stores that were still open. Following the street, she headed toward Boston simply because it was familiar territory. Where should she go? She had to find a motel, one where no one could see Wes get out of the car. If someone saw him they might ask questions. She glanced over at him and saw that his head was lolling on the back of the seat. Lights glared luridly on his pale, sweat-slicked face and then slid away.

Stopping at an all-night drugstore, she bought gauze pads and tape and Mercurochrome and a pair of small sharp nail scissors, almost screaming with impatience as the clerk had trouble working the cash register.

Weston's eyes were still closed when she got back to the car. She touched his face softly with her hand and said his name.

"Yeah," he muttered. Then his eyes opened. "Daphne."

"Yes, I'm here. I'm taking you to a motel, okay? You'll be able to rest soon."

She found herself sweating in the car and sticking to the vinyl seat. Her hands felt slippery on the steering wheel and her neck ached with tension. How far did she need to go? She was heading vaguely south, toward Cape Cod. She was sure no one had followed her.

At Quincy, south of the city, she got off the expressway and looked for a motel. The clerk stared at her curiously and then she realized there was blood on the front of her dress and on her hands and her feet were bare. "My husband cut himself," she said, rattled. "He's in the car."

Blindly she filled out the registration card, making up the name and license number and address, and took the key. The room was cool and musty smelling and the air conditioner whirred and rattled in the window. She half dragged Wes out of the car, bracing herself against his weight, and almost falling through the door when she finally got it open. She let him sink back on the bed, as easily as possible, but her arms trembled from the strain.

"Wes?"

"It's okay," he replied in a slurred voice.

"You can rest now, but first I'm going to clean your head. It might hurt."

His eyes flew open, clearing for a moment. "No police," he said firmly.

"No, no, I promise."

"Okay..."

She took his shirt off him, grunting with the effort of rolling him over to get his arms out of the sleeves. Then she stuck it in the sink in cold water to soak the blood out. After shoving towels under his head she tried warm water, gently, to remove the caked blood. Head wounds bleed profusely, she remembered. Maybe it wasn't so bad, then. Next came Mercurochrome, and then she carefully clipped the hair from around the furrow in his scalp. He needed stitches at the very least, she was sure. Then a thick gauze pad, held in place by a bandage wrapped around his head.

The wound seemed to have stopped bleeding. Daphne sat on the edge of the bed and studied his face. He looked drawn and gray. His lashes, too long for a man, lay on his cheeks. His mouth was stubborn even in sleep.

Exhaustion bludgeoned her abruptly. She pulled Weston's shoes off and covered him with a blanket from the other bed. Then she undressed tiredly, tried to sponge the blood off her dress and hung it up on a hanger to dry. His shirt. She wrung it out and hung it up.

If she could only sleep... but she was afraid to. What if he... She wouldn't consider that possibility.

Curious, she thought, turning off every light but a dim one by the bed. Here she was in a bra and panties in a motel room with a strange man, and yet she felt not even a vestige of shyness. Lying down next to Wes, Daphne put an arm protectively over him, in case he moved or woke. Her eyes closed but her body thrummed with anxiety. She deserved it, she thought, despising herself. She'd been the cause of this disaster in the first place. But Wes didn't deserve it. She lay in the dimness, conscious of the shallow rise and fall of his chest, and listening to his occasional mutterings. Tears gathered and slowly, hotly, slid out of the corner of her eyes and dripped onto the pillow.

Once she dozed and jolted awake when Wes moved restlessly, mumbling. "Hubert," he said and then, "Dodie." Who was Dodie?

The night passed in oddly spasmodic time, jerking along nightmarishly.

LIGHT IN HER EYES woke her with a start. It was morning. Wes. She moved carefully, trying not to disturb him.

"I'm awake," he said perfectly clearly.

Daphne sat up quickly. "Wes? Oh, damn, I fell asleep." She felt woozy and heavy-headed.

He was struggling to sit up and she helped him, totally unaware that she was half naked. "How are you?"

"A little the worse for wear," he joked feebly.

"Does it hurt?"

"Like a sledgehammer." He eyed her for a moment and then turned away.

It struck Daphne like a thunderbolt. "I . . . I'm sorry," she stuttered, pulling a blanket off the bed and wrapping it around herself. "My dress was all bloody. It's drying. And your shirt. I didn't mean . . . Last night it didn't seem to matter."

"You did real well, Daphne," he said quietly, his face averted. "Think you can get me to the bathroom?"

She flushed. "Sure. Let me get dressed first."

The blue flowered sundress was still damp in front when she donned it. It didn't matter. By then Wes was sitting on the side of the bed, his head in his hands. She helped him to the bathroom, struggling to hold up his weight, but he seemed a little better. "If I fall in, you can come save me," he said, trying to grin.

When the bathroom door opened she hurried to him. He groped for her tiredly and let her put on his half-dry shirt.

"We're going home, Wes," she explained.

"Where are we?" He seemed so confused.

"Quincy, not far from Boston."

"God, I can't remember…" He felt the bandage on his head. "How'd I get this?"

"I did it."

He was terribly thirsty but she only let him sip slowly. Something she recalled about nausea. When she supported him out to his car, a family loading up their station wagon gaped at them. She ignored them pointedly.

Wes seemed to slip in and out of sleep on the drive to Woods Hole. Daphne almost sobbed in frustration when they got held up by construction on the Southeast Expressway. "Take it easy," mumbled Wes, opening his eyes to find her pounding the steering wheel.

Getting him onto the ferry was utterly exhausting. Everyone stared and gave them wide berth as if they were criminals. Daphne propped Wes up on a bench in a corner and sat close to him, supporting him as she held his hand tightly. The ferry wallowed, causing Wes to sway against her. Finally she gave up and put both arms around him, holding him, not caring that people gawked.

She left him in the ferry building on the island side and ran to get her car. She pulled it right up in front, disregarding the No Parking signs.

Almost there. She didn't know what she'd do alone with a wounded man, but home was safe, secure; she could breathe there and plan. Maybe even call old Dr. Stevens, who was retired now. And Audrey would come from the club and help. She wouldn't be so terrified anymore.

Home. She drove as quickly as she dared, glancing nervously at Wes every few minutes. He looked awful.

Audrey's Saab was parked in front of the house. She should have known Audrey would disobey any direct order. Stubborn! But Daphne thanked heaven for her irrepressible mother. There was someone to help her now.

Wes leaned on her heavily as she stumbled up the front steps. His feet dragged and his breath whistled through his teeth. She kicked open the front door, lugged him through the vestibule and toward the living room. She felt sick with sustained fear and exhaustion.

"Audrey!" she yelled. "Mother!"

Around the corner into the living room. Audrey could help her get him to bed.

In a minute, thought Daphne, she could ease Wes down onto the couch and unburden herself. He was so very heavy. She looked longingly at the couch, stumbled, then edged forward a foot.

"Audrey!" she cried.

There were footsteps behind her, on the staircase. She turned her head. "Audrey, help me!" But it wasn't her mother. No. Suddenly all the blood drained from her face and fear tore at her stomach.

It was Hubert.

CHAPTER NINE

PARALYSIS GRIPPED DAPHNE. Hubert! There in the house! Her thoughts spun futilely as she stood with Weston's weight dragging at her while she stared directly into the traitor's eyes.

"Who's that?" came a voice from somewhere downstairs. "Sam," called her mother once more, "who's out there with you?" And then Audrey appeared from the kitchen, wiping her hands on a towel. She stopped short alongside Hubert. "Daphne? You're here already? And what's happened to Wes? Good grief!"

Everything went haywire then. Daphne breathed, "He's been shot," and Hubert and Audrey relieved her of his burdensome weight and got him to a couch. For a minute, Daphne stood frozen, feeling a fist of fear clench in her stomach. Hubert was there and they were helpless. Then slowly she forced herself to move, to act. She edged over to the fireplace to pick up a poker.

Audrey executed a classic double take. "What *are* you doing?"

Weston was muttering unintelligibly. Daphne took isolated looks at their three faces, the poker still gripped in her hand. She shook her head in confusion; fear was still clogging her thoughts.

"Put that thing down," said Audrey, "and get the emergency medical kit out of the kitchen cupboard."

Hubert was kneeling by Weston's side, unwinding the bandage. "What happened?" he rasped, turning to her.

"I don't know," she said carefully. "I went into Boston because I was worried about Wes and I found him lying on the floor in his apartment . . . like that." She gestured vaguely at Weston's recumbent figure.

Hubert turned back to Weston. Hubert's hands were shaking, Daphne noticed. Slowly, trying to grasp the situation, she lowered the poker and set it down. She looked dubiously from Hubert to Audrey and then went into the kitchen and found the medical kit.

If Hubert had shot Wes, then what was he doing back here? And if he'd returned to permanently silence Audrey and Daphne, then why in the devil was he kneeling alongside the couch, tending to Weston's wound, obviously distraught?

When Daphne returned and handed Hubert the kit gingerly, she said simply, "You better explain what you're doing here."

Hubert continued working on Wes. Without looking up from his task, he replied, "I never left the Vineyard. I just walked for a long time. When I got back here, the place was locked up and empty. I jimmied a window on the beach side and waited for you."

"Sam didn't know where we'd all gone off to," put in Audrey helpfully.

"I tried Weston's number in Somerville several times and finally I fell asleep."

"I woke him this morning," explained Audrey.

"So you came back to the house, then." Daphne gave her mother an admonishing look.

"Only to pick up my blow dryer." Audrey shrugged. "And as long as old Sam was here, well, I stayed."

Hubert looked up at Daphne, his expression grim. "You thought I shot him," said Hubert sadly.

"Yes," Daphne replied in a small voice. "I was certain you'd done it."

"The first morning ferry hadn't even run yet when I found Sam here. He couldn't have been in two places at once," added Audrey.

"I realize that now," Daphne replied tiredly. And then an awful thought slammed into her mind. "If it wasn't Hubert, then who did this to Wes?"

Hubert glanced up into her wide blue eyes. "The man who murdered Brady, the one who sold out his country, Daphne." His eyes locked with hers for a moment, and Daphne felt the truth his gaze held. No, Hubert was not the one.

"Now," said Hubert briskly, "tell me the whole story, every detail."

So Daphne told her story as well as she could, reliving the terrible night. When she was done, Hubert asked a couple of pointed questions, nodding to himself. Suddenly she felt better, as if a burden were lifted from her. Then, relieving her even more, Hubert confirmed Daphne's own diagnosis: Wes had received only a deep graze and the bullet had not penetrated.

"Of course he should see a doctor," said Hubert, "but I suppose you understand why it's not advisable at this time?"

Daphne nodded, biting her lower lip. "It really bled," she explained.

Audrey hugged her daughter. "What a time you must have had, baby. But it's all right now."

"Is it?" Daphne sank down into a chair. "Wes is wounded and here we all are, sitting ducks." She shivered involuntarily.

While they helped Wes up the stairs and back into Felicity's room, Hubert said, "You realize that whoever shot Wes must have thought him dead. At least he didn't come back to finish the job."

"I thought of that. Maybe he got scared off." Gently, Daphne propped a pillow beneath Weston's head. "Is he going to be all right, Hubert?"

"He'll be just fine. I wouldn't hesitate to take him to a doctor if I thought there was any real danger. I imagine he got himself a whopper of a concussion."

Hubert pulled Weston's shirt off and then began stripping him of his pants. "Sorry, ladies," he said brusquely, "but there's no room for false modesty here."

Audrey watched impassively, but Daphne flushed and was glad when Hubert pulled the sheet up over Weston's torso. Still, the image of his lean body remained in her mind. He was wearing red bikini underwear. His stomach was so flat and hard and she couldn't help noticing the line of fine brown hair that widened just over the waistband of the pants.

"When do you think he'll wake up?" asked Daphne in a strained voice.

"Hard to say. A day or two, maybe. Concussions are unpredictable."

"Hubert," Daphne said, "I'm sorry for all this trouble I caused."

"It wasn't you." He stood at the door, ready to leave Weston to rest.

"But it *was* me," Daphne admitted, unable to meet his eye. "I was the one who stumbled onto that box of your old checks." She blushed guiltily. "Not Wes. He wasn't even there. I was hunting for your tennis racket in the garage. I just got too nosy. Then I thought . . ."

Hubert waved a hand in the air. "It doesn't matter anymore."

Daphne wondered just what those large cash withdraw-
als from his account had been for, but she wasn't going to
ask. She'd done enough harm already. And besides, it was
obvious he wasn't paying off a Russian blackmailer or
anything. If that had been the case, none of them would
have been still alive. Relief flooded her to know that it
wasn't Hubert.

But then who was it?

Hubert interrupted her thoughts. "We'll get Brady's
killer. We'll do it somehow." Then he left with Audrey, full
of questions, hot on his heels.

How were they going to uncover the traitor's identity?
If only, she thought, Wes would wake up and help. He'd
think of something. Yet she realized how short the time
was becoming. In just over two weeks the Labor Day
crowds would storm the island for that one last summer-
time escape and Gorvieski would step off the plane in
Boston. The thought of what the Russian diplomat would
face was too chilling to contemplate.

She sat on the edge of Weston's bed and pushed aside
the sandy hair that had fallen onto his bandaged brow.
She'd let him rest now, but her heart cried out for him to
wake up and talk to her.

By the middle of the steamy afternoon, when not even
a faint breeze lifted the lacy curtains that were drawn
across the window and the air was heavy and too close,
Weston had still not come around. Daphne kept watching, dozing off several times in an overstuffed chair, waking with a start only to find that mere minutes had passed
and nothing had changed.

She even tried writing, but with no success. Her mind
was sluggish from heat and tiredness, and her trusty pen

felt like lead in her hand. She put the papers on the floor next to her and her head lolled back against the chair. To-morrow, tomorrow she'd call her editor and tell him she needed an extension. Tomorrow...

Around three, Wes broke out in a sweat and began mumbling gibberish and thrashing around the double bed.

Daphne tried to hold him still. "Shh," she whispered, "take it easy, Wes. Everything's okay. Shh."

She mopped the beads of sweat from his brow with a fresh, cool cloth. She loosened the thin coverlet that had become tangled around his torso during his tossing and then ran the cloth across his chest and down along the flat plane of his bare stomach to cool his feverish flesh.

The sun had drifted across the lazy white sky and was now on their side of the house, striping the room with shadow and gilt. A shaft of afternoon light stole through the drawn curtains and fell across the mahogany head-board, caressing the polished wood, and reflecting onto one of Weston's naked shoulders, bronzing it.

He was beautiful. Whereas Brady had been long and thin, Weston was more compact, more sinewy and curved. She couldn't resist sitting on the edge of his bed a little longer and running the cloth along those lean, corded muscles. Yet she felt guilty as her hands stroked him pos-sessively while he was unable to consent to her ministra-tions.

How *would* he react to her touch? Would he take her in his arms, press her breasts to that lovely, bronzed chest or would he reject her in disgust?

He was so weak and she wanted him strong again, but a part of Daphne wished she could keep him like this for-ever. Her prisoner.

She rose, walked to the window and pulled aside the curtain. What did she want? Brady, of course, Daphne told herself. She would always love him; even in death he never seemed very far away. It almost felt as though he were pushing her and Wes together, as if he were the catalyst and they the two elements to be combined. Brady was dead but life teemed around her, thundering out there in the blue ocean, touching the land with a soft green hand and pulsing red and hot in her veins.

She dropped the lacy curtain and leaned against the wall, looking at Wes with a sob catching in her breast. She wanted to be alive, to be rid of guilt and fear and get on with things. And yet when this ordeal was over—as one day it must be—where would she go from there?

Weston's breathing was easier; she could see his chest rising and falling gently in restful sleep. *I want him,* she thought. She wanted every sinew, every bone, all that smooth flesh to herself. Brady had always said how possessive she could be. And yet if she had Weston in that way, would it merely be on the rebound, an attempt to purge Brady from her heart, a way of rejoining the living? Was that what she was so urgently seeking?

Late in the afternoon, Audrey tiptoed into the room. "How is he?"

Daphne tried to smile. "Better, I think."

"Do you suppose he could eat anything?"

"Maybe later. Soup or something liquid."

"Chicken soup it is, then."

"Where's Hubert?" asked Daphne.

"Oh, Sam's been doing what he calls 'securing the old place' all afternoon. Drawing curtains, fixing that window he jimmied."

"He's afraid that whoever shot Wes will come for us."

"I guess. Anyway, he's awfully upset. Wouldn't even go for some tennis."

"How can you think of tennis, Audrey? My God, someone shot Wes and we'd be foolish to think we're safe for even a minute."

Audrey sighed. "So? What should I do, sit in a corner and quake? Not this islander," she declared, smirking.

"We'll have to think of something, a way to protect ourselves and get the traitor, too. I just can't see how."

"What time is it?" came a parched croak from the bed.

Daphne spun around to see Wes trying to sit up.

"There," said Audrey, "you see? Wes will take care of everything."

"Don't try to sit up," said Daphne, trying to press him back down gently. She turned to Audrey. "Get Hubert, will you?"

Weston's eyes were still glassy and a thin sheen of perspiration dampened his unshaven upper lip. "Hubert's here?" He took a swallow of water from a glass that Daphne held. "I kind of remember him trying to get me up some stairs. What time is it?" he repeated.

"Around five. In the afternoon."

He looked blank. "Hubert?"

"It's a long story, Wes," said Daphne. "Hubert never left the Vineyard. He came back to the house yesterday, found us all gone and simply waited here."

Weston reached up and felt his bandaged head. She wasn't sure he understood.

"Boyo," said Hubert as he crossed the carpet briskly, "it's good to see you awake."

"Yeah, well..."

A moment of awkward silence followed and Daphne wondered if she shouldn't leave the two men alone, to talk, to possibly patch up their differences and the awful mess she herself had caused.

But then Hubert spoke up. "I'm afraid I've got some explaining to do," he began uneasily. "I've been thinking about it since yesterday, on the beach."

"You don't have to," said Wes quickly, and Daphne could see the strain on his face. They should all leave him alone to rest.

"It's been on my chest for too long." Hubert shook his gray head. "For far too long."

Daphne began to edge toward the door. "I'll help Audrey with the soup," she said uncomfortably, nudging her mother.

"No," said Hubert. "You might as well all hear this. It doesn't matter anymore. I'm through with it." He spoke as if to himself. Daphne was embarrassed, but Audrey blocked the door effectively, unbudging, her brow creased in lines of concern.

So, thought Daphne, for all Audrey's glib tongue and teasing, she really did care a little about Hubert Samuels.

"You'll remember, Wes," he was saying, "it all began about fifteen years ago when I was in that auto accident with John Fuller."

"Fuller was killed."

"Yes. And I'd been driving. But what no one knew—at least I thought no one knew—was that I was drunk. Blind, roaring drunk."

"Hubert," said Weston, "if you'd rather not..."

"Let me finish." He stared past Weston's shoulder sadly and went on to explain that the Boston police had made only a cursory investigation of the accident because of Hubert's Secret Service status. He'd walked away with only a cut lip and a hangover and John Fuller, another agent, had been carried away in a plastic bag.

"No one asked me if I'd been boozing," recalled Hubert. "Not even the chief. Although I'm sure anyone could have found out. The chief..."

"Jerry Gallent?" Daphne asked quietly.

"No, no. Jerry was an assistant back then. Still, it was around that time that Gallent was being considered for the top job. Anyhow, I joined A.A.—" Daphne saw Weston nodding, remembering "—and I knew I'd have to live with Fuller's death on my conscience. Then one day I got this call."

"A blackmailer," said Wes softly.

"Exactly. It was the guy who owned the nightclub where Fuller and I had been drinking. First he asked me to help him out. His daughter was having a problem with an ex-husband who was bugging her all the time."

"What did he think you were, some kind of Spenser for hire?" threw in Audrey.

Hubert shook his head. "I don't know. The point is, I was able to tail this ex of hers and persuade the guy to lay off. But it didn't end there. Next thing I knew, it was a small loan—the club owner was cash short. He never paid it back, of course."

"And it snowballed," said Daphne, half to herself.

"It sure did. Every year or so I'd get a call from him. Money. Then last year, he asked me to pay him off, five hundred a month for a year. He swore that would be it."

"And you believed him?" gasped Audrey. "Poor Sam."

"The guy's getting older and his nightclub went under years ago. He needed it, I suppose."

"Hubert," asked Daphne pensively, "why didn't you just tell him no? I mean, the accident happened fifteen years ago and you say you've been sober since. Why couldn't you have gone to Gallent and told him the truth? Surely—"

"Daphne," interjected Wes, "you don't get it. The Service is not your friendly neighborhood grocery store. Gallent would have had to cut Hubert's pension. It's just the way it is."

"I figured," said Hubert, "that after the end of the year if the guy asked for more, I'd tell him where to get off. Maybe he never would have gone to the chief. Who knows?"

"Are you still paying now?" asked Audrey.

"I'm afraid so."

"Boy, it must really strap you," Audrey said bluntly.

Hubert shook his head. "Not as much as losing my pension would. If the chief knew..."

"I don't think," ventured Daphne, "that after so many years, this guy would actually go to Jerry Gallent."

"He might," Wes said. "I assume Hubert didn't want to risk it."

Hubert's eyes narrowed and his fingers moved through his beard in agitation. "I'm done paying, like I said, boyo. I was stupid not to face up to it years ago."

"Good for you," said Audrey. "To hell with this creep."

Hubert grimaced.

"Look," said Weston quietly, his voice trailing away, "you know that whatever happens, Hubert, I'll stand by you the whole way." His eyes closed slowly.

That evening, Daphne tried to work again on a new recipe she'd received from a friend of her mother's: creamy Vineyard corn chowder. The problem was, as always, how to tie in the recipe to local lore so that the reader, the cook, could stand in her kitchen, chop vegetables and be entertained by the story behind the recipe at the same time. It had to be light and fun and informative all at once. Daphne did not feel "light and fun" right then.

She walked down the hall and checked in on Wes at eleven. He was still sleeping peacefully. It felt strange to Daphne to be constantly checking on him in the privacy of his bedroom, to watch him sleep or toss or just roll over. He was breathing deeply, almost snoring: she lowered the open window slightly and then pulled the sheet up around his chest. He was like a child to her, an innocent creature needing care.

And yet, somewhere inside his body existed the man she was beginning to like a little too much for her own comfort—the strong, gentle man who'd been through a lot of pain in his life. He was a man of staunch loyalties who would do anything for his friends, a man of principle, expert at his job, full of energy and confidence in his chosen field. Then there was the other side of Wes Leroux, the hidden side that she could only begin to guess at—the aloofness beneath the easygoing surface that was Weston's method of protecting himself from the pain he was afraid of suffering all over again.

Could anyone break through his smooth, pleasant barrier? She thought maybe she had—slightly—a couple of times. In San Francisco, perhaps. Or was she flattering herself to think she could be the one? Didn't every woman think she was the one who could get to a man?

A thought angered Daphne suddenly as she stood over his sleeping form; hot waves of rage washed over her to think that his mother was out there somewhere with a new family and couldn't even bother to send him a Christmas card. What kind of woman would do such a terrible thing to a child, to any human being? Could Wes think all women capable of such blatant selfishness? Did Wes lump her into the same category?

Daphne took one last look at Weston before quietly closing his door. She knew that the image of his strong wounded body lying there would haunt her long after he was well and this ordeal was history and he was gone from her life.

Hubert glanced up from his magazine when Daphne entered the living room. "I thought you'd turned in already."

"I was checking on Wes. Now I *am* going to bed. I just thought I'd see if you need anything."

"I'm fine. Audrey made me a pot of coffee before she went upstairs."

Daphne sat on an ottoman for a moment. "I hope Audrey isn't driving you too crazy," she ventured.

He shook his head. "At first she did. But now I'm kind of getting used to the things that come out of her mouth."

"Yes," reflected Daphne, "she can produce some pretty incredible statements."

"I don't think she means half of it."

"Oh, she doesn't. It's her way of thinking she's staying on top of it. Getting in the last word and all." Then she started to rise but sat back down again. "You know, Hubert," she said slowly, "we are all behind you on this blackmail business."

"Thanks," he murmured uneasily. "But it's my problem."

"Well, at least you had the courage to quit drinking."

"I don't know if I'd call it courage. It's more like I didn't have the guts to keep *on* drinking."

She smiled. "Anyway, if there's anything we can ever do, myself or Audrey..."

"Again, thanks. But for now you'd better get some rest."

"I'm going to. But there's something else before I go up. It's been sort of coming to me all day."

"What's that?"

"How we're going to flush the traitor, Hubert. What if," she began, musing aloud, "we could make him show his hand. You know, lure him to us?"

He cocked his head and regarded her questioningly.

"It might not be hard. Let's say he thinks Wes is dead. And I assume he must because surely he would have come back to Weston's to finish the job otherwise."

"Maybe," Hubert said carefully.

"Well, then he must know a lot about what's been going on. He must know I'm involved."

"That's why I'm being extra cautious tonight, Daphne. It's more dangerous now for you than it was before. Whoever it is, is on to you and Weston. He must feel you two were getting close to him."

"Good," she said pensively. "So what if we could get him to the island . . ."

Daphne did not go up to bed then; her mind was awake and churning and Hubert was leaning forward in his chair, listening, interjecting, nodding raptly.

It was after one in the morning when she finally climbed the stairs, but even then the thoughts kept coming to her, the plans and contingency plans. She felt afraid, for her idea was dangerous and yet, strangely, there was a kind of excitement growing within her.

She closed her eyes and saw herself: barefoot islander, cook and author, and now she added something else to the picture—sleuth.

CHAPTER TEN

WES AWOKE STARTLED. Sweat dampened the sheet that was twisted around him, and his stomach lurched with nausea. He blinked his eyes a couple of times and licked dry lips. The pull of a half-drawn shade tapped against a windowframe in the moist breeze.

Why did his head hurt so much? And his stomach... He felt as if he had a giant hangover but he hadn't had one since he'd been in the Marines, and he hadn't been drinking, had he?

Lace curtains billowed picturesquely on either side of a tall window. The air smelled fresh. How did he know it was morning?

Frighteningly, he realized that he didn't know exactly where he was. Or rather, he was sure he knew but he couldn't put a finger on it.

What in hell was going on?

He started to sit up and grimaced, his hand going automatically to his head. There was a bandage there and gauze wrapped around it. The spot was too sensitive to touch and his skull felt as if it was splitting.

Disconnected images came to him: Daphne in a blue flowered dress with blood on it, *his* blood, he knew somehow. Car lights smashing into his eyes at night, the sound of glass breaking, strangers' faces gawking, slack with curiosity.

The confusion in his mind unsettled him. It cleared slowly, leaving wisps of ignorance, like a fog reluctant to disperse, clinging in stubborn tatters to hollows. He decided he was at Daphne's house on Martha's Vineyard. He didn't remember getting there, only Daphne's voice urging, murmuring in his ear. Attempting to work backward from there, he recalled getting to his apartment. He'd been walking into his flat; he'd been angry at Hubert, angry at himself, at Daphne.

Glass breaking. A shot. He'd been shot. And somehow Daphne had found him and brought him back here. Then abruptly he remembered the conversation of the day before—Hubert's confession, everything. Or had it been the day before?

He rose from the bed, tottering like an old man. It occurred to him that he had on only his underwear. His clothes were nowhere in sight. He looked around, shrugged, and then pulled the sheet off the bed and wrapped it around himself.

Holding on to the bedpost and a dresser, he made his way toward the door, opened it and leaned on the doorframe for a second, fighting down the nausea.

He heard footsteps down the hall, quick pattering bare feet and then Daphne's voice. "Wes! You shouldn't be up!" She held his arm, steadying him, and led him back to the bed.

"I was just coming up to see if you were awake. Audrey's making you a poached egg and tea, and Hubert's fast asleep."

"Whoa," he said weakly. "I just remembered who I was. Before anything else, tell me what day it is. How long since I was shot?"

She looked at him, astonished. "But yesterday you were okay. You talked to us and I thought I told you . . ."

"Enlighten me, please. I have a helluva memory these days."

"I found you the night before last."

Wes whistled. A whole day was gone. "How did you get me back here? And why were you at my place, anyway?"

Daphne looked away, a faint pink staining her cheeks. "I was worried and I couldn't bear waiting. I was afraid Hubert and you... So I took the last ferry that night and got a ride to your flat." Her eyes filled with tears. "You were on the floor. Oh, Wes, I was so scared. I thought you were dead at first. I didn't know what to do."

"Looks like you did fine," he said softly. "I suppose I didn't thank you."

"You don't have to *thank* me," she said indignantly.

"When someone saves your life you usually thank them."

"Wes, really, I didn't save your life. I dragged you around as if you were a rag doll. And after I'd accused Hubert... It was all my fault."

"Daphne, don't blame yourself. For one thing, I was careless, and for another, you couldn't have stopped it. Whoever took a potshot at me must have waited there for a long time."

"You're trying to make me feel better."

"Don't you want to?" he queried.

She pursed her lips.

"And by the way," he asked, "where are my clothes?"

She blushed too easily. "Audrey washed them. They're downstairs."

"Do you suppose I could have them back?"

"Of course. I'll bring them up with breakfast. Oh, Wes, you seem much better this morning. I was so worried..."

"I've got a hard head, Daphne," he said lightly, touched by her concern.

She insisted on helping him down the hall to the bathroom. To tell the truth, he was glad of her strength. His legs were like macaroni and his head pounded.

When he was through she was waiting for him. She gave him a bathrobe of Hubert's to wear. It was much too short, but it was better than the sheet. His shirt and pants were folded neatly on a chair in his room, breakfast awaited on a tray and his pillows had been fluffed.

"Hubert said you shouldn't eat much," Daphne explained, setting a tray in his lap. She wore red-and-white striped shorts and a red T-shirt with a scoop neck. Bare feet. Her hair was tousled. She looked very fresh and young. Wes glanced away from where she sat on an old pine rocker and sipped his tea. A kind of wonderment seized him; this girl—this woman—had done as good a job as a professional, gotten him cleanly away under the most trying circumstances. She hadn't lost her wits or her nerve.

"You'll have to rest a lot, Hubert says." She was trying to look stern.

"Hubert says, Hubert says," Wes mumbled through a mouthful of egg. "You realize, Daphne, that I've lost a day and there's a week and a half left till Labor Day?"

"Yes." She averted her face and stared out of the window. "You have any ideas?"

"Not at the moment. I'm still a bit dingy," he said dryly.

"Hubert and I have one," she said too casually, looking at her fingernails.

"Oh?"

"Would you like more tea?"

"Daphne, what's this scheme you and Hubert have cooked up?"

"You were sort of out of it so I...we thought of the most obvious thing. The traitor thinks you're dead, right?"

"Theoretically."

"So I'm the only one left who's a real threat."

"So?"

"This person has to be flushed out, Wes, and soon," she said carefully.

"I won't allow it, Daphne."

"Won't allow what?"

"You two have cooked up something dangerous."

"Not *very* dangerous," she answered. "Look, Wes, you're in no condition to do anything. Somebody's got to."

"Not you."

"But I'm the only one who can do it. We lure him, you see. Oh, we haven't decided on all the details yet. He'll come to get me but you and Hubert will be here. That way I'm protected and he shows his hand and we've got him."

"I don't like it, Daphne. You'd be exposing yourself. These things never work exactly as they're planned. There are always unexpected problems, dangerous problems."

"Look, Wes," she said in a suddenly hard voice, "this man killed Brady and nearly killed you and I'm not going to just sit around on my rear end and wait until he kills someone else!"

"And Hubert agrees to this?"

"It's the only way."

Wes rubbed his eyes with a thumb and forefinger. "Let me think about it. There must be another way."

"There's no time," she reminded him.

"Damn!" he muttered. His head hurt like the devil, and he couldn't think straight with that infernal pounding on his brain.

"Um," began Daphne timidly. "There's something else I'm a little worried about. Your window. It was broken. Isn't it dangerous to leave it like that? I mean..."

His window. He tried to think. His head ached so. "I haven't even got a TV set," he began. But an idea struck him. "It's got to stay broken, Daphne, so that if—when— the killer checks, he'll see it's still broken and figure I'm dead."

"I was just worried about your stuff, but I guess you're right. Well, then, I'll send Hubert in when he wakes up. He was up all night on sentry duty," she said. "Try to rest. You don't look so good."

He essayed a smile; it was crooked and halfhearted. "Yeah, I bet. I feel like death warmed over."

She started out of the room, her saucy red-and-white shorts stretched distractingly over her round bottom as she exited.

"Hey, Daphne," he began.

She stopped and turned to him questioningly.

"Thanks."

She reddened and turned away. "Get some sleep," she murmured.

He dozed off, unable to concentrate on the problem at hand. When he awoke Hubert was sitting in the old rocker eating a fat sandwich.

"So, me boyo, how's the head?" Hubert grinned.

"Hurts like hell."

"And well it should. You're lucky, Wes."

"What's this plot you and Miss Farway have cooked up?" he asked grumpily, pushing himself up in the bed.

"All her idea, Weston. That girl is a paragon among fe- males. She sets herself up as bait. The guilty party comes, tries his trick, we nab him. It's simple."

"Real simple," he grumbled. "And Daphne's neck is at stake. No way, Hubert."

"It's the only way, Wes," said Hubert soberly. "There's no time for anything else. You tried and it got us three suspects. Well, four actually, but one—" he pursed his lips and looked down "—conveniently cleared himself."

"Hey, I'm sorry about that. I never believed..."

Hubert waved a hand in dismissal. "Not another word, boyo. It's a closed file. Anyway, we have three suspects. We have to narrow it down pronto."

"There must be some other way!" railed Weston.

"She can handle it," said Hubert quietly. "Let's face it, our Miss Farway has the instincts of a real sleuth. She hasn't made a wrong move yet."

Wes didn't like the idea at all but he couldn't see any way out. They were both right, of course. Daphne was the perfect bait. His mind began sifting possibilities. He cursed his helplessness.

"You hungry?" asked Hubert.

"A little."

"Good sign. I shall inform room service."

"Damn, I hate being a burden," objected Wes.

"One must learn to give in gracefully," intoned Hubert.

Audrey brought up a tray for Wes. Chicken soup, Jell-O, a glass of milk.

"Hospital food," said Wes dubiously.

"And that's exactly where you should be, young man," Audrey replied smartly.

He shut up and ate. Hubert finished his sandwich while Audrey pulled up a chair and sat herself down.

"Are you watching me eat?" asked Wes finally.

"I'm watching you improve," said Audrey. She turned to Hubert. "Isn't he looking better, Sam?"

"He certainly is."

"All this excitement," breathed Audrey. "I haven't had so much fun in years."

"This is very serious, Mrs. Farway," said Wes.

"I know, that's what makes it so much fun. It's like a Wimbledon final with matched sets and a deuce going."

Hubert looked at Weston and winked drolly.

"You know," said Audrey, leaning back and crossing trim legs, "your friend Sam here isn't a bad tennis player. Out of practice, but he's got a fair backhand."

"I only lost by one game," said Hubert angrily, "and the name's Hubert, not Sam."

"That's what I said." Audrey was unperturbed.

"Where's Daphne?" asked Wes.

"Doing some work. She's got a deadline in two weeks."

"Uh, Mrs. Farway, if she's not too busy, could you ask her to come up? I have to talk to her."

"If she's too busy to talk to *you*, she's stark raving mad," declared Audrey.

Wes had dozed off again when he heard his door swing ajar quietly. He opened his eyes to find Daphne standing indecisively on the threshold.

"Come in, I'm not asleep," he said.

"Mother said you wanted to see me."

"Sit down."

She sat.

"I'll consent to your plan," he said, almost harshly.

She nodded soberly, her eyes wide.

"You will do exactly as I say. No winging it, Daphne. This man will be out to kill you."

She shuddered delicately.

"You will call each man: Mike Toth, Walter Greenburg and Jerry Gallent. You will introduce yourself, then tell each one that you know he killed Brady to cover up his own treachery. You can go into details if necessary, the things Brady really did tell you—like where the itinerary was handed over, to whom and so on. You will make a date for each of them to come out here to see you because you want to 'talk it over.'" He paused, licking his lips.

"The innocent ones will come to clear their names and the guilty one will come to kill, or at least to case the place—and you."

"Hubert and I will be hiding. I think before long it'll be pretty obvious who the guilty one is. If he tries something right then, it's simple. If not, we just have to be on guard for whenever he does try."

"When do I do this, Wes?" she asked.

He leaned back against the pillows and felt his head throb. "As soon as possible," he said tonelessly.

"And what do I say when they get here?"

"That's what we'll work on next," he said tiredly.

"Oh, I'm sorry. You're exhausted. We shouldn't be discussing this now."

"It has to be done," he said.

"But you're so... you're so... I mean..." She stopped short, overcome by some emotion Wes dared not name to himself.

"I'm okay, really," he attempted.

"You're not okay. You were half-dead when I found you. Bleeding. It was so scary. Oh, Wes..."

Were her eyes filling with tears? It couldn't be. Not over him. He suddenly felt uncomfortable, hemmed in, afraid to hear one more kind, caring word from this woman. Afraid of what? he asked himself. Afraid that he might return her feelings and leave himself wide open to intolerable pain? He shut his eyes, willing her to leave him; he was too weak right now, too vulnerable to her solicitude.

When she left, he got up. He needed to test his strength; he had to feel in control of the situation. He felt a little better than he had that morning, a little stronger. It would take time for him to heal completely, but time was the one thing he didn't have.

He cursed himself again and walked around the room, despising his shakiness. He stood at the window and looked out, squinting, over the sand dunes to the sea, where a wavering line of white foam crept relentlessly onto the shore.

A figure in a bright blue bathing suit picked its way down a narrow path to the beach, a shocking pink towel over its shoulder. Daphne. She walked steadfastly out through the surf and then plunged cleanly into the water and began to swim. The sun glinted off each of her elbows in turn as she stroked and the droplets of water flashed like streams of diamonds from her arms. Her head was a seal-smooth cap of wet gold.

He recalled with sudden clarity, without any connecting thought, Daphne in a bra and panties, leaning over him. Where? Why? They hadn't . . . It escaped him.

She came out with water sluicing from her body, sleek, unself-conscious. He felt himself grow hard at the sight. Confused, guilty, he turned away from the window. Disgust was a worm eating away at his innards.

That evening Wes insisted on descending the stairs to have supper with the others. He felt much better when he had showered, carefully avoiding getting the bandage wet, shaved and dressed.

Hubert followed him downstairs—"in case he got weak and fell." He felt foolish and decidedly embarrassed at being the center of attention, especially when Daphne and her mother met him with applause at the bottom of the stairs.

Audrey had a glass of wine in her hand but Daphne had to make the phone calls and Hubert didn't drink and no one would consider letting Wes imbibe any alcohol yet.

"Party poopers," pouted Audrey.

Daphne sat down in front of the telephone, and Wes went over her lines with her once again. Finally he leaned back in his chair, folded one leg over the other, rubbed his temples and looked at her. "As Audrey would say, 'the ball's in your court now, Daphne.' "

DAPHNE REALIZED that she'd be lying if she told herself she wasn't nervous. But she'd been over and over it in her mind, and the plan still seemed sound. The question remained, however: just how good an actress was she? She was thinking of herself as a black widow spider, enticing men to her to destroy them.

She felt Weston's eyes on her as she reached for the telephone. Her nerves were raw, jumping under her skin. She held a slip of paper with numbers on it in her hand and knew her palms were perspiring. Then, to make matters worse, Audrey and Hubert popped into the room.

"What is this," she snapped, "center stage or something?"

"You don't have to be so touchy," said Audrey loftily. "I was only going to ask who's paying for these calls."

"Mother!" said Daphne.

"Send the bill to the office," put in Hubert hastily, "*after* this is all over."

"Don't think I won't," warned Audrey.

"Will you all get out of here and leave me alone?" demanded Daphne. "I've got stage fright."

Hubert and Audrey left, trading witticisms, but Wes stayed, slumped in his chair, looking pale.

"Go on," he said. "Get it over with."

She dialed Mike Toth's number. It rang five times before he answered, and she was breathless by the time she heard his voice.

"Mr. Michael Toth?"

"Yes."

"My name is Daphne Farway, Brady Leighton's fiancée. You remember Brady." She tried to keep her voice very cool and impersonal. "He was killed."

"Miss Farway. I am so sorry. Yes, Brady and I—"

She cut him off. "I happen to know that you murdered Brady, Mr. Toth."

There was a moment of stunned silence on the phone. Then she heard, *"What?"*

"You murdered Brady because he found out about your deal with the Russians."

"What deal? Are you crazy, Miss Farway? Is this some kind of joke?"

The hardest part was getting him to take her seriously. Eventually he promised to be there at two the next afternoon.

"I'll look forward to seeing you, Mr. Toth," she said, and hung up.

"Good," said Wes. "Next one."

Jerry Gallent was next. She got him away from the dinner table and he sounded irritated. "Oh, Miss Farway, how are you?" he said in his hearty, smooth voice. His tone changed when she recited her lines. "You are unhinged, Miss Farway. You need help," he croaked.

"I'd like to talk to you as soon as possible," she said emotionlessly. "Maybe we can come to some arrangement."

The date was made. She wondered if either of the two men had been truly shocked or just frightened at being found out.

Walter Greenburg was not home. She'd have to wait and try again later. She was filled with equal measures of relief and frustration.

Supper was salad and rolls and broccoli quiche. The conversation was mostly about whether the house was secure and who would stay up to watch that night. Wes offered but everybody shouted him down. He was barely ambulatory, Audrey snapped.

"I could *sit* all night," he offered but they all decided he was too much of a risk as a guard.

"I guess I should try Walter again," Daphne offered, sighing.

Walter Greenburg answered immediately, a thin-voiced man who spoke very quickly and intensely. Of the three, he sounded the most upset. "I wouldn't murder anybody!" he yelled. "You've lost your mind!"

"Why don't we discuss it, Mr. Greenburg, at my place?"

The date was made. All three were coming.

"You did well, Daphne," said Wes.

She grimaced. "I'm getting great at lying. What a talent."

"This was your idea, remember?"

"Sure. I forgot for a minute there." She gave a shaky little laugh.

"You didn't have to make those calls."

"I *did* have to make them. It's just that, well, it was a little different from what I'd imagined. These are lives we're playing with, and two of them are innocent."

"It's always like that, Daphne," he said gently. "Forget it for now. Come on, take me for a walk. I'm sick of four walls."

"Oh, sure," she said derisively, "so you can do push-ups on the beach."

"No push-ups, I promise."

"I don't think you should be exerting yourself."

"Well, a walk on the beach is hardly exerting myself. I need the air. For pete's sake, they let heart patients out of bed right after surgery. I'm not an invalid."

"But is it safe? It's getting dark."

"You just talked to our three suspects in Boston. I think we're safe for now."

Daphne looked doubtfully at him for a moment before she pushed open the porch door. "I'm not carrying you back up the dune, though," she said, smiling, as she led the way.

The sun was setting, reflecting orange and purple streaks off a cloud bank. The tide was out, leaving a broad hard-packed sandy swath that made easy walking. The evening air smelled of the sea, salty and pungent.

"It's going to rain tomorrow," said Daphne.

"How do you know?"

She pointed. "Those clouds." Then she pulled off her sandals and walked along the edge of the water. "I love bare feet and I love squishy sand between my toes." She regarded him seriously, her head cocked. "You know, you look a little like Yankee Doodle with that bandage."

He laughed. Then he took his loafers off and waded into the shallow water. The sun's rays burnished a path across the waves from west to east. Sea gulls dipped and soared through molten bronze swells, flashing white, then gold, then white again. Their harsh calls cut the air like the cries of damned souls. Daphne stood, ankle deep in the water, her head thrown back, watching the birds and the sky, feeling the breeze caress her face and wash away the ugliness and deception.

THE WATER GURGLED over Weston's toes, cool and silky, then sucked away, tickling and leaving his feet deeper in the sand. It had been years since he'd felt anything like it. Had he really been so cut off from physical pleasure?

Daphne stood like a statue. He knew she was feeling something that he never could and he was jealous of her ability to be so natural, to draw strength from her surroundings.

She stood there, spontaneous and relaxed, until the sun set completely and the western sky turned to a dark blue. Finally Daphne looked down, wiggled her toes in the shallow water and remarked, "I make you very uncomfortable. I can tell."

"Not at all..."

"You don't have to lie."

He was struck silent, like a chastised schoolboy. The water ran seaward between his toes, pulling at the sand. Out on the ocean the running lights of a boat cut through the darkness. It was very still. Daphne was a shadow against the water. He felt that she was very far away, and it saddened him unaccountably.

"I'm uncomfortable with a lot of people," he finally said. "Don't take it personally."

"You're not with Hubert or my mother or your sister-in-law," she retorted.

"They're safe," he said without thinking.

"And I'm dangerous?"

He didn't answer.

"Who's Dodie?" she asked abruptly.

"Dodie? What?"

"You talked about Dodie that night in the motel. You mentioned other names, too, but I knew them."

"Dodie is Hubert's daughter."

"Are you uncomfortable with her?"

"Dodie? We lived together in the same house. Like brother and sister. She's married and has three children."

"Oh."

He wanted suddenly to tell Daphne how he felt about her, to unburden himself of the guilt he felt and receive her absolution. It was unthinkable. And yet the thought of keeping his feelings from her, of hiding those terribly dangerous sentiments he harbored was equally anguishing.

She could heal him, he sensed instinctively, make him happy and whole as he'd never in his life been. He savored the possibility of loving her like a morsel of the most delicious chocolate, tasting it until every bit was melted away.

Yes, she made him uncomfortable, he wanted to shout at her. She made him crawl with desire.

She came to stand next to him, and he swore he could feel the heat radiating from her skin. It was as if she were deliberately provoking him.

"Do you think we'd better go back?" she asked. "You have to climb that hill."

"Don't mother me!" he commanded harshly.

"I . . . I'm sorry, Wes." Her voice was hurt.

He took a deep breath and felt a stirring in his groin. He turned away. "Sorry," he muttered.

Her hand touched his arm lightly; a shock went through him, as violent as an electric current.

"Did I do something to make you mad?" she asked in a small voice.

A strangled noise came from his throat and he jerked away from her touch, turning to face her in the darkness. He wanted to tell her to leave him alone. He wanted to warn her, but his voice died before reaching his lips. He could only look at her face, a pale oval in the dusk. Those lips, to touch those soft pink lips and feel her skin again.

She put a hand out and brushed his face, a butterfly-light stroke. He groaned.

"Wes . . ." she began, "I . . ."

"Please don't say anything." He felt that he was bursting with need, bursting to pull her into his arms and savage her, to possess every ounce of her.

Again, she stroked his cheek, tenderly, reluctantly. He felt the ache in his groin and cursed it silently. "Damn," he mumbled. Then, in a swift, defiant motion, he pulled her up against him. "This is no good," he said, before his mouth caught hers in a hard, tormented kiss.

Desire, so long repressed, flared within him. Daphne responded in kind, reaching her arms around his back, pressing those full breasts to his chest, opening her mouth to receive the urgent thrust of his tongue. He felt his hardness burn against her pelvis, and her sharp intake of breath as their lips searched each other's, twisting and groping.

A thought, unbidden and ugly, flashed through his head. Brady. She'd kissed Brady like this, pressed her round woman's body to his, accepted his love, given her own.

He pulled away, tortured, dropped his hands and drew in a painful breath.

"Wes," she said softly in the soughing darkness. "Don't pull away from me."

But he couldn't speak. Silence encased them horribly. Brady, he kept thinking. Brady Leighton had made her happy. Utterly, wholly content. And good ol' Weston Leroux? He'd never in his life made anyone happy.

"Please don't do this to us," she was saying, "please, Wes."

His voice came out a hoarse whisper. "I need to be by myself." He turned then, as if in shock, and headed back toward the house.

CHAPTER ELEVEN

IT RAINED the following afternoon, the afternoon that Michael Toth was due to arrive at the Farway house. The dismal weather did nothing to lighten Daphne's mood. She looked down at the half-finished recipe in front of her. Vineyard Corn Chowder. She cleared her mind and launched in.

Even as Felicity Hawthorne thickened the pot with a half cup of sweet butter, a quart of cream and a cup of flour, she knew the storm was worsening at sea and that Edmund Hawthorne was out there somewhere, his whaler tossing about like a bit of flotsam on the turbulent ocean. Edmund, her heart cried out, make safe port, my love. She peeled five potatoes and cubed them, enough hearty fare for her six children and Edmund. She placed them in the pot as the wind howled and moaned and flung the island foliage about. One onion, diced and sautéed, went into the pot. Two cups of corn. She salted to taste and ground pepper into the slow rolling liquid, crumbled bacon into bits and added that fifteen minutes later. In an hour, when Edmund did not arrive in time for the meal, she supped with the children. But Felicity had no appetite, so great was her fear for her brave husband, Edmund Hawthorne of the whaler *Gracious*. The knock on the door came just after the children were abed.

Edmund was lost at sea. The following morning, as a bright sun and a calm sea prevailed, Felicity was found on the beach, drowned—gone, the mournful children were to say, in search of her beloved Edmund.

It is related on the Vineyard that sometimes when a good wife prepares corn chowder, a haunting moan can be heard coming from the sea as the family seats itself around the supper table. It is Felicity, mourning her loss for all eternity.

Daphne put down her pen and sighed. Felicity's story always touched her. Audrey, of course, was the first to tell visitors to the Farway house that Felicity and Edmund Hawthorne had occupied the house during the 1860s. They had slept in Weston's bedroom.

"Daphne?"

She started and spun around in her chair. "Oh. Wes," she breathed, a hand going to her chest.

"Seems I'm always scaring you," he said. "Did I interrupt your train of thought?"

She shook her head. "Not really. I need to put this aside and rewrite it later."

"Well, I was just checking. We haven't seen you for an hour or so. Audrey has lunch ready."

"I'll be right down."

He turned to leave, and then hesitated. "About last night..."

Daphne could feel heat rising up her neck. "Yes?"

"I didn't mean for that to happen. I guess I'm apologizing."

She looked at him searchingly. What did he want from her? Did he require her to apologize, too, to tell him that she hadn't meant it to happen, either? But that was a lie.

Perhaps Wes could deceive himself, but it was time for her, at least, to be honest.

She cleared her throat and sat up straight. Once again, irrelevantly, she noticed the length of his lashes. "I'm sorry you feel that way," she said frankly. "I guess what I mean is that I wanted it to happen. I wanted you to kiss me. I won't lie."

He leaned against the doorframe as if dazed. "Daphne, I ..." he began.

"Let me finish," she said. "I can't help it if I like you. I'm human, Wes, and I'm alive and I need to be held and kissed and ... loved," she dared to admit. "That doesn't mean that I'm asking for a commitment or anything of the kind. I'm lonely and, well, you're here and ... Brady can never be here again."

"Daphne—" his green eyes searched her face "—I'm not the one."

"Wait a minute," she said quickly. "I'm not asking you to be the *one*. There may never be anyone that special again. I don't know. But I'll be damned if I'm going to stop looking or give up my dreams because Brady's gone. Emily Dickinson I am not." She knew her voice had risen and become choked and she tried to calm herself. "So go on your merry way, Wes. I'm not going to latch on to you like some infatuated schoolgirl."

"Daphne ..."

She put up a hand. "But if you don't want me, then we'll be friends. I'm a big girl. I can handle it."

"What can I say?"

"Nothing. Just go down and have your lunch and forget it. I'd be the last one to try to chink away at the barrier you've set up."

His back stiffened perceptibly. "Okay, I'll leave you alone. I am sorry, though, that I can't fill Brady's shoes for you. It will take a pretty exceptional man to do that.'' He turned and walked out the door and she could hear him striding down the hall, his steps slow and resigned.

He *was* exceptional, she thought, but he'd be the last person to recognize it. She wondered what in the devil had gotten into her. Was she that frustrated and aching that she had to take it out on Weston? Couldn't she leave him out of it, leave him alone? Yet Daphne knew that it wasn't in her nature to simply let those she cared about slip away so easily.

The next move was his, she thought, as she made her way downstairs to the living room. That is, if there was going to be a next move.

It was a few minutes past two when Audrey sounded the alarm. ''There's a cab coming!'' she shrieked loudly enough to wake even Felicity.

Daphne's heart quickened. *Toth was here.*

Suddenly she couldn't remember the first thing Weston had told her. Her lines were gone completely, and her mind was as blank as if they'd never existed.

She stood in the vestibule at one of the long windows with its uneven whorled glass and stared out into the fog and mist and grayness. Horrible island weather. Obviously Moshop, the legendary Indian giant, had lit his pipe and settled down for a smoke. Or so the islanders liked to tell visitors. She could see the taxi bumping slowly toward the house and hear the others taking their places.

Her thoughts flew in a frantic whirl, and her mind kept picturing Brady that hot July night. He had been going to face...who? Had it been Mike Toth?

She knew Audrey was slipping out the back door, making her way through the undergrowth to her Saab, which was parked out of sight on the main road near the entrance to the Farway drive.

Hubert was in the next room behind the Chinese screen, and Weston took his place behind the door leading from the living room to the hallway. Both men had their guns loaded and ready. Everyone was set, except for Daphne, who couldn't for the life of her remember a syllable of Weston's patient coaching.

She was frozen to her spot. A man whom she assumed to be Mike Toth was instructing the taxicab driver. Then he turned, scanned the three floors of the old sprawling Victorian and began heading toward the front door.

Dear Lord! Daphne thought. What was she supposed to say?

He rang the bell. Her heart squeezed in fright. Images tormented her: Toth would see Wes or Hubert in their hiding places, she would suffer and fumble and not make the least bit of sense to Toth, Toth would pull a gun on her and Weston wouldn't be able to get to her in time!

She took a deep breath, straightened her navy blue sweater, adjusted her blue denim skirt and pulled open the front door.

"Daphne Farway?" he said, standing there in a suit, hat and raincoat, his shrewd blue eyes taking her in cautiously.

"Yes," she managed, her mouth cotton dry, "you're Mr. Toth. Come in, please." Oh, no, she thought, Wes had told her to be hard and callous. She'd have to alter her behavior.

She led him into the living room, and almost offered him a cup of coffee, for goodness' sake, but then she checked herself.

"Sit down," she said, "if you want." There, that was better.

He removed his hat, revealing a shaven head and, after searching the room for a minute to case his surroundings, he finally sat. She held her breath.

"You alone?" He had a very faint foreign accent.

Daphne shrugged. "Sure. I wouldn't want my mother to hear this. She's off running errands." Daphne had almost said, "playing tennis," as previously planned. Tennis, in the rain?

"Let's get down to business," said Mike Toth in a coldly impatient voice. "I have a cab waiting."

"Okay, I'll give it to you straight, Mr. Toth." Daphne sat down opposite him, her back to where Wes and Hubert were hiding so she wouldn't be tempted to keep glancing in their direction. She gulped and plunged in. "You killed Brady because he discovered that you were giving information to the Russians."

"Me?" He laughed. "Don't you know Hungarians hate the Russkies?"

"But not all of them do," she said.

"What's this information I was supposed to have given them?"

"Gorvieski's itinerary."

"What the hell for?" Toth seemed calm. Maybe they were wrong about him...

"To assassinate him."

"Holy cow, lady, that's pretty farfetched." His vaguely Slavic features pulled into a frown.

"You must admit, Mr. Toth, that you appear very suspicious. There are your Hungarian connections, which are hardly on the side of freedom and justice for all."

His mouth formed a thin line. "How do you know about that?"

"I know what Brady told me before he died," she said coolly, but all the while her heart pounded frighteningly.

Toth jumped to his feet, sudden anger darkening his square face. "You *are* out of your mind, lady!"

Fear clutched at Daphne's stomach. She'd pushed him over the edge. Desperate, she longed to turn and look in Weston's direction to reassure herself, but she knew she didn't dare.

Toth began to pace the carpet. "I don't believe this. Brady told you I'm a traitor! This is crazy!" His accent intensified as his anger grew. "I'm supposed to come all the way out to this godforsaken rock and listen to this garbage!" He spun around on her like a trapped animal. "I refuse to believe it!"

"You might as well come clean," she said, positive that he was going to attack her at any second.

Toth was still glaring at her, his head thrust forward menacingly. "Come clean?" he repeated. "You want me to stand here and admit I'm a murderer and a traitor?" Suddenly he cast his eyes around the room. "What have you got—a hidden tape recorder or something?" He began moving around the room again. "Who's here, the police? Maybe even my chief?" He walked toward the Chinese screen.

Daphne almost fainted from panic. "No, don't be silly."

"Then what are you after?"

"Money," she said flatly. She was watching him like a hawk, terrified that he was going to discover Hubert. "Money," she said again, "that's all I want. I don't give two hoots about Gorvieski. And as far as Brady is concerned…" She had not rehearsed this part; it just came out logically. "I feel I should be compensated."

That stopped him in his tracks. "Compensated?" he breathed. "You are quite a woman, aren't you, Miss Farway? Quite a woman."

Daphne felt dirty and ugly, but she couldn't afford to let him see how frightened she was. She covered herself by laughing. "Call me what you want, Mr. Toth. I don't care what you think, really. Just consider what I've said and you and your friends can walk away from this home free. It's a small price to pay, actually. I want a hundred thousand dollars. Tell your Communist pals. Now I think you better go."

"I'll go, all right," he said acidly. "But you've got the wrong guy. I don't give a damn what Brady told you. It's not me. For all I know, you've made this whole thing up. You could be crazier than hell, lady."

"I think you know better." She came to her feet as if to walk him to the door but she kept wondering: was he going to try to kill her then?

He looked suspiciously around the room again. No, Daphne thought, he wouldn't try to harm her right now. But later, when he felt it safe to sneak back into the house—today, tomorrow.

At the door, Mike Toth turned to her. "If you don't get this money," he asked, "what do you plan to do?"

"I plan to go to the authorities, to your chief."

"Even if I'm innocent and someone has made a pretty goddamned serious mistake?"

He sounded so sincere, so sure of himself, that she could almost believe him. "You'd have to prove your innocence to me, wouldn't you?"

He nodded slowly, his slightly slanted blue eyes fixed on her, chilling Daphne to the bone. "I would. And I could prove it. But not until my career was finished and my family disgraced."

Daphne shrugged eloquently, reminding herself that it could be Toth; he might have been the one who shot Brady down in cold blood and then tried to kill Weston. "That's your problem," she replied. "For now, you think about that money and I expect you'll be calling me, Mr. Toth."

"Oh, you'll hear from me, lady, I promise you that." He ducked his head against the cold slashing rain and headed toward the taxi.

Daphne closed the door with a quiet click, heard the cab pulling out of the sandy drive and leaned against the door in exhaustion. "He's gone," she whispered. Then more loudly she called, "You can come out now. He's gone."

Wes was by her side quickly. "Are you all right?"

A sob caught in her breast. What a stupid question to ask! Was she all right? Of course she wasn't! She'd lied, threatened, blackmailed, thrown herself out as bait and dirtied Brady's memory.

Daphne looked up into his concerned face and loathed him. She hated them all. Then suddenly he was reaching out to touch her, and she ached to be held in his strong arms and comforted. But that, she knew, would be the final betrayal. Unable to endure another moment of the sordid charade, Daphne turned and fled up the staircase, locking herself in her room, away from Weston and his blasted pity.

For a while she merely cried, pounding her fists on her quilt and feeling sorry for herself. Then, when the telephone rang below, she picked up the extension in her room and listened.

"I followed the cab just like you said." It was Audrey. "Toth got out and paid the driver and got on the ferry."

"You saw it pull away from the dock?" Weston asked on the other end.

"You bet I did. He won't be back...at least for a while."

"Thanks, Mrs. Farway. Come on home now."

Daphne showered, a long steamy shower, to ward off the chill she felt. Then she rubbed a clear circle in the mirror and stared at herself. She was red and puffy eyed, like an ugly old lobster. She splashed cold water on her face and looked again. Still awful, just like a child after a crying jag.

She put on powder and eye shadow and slipped into khaki slacks with big pockets and a long wool shirt that she sashed with a wide belt. She fluffed her short curly hair with her fingers and put a smile on her lips.

She'd asked for it. She'd been through Brady's death; she'd chased all over the continent hunting down clues to a traitor's identity, and then set herself up as bait for a killer. She was not about to lose it now. Oh, perhaps a little self-pitying cry was forgivable, but she was going to see this through to its conclusion.

Wes was sitting with Hubert in the living room when Daphne padded in. He looked up with a raised brow, no doubt expecting her to lash out at them.

"Hi," she said brightly. "Audrey back yet?"

"She's in the kitchen," said Hubert, exchanging a glance with Wes.

"I'll just go help her with dinner, then. See you." She smiled, noticed Wes staring at her in puzzlement, and made her exit.

Audrey was peeling carrots in the sink, humming to herself.

"Hi," said Daphne. "Need some help?"

"Oh, you're back to normal, I see."

"Now, what does that mean?"

"Oh, Wes said you handled that Toth guy really well, but that you were kind of shook up afterward."

"I was upset." Daphne found another peeler in the utility drawer and began scraping potatoes for Audrey's stew.

"You never were much of a liar," remarked her mother. "Even when you were a kid, you used to tell me that you hadn't been out playing in the sand when your face was caked in it and you'd turn red as a beet."

"It was dreadful today. Worse than anything I'd bargained for. It kept running through my head that Mike Toth might not be the one."

"Hubert said that he called this friend of his in New York and found out that the relief organization Toth sends money to is on the up-and-up."

"He did?" Daphne was aghast. "Well, why didn't anyone tell *me* that?"

"Wes said this morning that you should believe Toth guilty. The more so, the better. I guess he didn't want you going all soft on Mike Toth." Audrey shrugged.

"That's interesting," said Daphne, annoyed that Wes had withheld information from her, and feeling like a heel for what she'd put Mike Toth through.

"Excuse me," came Hubert's voice from the door. "Am I interrupting?"

"Oh, Sam," said Audrey sweetly, "come on in and help us women. The company would be marvelous."

Daphne swallowed hard. "If you'll excuse me," she said, "I think I'll join Wes in the living room."

"He's on the porch," called Hubert. "It stopped raining."

Daphne found him putting out the dry cushions on the bamboo furniture. "Hello," she said, stepping out into the golden afternoon light. "Need help?"

"All done." He looked at her and Daphne's heart did a flip-flop.

"Sit down," he said, "and let's talk. I'll get us something to drink."

"All right." She watched as he disappeared into the house and then returned with two glasses of iced tea. He was his old self once again, charming, gentlemanly, pleasant. He'd rebuilt his walls against her, she realized sadly, shutting her out, shutting himself in.

Was he totally unaware of his attractiveness? Those beautiful green eyes, the imperfect, broken nose, the cleft chin, the beautifully carved lips, the sinewy neck. To some he might not appear so handsome, she realized, but to her, looking at him was like gazing on a work of art, perhaps a sculpture of an ancient Greek, slim and muscular, powerfully aesthetic.

"Penny for your thoughts?" he asked.

"I was thinking about the Greeks." She smiled and the late light touched her blue eyes, softening them, turning their color to that of deep Atlantic waters.

"The Greeks, is it?" He sat back in his creaky rocking chair and studied her. Everything about the scenario conspired to make Daphne's flesh tingle—the gilded light spreading from horizon to horizon, the breakers, white-capped in the storm's aftermath, the sand that was pink tinted now, the quiet on the porch...and Weston. Most especially Weston.

"I'm sorry," she finally said, "if I fell apart on you earlier."

"You were entitled. That was a darn good number you did on Mike." He looked past her for a moment and then back into her eyes.

"He's your friend," she said softly.

Wes nodded. "There's something I should tell you. Something I kept from you earlier."

"Go on."

"About Mike. Hubert checked on the relief organization he donates to. It's legit."

"I know," she said, "Audrey told me."

"Are you mad at me?"

"Yes." She mock-frowned at him and then asked, "How does your head feel?"

"Prudently changing the subject?" He laughed and reached up to touch the bandage. "It's okay now. But I darn near passed out hiding behind that door when Toth was here."

"Wes!" she gasped, recalling how afraid she'd been, and then how reassured when she'd thought of him so close by.

"I knew I shouldn't have told you that," he said sheepishly.

"Maybe we should call the whole thing off."

"Too late now. We've got Mike running scared and we've already alerted the chief and Walt, too. We haven't got any choice."

"But your head?"

"I'll live."

"What if . . . if it's Toth and he returns to the island and you pass out?"

"Hubert. He's great backup."

"I understand, but I sure wish there were two of you handy."

"There are." He leaned forward, cradling his glass in his hands. His eyes, suddenly warm and soft, fixed on hers. "I'd never let anything happen to you."

Unconsciously Daphne looked down at his mouth, the mouth that had possessed hers with such burning passion, the lips that had pressed on hers, intimate and disturbing. She tore her gaze away and looked up. He knew. Of course, he knew.

She felt his eyes on her, searching, yet a little reserved. What went on in his head? How did he manage to put out of his mind everything that had gone on between them?

Daphne wasn't able to do that. Every time she saw Wes or thought about him she quivered all over, felt her knees grow weak, her heart pound, her skin burn. And she knew Wes could see it. It made her feel so ridiculously young and out of control. She'd never felt that way with Brady. With him it had always been warmth and closeness and comfort.

Was this love? This awful, shattering, crazy tangle of sensations?

But worse than that, worse than what *she* was feeling, was the question that never left her mind: what was Wes feeling?

CHAPTER TWELVE

DAPHNE AWOKE EARLY, her mind instantly aware, remembering that Jerry Gallent was due to arrive that
afternoon. She would have to go through the same awful
routine as she had with Toth. The notion was unsettling
and distasteful; to accuse innocent men of such terrible
acts was unconscionable. And she couldn't forget that two
of them *were* innocent.

Audrey already had bacon and eggs cooking when
Daphne appeared in the kitchen. Weston was there, too,
drinking coffee and chatting with Audrey. His bandage
was gone.

"How do you feel today?" asked Daphne.

"Much better, thanks."

They ate breakfast, and Daphne declared that she
wanted to go for a swim to clear her head and try to relax.

"I'm not sure it's wise," responded Wes to her announcement. "It's too hard to cover you out in the open
like that."

"I went the other day."

Weston looked down at his feet. "I know you did."

He did relent, however, and walked down to the water's
edge while Daphne dove into a breaker and came up
through the foamy backwash, laughing, her skin tingling
from the sudden cold plunge.

It was low tide. She stood out past the breakers and
waved at Wes, signaling for him to come in. At first she

could see him shaking his head, and she knew that he was probably right, that he shouldn't exert himself so soon after being wounded. On the other hand, she recalled, all islanders considered a good saltwater soaking extremely beneficial for almost anything that ailed them. She raised her hand and waved at him once more.

"Come on in!" she called through cupped hands.

For a minute he looked doubtful. Finally he shrugged and glanced up and down the shore and behind him to the dunes; there was not a soul in sight. Then he undid his shirt, peeled out of it and tossed it behind him on the sand. Next came his trousers, leaving him standing there unashamedly in his sporty briefs.

Unlike Daphne, Wes entered the water slowly and gingerly, turning his back to the breakers and hollering at the icy cold New England water. Then he moved past where the waves were breaking and came to stand on the sand bar next to Daphne.

"Chicken," she declared, laughing. "You didn't even get your hair wet!"

"You're absolutely right. This isn't Florida. And the salt water stings my head."

He did swim, nonetheless, keeping his head above the rolling water as he moved fluidly up and down the beach. Daphne swam, too, watching the flash of his bronzed arms in the sun, the way his shoulder muscles flexed, the silent wake he made through the water. If it had been Brady swimming alongside her, she knew, they would have engaged in some real water sports: dunking, chasing, a kiss stolen beneath the hot island sun. But this was not Brady.

They emerged, dripping, onto the sand and Daphne offered Wes her towel to dry off. She stretched out on the warm sand, shaded her eyes and looked up at him toweling his lean torso.

"Swimming in your undies," she teased. "What will my mother think? Or Hubert?"

"Were they watching?" He ran the towel across his back and down his taut thighs, then pulled on his slacks and sat in the sand beside her. "This is a beautiful spot," he said quietly.

"Umm..." The sun dried the salty water on her skin, leaving white splotches behind. She brushed at them casually, and then reclined onto her back.

"You're a good swimmer," he remarked offhandedly, turning his head to look down at her.

Daphne closed her eyes and sighed, feeling his glance rest on the curves of her breasts, knowing her nipples were still hard beneath the cool wet nylon. Time became isolated and stretched out lazily; his gaze was like a touch on her flesh, hesitant and warm and arousing.

Her lips parted slightly as she imagined him leaning over to kiss her. She dared not open her eyes and break the spell. She sensed his nearness, the cool shadow he made as he poised over her. Before she could take a breath he was touching his lips to hers so gently, so softly that it might merely have been a late summer breeze. Then the shadow moved and sunlight filled her inner vision.

"We better go." His voice drifted down to her, caressing yet cautious.

"All right," she breathed, forcing herself to sit up. And as they walked the sea-oat-lined path, she wondered if he had really kissed her at all.

Chief Gallent arrived in a taxi directly after lunch. Daphne stood in the foyer as she had done the day before, waiting in dread, forgetting everything she was supposed to say to him.

When he seated himself in the living room, his glance unflinching yet wary, his stocky form took up the entire chair. He had seemed so fatherly when she'd spoken to him in Boston. Now he was merely stolid and intimidating.

"I've come a long way to hear this outrageous tale of yours, Miss Farway," he stated with false indulgence, "so let's have it. I'm a busy man." His stare did not waver from her for a moment.

"But you *did* come," she said smoothly.

"You call me with some cockamamy tale that you have proof that I killed one of my own agents? Miss Farway, it was too ludicrous to ignore. This I have to hear."

"All right, Mr. Gallent, but you won't like it."

She did her best, but he was a hard man to rattle. He sat there, his bulky frame relaxed, his head sunken into his thick neck, his liquid brown eyes fixed on her.

Daphne tried to catch him off guard at every turn, using tidbits of information Brady had told her. Then she informed him that she knew about the huge deposit in his checking account and that it was quite obviously payment from his Russian hawk friends.

"Payment?" His bushy brows raised. Then he smiled tolerantly. "You're right, of course, it was a payment. Although how you got access to that information..."

"I know some people," said Daphne casually. She paused. "So you aren't denying it?"

"That some Russian gave it to me? You bet I'm denying it. If it means anything at all to you, it was a debt owed me for a very long time."

A sinking sensation pulled at Daphne. A debt. Was it a gambling debt? She recalled the people in St. George telling her about the chief's gambling habits. Was he telling the truth, then?

"If you ask me," the chief was saying, "you've got quite an imagination. Gorvieski's itinerary, someone selling it to the Russians. Brady naming me as a traitor. Really," he said, his lips pulling back in a grimace. "I think you ought to seek some professional help. Losing Brady, I'm afraid, has really upset you, Miss Farway."

He just couldn't be budged, she thought. He was too cool, too collected. And everything he said made perfect sense.

"Don't try to twist things to suit yourself," said Daphne, growing uncomfortably anxious. "You see, I know I'm not crazy. I know you killed Brady and are helping the Russians plot Gorvieski's assassination."

"What proof have you got?" he taunted quietly.

An idea struck her as she met his gaze levelly. She plunged in. "Brady took pictures." He tensed just a little, didn't he? "Brady gave them to me to hold. He photographed you giving copies of the itinerary to a known hawk, Mr. Gallent."

He came to his feet. "That's a..." He swore, then caught himself. "A lie. You're out of your mind and so was Brady. Let me see this film."

She watched his control slipping and the effort he was making to regain it. "Now you know I can't do that," Daphne said in an intractable voice. "It's my protection against you."

"Look, Miss Farway—" he ran a hand over the bald shiny surface of his head "—I don't know what this is all about and I can't for the life of me figure why Brady would have told you such a thing. It's too crazy. Maybe," he said pensively, "Brady was joking with you, making up spy stories to entertain you. Damned if I know."

"So why was he killed?"

"For Lord's sake, it was a burglar! When are you going to accept the facts?"

"Never," she breathed ardently.

"I'm going back to Boston now," he said, "and if it makes you feel any better, I'll check again with the police to see if they've come up with anything more on Brady's death. But as far as a traitor—me or anyone else—" he shook his head patronizingly "—there is no such animal. Brady was obviously playing games with you. Go see someone, Miss Farway, a counselor. Stop reaching for straws and looking for scapegoats."

Daphne was getting absolutely nowhere. Either the chief was completely innocent or he was one smooth liar. She tried her final ploy. "I want a hundred thousand dollars, Mr. Gallent," she said, "to keep me quiet."

He seemed not to know whether to laugh or cry. "You *are* unbalanced." He took up his hat and strode to the door. "I'll see you, Miss Farway," he said. "I can't say this has exactly been a pleasure."

"A hundred thousand dollars," she pressed, "or I'm going to Washington, to your superiors, with this."

"You know as well as I do that there's no hidden film. Go to Washington, Miss Farway. See my superiors. They'll laugh you out of their offices." He opened the door and headed toward the waiting taxi.

"You call me!" she said. "I'll be waiting to hear from you." But he'd stepped into the vehicle and closed the door.

"It's not him," she said flatly to Wes and Hubert. "You heard the whole thing. It just can't be him."

Hubert pulled on his beard thoughtfully. "He was pretty convincing."

"What do you think?" Daphne turned to Weston.

"What?" He looked as if he were shaking himself into the present.

"I said, what do you think? Could it be the chief?"

Wes was silent for a long time. "Gallent," he said finally, "has always been a cool customer. He's smart. But I don't know if he's *that* smart."

"So what do we do?" asked Daphne anxiously.

"We wait."

Audrey returned from making certain Jerry Gallent had left on the ferry and the afternoon waned. Dinner was cooked and the dishes cleared away. Hubert napped, as did Weston in the early evening. The hours ticked by slowly, and the strain of the vigil began to wear on them all, causing tempers to flare.

Wes appeared downstairs shortly after nine. He was early for his watch, and Daphne knew there was something on his mind. It showed in the rigid set of his shoulders, in his stance and the worried lines etched on his face.

"I couldn't sleep," he offered.

"You need your rest," advised Hubert.

Daphne saw the circles beneath Weston's eyes and his sleep-tousled hair. "Hubert's right," she said, concerned that he'd have a relapse.

"I'm okay—just need some coffee. Why don't you go on up and sleep now, Hubert?"

Hubert shook his head. "Think I'll read awhile. I'm not sleepy."

Daphne rose. "I'll get you some coffee, Wes." She went to the kitchen. Her back was to the door as she poured but nevertheless, she could feel Weston's presence as he came up behind her. She turned and handed him the coffee mug silently.

"Are you okay?" he asked. "I know what an ordeal this is."

"I'm all right. It's just a strain. I don't think this cloak-and-dagger business is really my line, though." She smiled tentatively. "It looks as if it's getting to you, too."

"A little" was all he would admit.

She wondered just how much he could stand. He still had to find the traitor, and then there was his job. If Gallent wasn't the guilty man, Weston's career was at stake. And, no matter how the whole thing turned out, one of his trusted friends *was* guilty. He couldn't win.

Or, wondered Daphne, was Wes thinking about them, about their curious relationship and the obvious strain of living in the same house, unable to deny the attraction yet unable to do anything about it?

It suddenly seemed too close in the house; the humid night air was too heavy to breathe. If only she could get away from it all. A movie in Edgartown, a walk on the beach, a drive. Anything...

Daphne pushed her damp curly bangs. "It's stifling in here," she said. "I don't suppose we could take in a late movie or something."

He shook his head. "Sorry. I'd like to, but by the time we drove somewhere, watched a movie... You understand, Hubert can't stay up forever."

"Oh," she said, disappointed. "And I guess a walk is out, too."

He smiled in understanding. "We shouldn't."

"Okay." Her voice fell. "A drive? Is that out, too?"

"Well..."

"Never mind. It doesn't matter. It's just so hot and stuffy." She shrugged, trying to be agreeable. "I'll go on up and take a cool shower." She began to walk past him, but his hand stopped her as he took her arm above the elbow, holding her.

"I'll tell Hubert," he said simply, "that we're going for a short drive. Okay?"

"Fine," she breathed, smiling.

Wes took great care even as they walked the few feet to Daphne's car. He turned off the outdoor lights, checked their surroundings, had his hand on his gun in its shoulder holster.

Daphne felt foolish. Obviously they were in more danger out in the open; she should not have been so selfish. But her feelings softened as she drove down the long sandy drive and turned left, heading toward Gay Head. It was good to be away from the house. It had been, what, four days since she'd stumbled in with Wes?

"Where're we heading?" Wes asked through the darkness.

"Just along the South Road, toward Gay Head."

"Gay Head?"

"The western point of the island. A very popular tourist attraction. I don't know if you can see them at night, but the cliffs are all striped with colored clay. They're beautiful."

They parked and walked along a rough path across a meadow and out onto the cliffs. Below, the sea tossed itself onto the rocks, sending plumes of froth into the moonlit sky. Mist enshrouded them, coming in waves, rolling silently across the grassy meadow. It was a hot August night and even there, outside, the air seemed too heavy to breathe.

Daphne put a hand to her throat and felt her flesh, warm and moist, soft in the sultry night.

Just then a bus drove up and disgorged a load of tourists who had come to see the cliffs by moonlight.

"Oh, dear," said Daphne, as the quiet night was broken by voices.

"We better go," he said under his breath. "It's not safe here anymore. Sorry about your walk."

"Maybe we could go to a cove I know that's not far from here," Daphne suggested. "We could walk on the beach there." Then she added, "If you want to, of course."

"That's fine by me."

She glanced up and saw his eyes, heavy lidded, the lashes spiky in the humid night. How could a masculine man have such lovely eyelashes?

Daphne had been afraid that her cove might not be deserted at all; there could have been kids with a bonfire or couples on blankets. There was no one, however, as she pulled the VW up to the end of a rutted road near the cove and parked.

They left their shoes and headed down to the spongy sand, letting the dying waves lick their toes. They ran from one large wave that ended up soaking the legs of Daphne's shorts.

"Darn!" She laughed. "I used to be quicker."

They walked again. Daphne wanted to reach over several times and take his hand; she sensed that he wanted it, too. Instead, they remained several feet apart, moving in and out along the uneven shoreline, avoiding a good drenching.

"I'd like a place here," Wes mused out loud. "Right here. I'd come down from Boston every spare minute."

"The land's too marshy to build on around here. But down the beach, near our place..."

"Did you come here with Brady?" he asked too casually.

Daphne stopped walking. "Is that what you've been thinking? Is Brady always on your mind?"

Weston's silence was answer enough. She felt anger growing in her and frustration and a dragging futility. Was Brady always to stand between them?

"I never made love to Brady here, if that's what you wanted to know," she blurted out.

"You don't have to tell me..." he began uneasily.

"Oh, yes I do! You'd go on wondering, wouldn't you? Oh, Wes," she cried, "Brady is gone."

They stood facing each other in the darkness. The sea swished and gurgled in the blackness and a warm, moist wind ruffled Daphne's curls. Her heart thudded in her chest. She wanted him so badly.

Weston's lean silhouette against the ocean was rigid. She could barely make out the gold in his hair where the moonlight struck it, the shadowed opaqueness of his eyes, the thin dark line of his mouth. Something inside her gave way like a dam breaking, letting her emotions loose; there was no way to stop them from seeking their own level. Daphne stepped up to him and put her hands on his smooth-shaven cheeks. For a terrible moment she thought he was going to push her away, reject her, but he only said something under his breath, a kind of reverent swear word. She was waiting, her hands on his cheeks, her fingers feeling the sticky salt of the night on his flesh.

Then his head bent to hers, slowly and hesitantly until their lips touched. He parted her mouth with his and twisted his lips against hers until Daphne's stomach knotted madly and naked pleasure shot through her, burning a trail of raw sensation that became a vortex of desire whirling in her abdomen.

"Wes," she breathed, stunned, trying to pull back for a moment, to gain her equilibrium. But it was too late. He merely brought her up against him, hard, forcing her breasts to his chest, until the buttons on his shirt pressed into her skin beneath the thin cotton blouse. She could feel his hardness against her and sense his urgency in his breathing and in the movement of his hands over her back and down her mist-damp arms.

Then he was pulling her shirt over her head and discarding it some distance from the lapping waves. She wondered crazily: were they going to make love right there, on the shore? But the thought drifted away as he bent to kiss her breasts and his hands cupped the two globes, soft and white in the moonlight.

Daphne's back arched. She moaned, feeling his hair in her fingers, feeling his hands leave her breasts to unfasten her shorts. Then she was free of them and out of her lacy panties. He was stripping down, also, tossing his clothes up onto the sand. Quickly he pulled her against him with force, his strong hands cupping her buttocks, molding her to him until the crispy mat of his hair moved against her, arousing, tickling, sensual.

Her knees felt like rubber. Passion was leaving her shaken and desperate; she needed him immediately, inside her, moving against her pulsing flesh, assuaging her. She cried out softly and his mouth covered hers once again, hot and burning and demanding.

Locked in fevered embrace, they kneeled down together in the cool wet sand, and Daphne felt the death of a wave on her knees. Even the touch of the water was heaven.

She was on her back suddenly, registering in some part of her mind that the sand felt strangely warm and smooth, that the stars shone through the misty night and the moonlight was gleaming on Weston's shoulders.

He kissed her neck and her breasts, sucking each nipple into her mouth in turn, teasing with his teeth, cupping her heavy breasts with a hand while his other stroked the flesh along her inner thigh.

She wanted to pull him closer, to tell him, Now, to find release. But Wes was patient, savoring her, driving her beyond madness.

He kissed the plane of her stomach, he whispered against her flesh, circling her skin with his tongue and sending chills over her in exquisite spasms. The water touched her legs, her hips, wet her hair and then receded into the expanse of the ocean. He pushed the damp curls from her face and held her head motionless for a second, looking down into her limpid eyes before his mouth covered hers.

At last he was poised above her, supporting his weight with his arms, and she parted her legs to let him enter. He was hard and hot, thrusting deep into her. Daphne cried out as her hips rose to meet him.

She rocked with Wes in the timeless dance of love, feeling herself lost in its grip, reaching for something, writhing and gasping and sweating. Searching.

Slowly the heat rose in her belly and she rocked more quickly, her hands holding his shoulders, her head moving from side to side, her lips parting to draw in air. Then her buttocks were rising off the sand and she could feel her thighs trembling. The hot pulsing deep within her reached a wild crescendo until an explosion shook her. She clutched Weston to her breast and sobbed, feeling him shudder above her, feeling his sweat-slick body glide against hers like silk until they both lay panting and exhausted and utterly sated.

It was the wave, half drowning them both, that broke them apart finally. Daphne sputtered and laughed and felt utterly happy. Even Brady had not... But she refused to finish the thought. She would not think about that this night. In the morning, perhaps, she would put it all in perspective.

Wes's arms tightened protectively around her as they lay together on the warm sand. She wanted to say so many things to him, to tell him of her pleasure and her feelings and the wonder of their lovemaking. But she sensed that Wes would have difficulty with her confession. So she only laid her head on his shoulder and snuggled closer to him, trying to let him know how she felt.

"It's so obvious what we were doing," said Daphne later, embarrassed, as they drove back. "My hair's all full of sand and so is yours. What will Hubert think?"

Weston laughed softly at her. "He'll think we just made love on the beach."

CHAPTER THIRTEEN

THE DAY DAWNED CLEAR AND COOLER, a relief from the heat. Weston slept all morning. Daphne wandered aimlessly around the rambling house, searching for something to do, something to take her mind off Weston. Working, she'd found, was not the answer.

He appeared at lunch, freshly shaven, crisp looking and smiling at her cheerfully. "Morning," he said, picking up a sandwich Audrey had made for him. "Or should I say good afternoon?"

Audrey looked him over carefully. "You *are* feeling better," she concluded.

"Certainly am." He exchanged a glance with Daphne, who instantly colored.

Hubert walked into the kitchen. "Oh, boyo, you're up," he remarked absently.

"Sorry. I meant to relieve you at ten."

"That's okay."

Daphne studied Hubert closely. He seemed distracted, not his usual self. She'd heard him making a couple of phone calls earlier. Had something happened? But then as they all sat down to eat lunch and the conversation grew lively, Daphne forgot Hubert and whatever problems he had. She forgot because she was too busy gazing at Wes, noticing the way the cool sea air came through the kitchen window and lightly lifted the sandy hair from his brow.

She wanted desperately to touch him, to show her feelings. They'd made love the night before. Didn't it count for anything? But Wes was being friendly and noncommittal and she knew he'd hate her to cling or moon over him. She swallowed her disappointment and tried to keep her eyes averted. There were other, more important, things to concern her, she told herself firmly. But her heart cried out for a word from Wes, a look, a touch.

Walter Greenburg arrived at two-thirty. Daphne was surprised at how easily she stood waiting for him at the door, how in control she felt this time.

She looked him over thoroughly as he entered the house. He was tall and lanky, with pale red hair and freckles. At one point, he'd had skin problems, but his ruddy complexion mostly hid the marks now.

He was nervous. Of the three suspects, Greenburg was the only one to have walked into the living room with his suit jacket slung over a shoulder and huge perspiration rings showing on his shirt.

He declined her offer to seat himself.

Daphne shrugged and placed a cool, impersonal smile on her lips. She spoke of Brady and Gorvieski's itinerary. Greenburg remained silent but developed a tic under one eye. He began to sweat more profusely, all the time pacing a small path on the carpet, restive and agitated, and never looking directly at Daphne.

"You're crazy," he said at last, his voice thin and brittle. "Why would I kill Brady? Why would I sell information to the Russians?"

"There was *one* Russian you were quite friendly with," said Daphne with deliberate coolness.

He spun around; there was a wild look to him. "What are you talking about?" he rasped.

"San Francisco. Vera Sherinsky, Mr. Greenburg. Your lover."

"But you're wrong! That's over! I swear to God, it was over a year ago!"

"You're still giving her information, aren't you?" pressed Daphne. "You're still in love and can't help yourself. And you had to kill Brady because he knew, because he'd photographed you giving information to..."

"No! No! No! You're crazy! Brady was crazy! No!" He'd slipped over the line of reason, and panicked completely. He stepped backward and bumped into a side table, causing a lamp to crash to the floor. He never even noticed.

Daphne held her breath. She'd pushed too hard.

"It's all lies!" he was shouting. "You'll ruin me, my career, everything! I beg you..."

Daphne never even attempted to hit with the part about the blackmail money. It was unnecessary to push Walter Greenburg any further. She bit her lower lip and braved a glance at Weston's hiding place. Greenburg did not notice, however; he was too consumed with his own distress. Finally he snatched his jacket and strode to the door.

He turned on her as he was leaving. "I beg you not to tell anyone about this! Please, let me have some time. I'll show you. I'll make you see." Then he was gone, and ducking into the waiting taxi, drenched in sweat, his color as blotchy as if he'd broken out in a case of hives.

Daphne leaned against the closed door and felt herself shaking. What had she done to that man? How could she have...?

"He very well could be the one" came Weston's voice in her ear. Then he put his hands on her shoulders, turned her and pulled her into his embrace. "It could be Walt, Daphne. Just keep remembering that."

She turned her face up to his. "It was ghastly."

"I know. I never thought Walt would lose it so badly."

Daphne took several long, deep breaths. "At least it's over now. At least I don't have to go through that part again."

"No," said Wes softly, "you don't. Now we just wait. I'm not sure which is worse."

But Daphne knew. It was the act of confrontation, it was the taking of a man into her hands like putty and twisting him until his pain was complete. She felt very dirty and very sick, and even Weston's arms encircling her, giving her comfort, were not enough to wash the bitter taste from her mouth.

Later that night, Daphne climbed the creaking stairs to her workroom and shut the door. Weston was resting up for the night's vigil, and Audrey and Hubert's wondering glances had finally become too much for her. Something must have shown in her face. She wasn't surprised.

She couldn't help imagining Wes lying on his bed in Felicity's room, stretched out, his flat stomach a hollow, his eyes closed so that his eyelashes made shadow fans on his cheeks. She yearned to enter the room and touch the smooth skin of his chest, to run her fingers down his legs, over the ankles, then up again.

She had to admit to herself, finally, that making love to Brady had never consumed her as it had with Wes. Never had she felt that powerful surge of passion, that incredible sensation of mixed tenderness and moaning desire and closeness.

It was good, perhaps, that Wes was away from her for a while. She sensed that he needed space—and time. It was desperately hard for him to get in touch with his feelings. They had time, though. She could give him time and then, maybe, eventually, he would feel comfortable with his own emotions.

When Audrey shouted up to her that there was a phone call, Daphne felt fear squeeze her heart. Who was it? One of the three?

She raced to the phone in her bedroom and snatched it up.

"Yes?" There was no click of the other extension, so she knew Audrey or Hubert was listening. She wished Wes were there. What if she said the wrong thing?

"This is Walt Greenburg."

Her heart thumped uncontrollably. "Yes, what can I do for you?"

"I want to meet you. To prove my innocence. I've been half out of my mind all day." His thin voice broke with tension; his words spilled out so fast that Daphne had to concentrate on them.

"Meet you."

"Yes, at Logan Airport. It's neutral ground. I swear I can prove to you that I had nothing to do with this terrible thing."

She thought frantically. Logan Airport. Crowds. He couldn't possibly harm her in full sight of all those people. Hubert and Wes could follow her. Yes, it would be all right. "Okay. When?"

"Noon tomorrow. Can you get there by then?"

"Yes. But where will you be?"

"At the American Airlines counter."

"American Airlines at noon. I'll be there, Mr. Greenburg."

"Thank God," Walter said fervently. Then there was only a buzz on the line.

Daphne hung up slowly. She prayed she'd done the right thing.

Hubert was waiting for her downstairs with a big smile on his face. "We've got him!" he chortled.

"Do you really think it's him, then?" asked Daphne.

"Sure. He's trying to get you away from here and pull something."

"So I did the right thing by saying I'd meet him?"

"Sure. Now we'd better wake Wes and tell him."

Weston was not nearly as enthusiastic as Hubert. "Look, crowded places aren't always safe. Sometimes you can't get to a person fast enough. And what if Walt went to my place to check and found that there was no body? He'd naturally suspect that I'd gotten away and that I was helping you. Everyone knows you talked to me that day at the office, and now all of a sudden you threaten him. He'd suspect I was here with you or behind your initial call, at least."

"We've got to do it, Wes," said Hubert.

Daphne was silent, looking from one to the other with trepidation.

Wes shook his head reluctantly. "I don't like it."

"Neither do I, but it's procedure. If a suspect makes contact you follow up. You know that, boyo."

"It'll be *Daphne* following up," remarked Wes cautiously.

"You know I have to do it, Wes," said Daphne gently. "Time's growing short."

He gave in, of course. There was no other way. "Hubert, as long as I'm up, let me watch and you get some shut-eye. I'll never sleep now. I've got to plan this thing out in my mind."

"Okay." Hubert yawned. "I could sleep for a year. I'm too old for these kinds of games."

Daphne roamed restlessly around the living room. "Are you tired?" she finally asked.

"Not right now. Don't worry about me, Daphne."

She guessed that he wanted her to leave him, but a force stronger than herself kept her there. She just needed to see him, to be near him.

"I'd like to keep you company." It hurt to beg, but she was beyond pain. She'd given herself to this man and he was rejecting her.

Wes sank down onto an antique Victorian settee and put his head in his hands. When he looked up, his expression was full of confusion. "I'm sorry. I don't mean to be cruel, but I've got a lot on my mind and I'm worried about tomorrow."

"It's okay, Wes. I'd just like to be with you for a while. I couldn't sleep now, anyway."

"God, Daphne, you're so damned good. You never get mad, you never play games. I'm afraid I'm not much of a bargain."

She sat next to him on the settee and put an uncertain hand on his arm. "I've got lots of faults. You just don't know me well enough to see them yet."

"You couldn't have any that would matter," he said gravely.

She smiled. "I'm meddlesome and stubborn and I hate to do dishes."

"Try again," he said wryly.

"Maybe you'll find out for yourself."

He looked askance at her. "Is that a proposition?"

"Maybe."

He tried to smile. "I've never been propositioned before by a lady."

"You should try it more often," she said lightly.

"Perhaps I should."

The night shadows crept out of the corners of the room, encircling them.

"You know, I really could believe Felicity haunts this house," said Wes.

"Her spirit does. Sometimes when I was a kid I used to go into her room—your room now—and sit there and imagine her suffering. Her husband out there on the sea. You haven't seen it in a blow, Wes. It's terrible. The waves came up nearly to our porch steps once. And Audrey remembers when the hurricane of '38 flattened Menemsha."

"I'd love to have known you as a kid," mused Wes. "Tell me what it was like growing up on this island."

"I think *your* childhood was more, shall we say, interesting."

He made a face. "Sordid. Sad. Lost."

"Tell me," she insisted softly.

So they talked in the dimness, telling each other half-forgotten stories, filling in the missing details for each other. Once, as Wes was relating a particularly unhappy incident in a foster home, Daphne spontaneously put her hand out to cover his. He did not pull away.

They sat there for hours, talking, and Daphne's hand remained enclosed in Weston's. Her heart broke for him as he related his childhood to her. And yet it soared, too, because he trusted her enough to tell her and because her hand stayed wrapped in his and his fingers stroked hers unconsciously, lovingly.

The small hours of the morning advanced, heavy with silence in the old mansion. Wes cupped her face with tender hands and touched her lips with his. Their tongues met and they explored each other's mouth. A tall clock ticked in the dim room, keeping vigil. Weston's hand moved over Daphne's breasts, warm and tender.

There was no urgency. As the tick, tock of the grandfather clock broke the quiet, they kissed and felt and held each other and grew close in the darkness. There was no need to consummate their passion that night—perhaps because they were both tired and consumed by the problem of finding the guilty man. But Daphne drew immense comfort from Weston's closeness and his opening up to her. Her heart floated on a cloud of poignant happiness, so piercingly sweet that it was almost pain.

She dared not tell herself he loved her, but he cared. And she knew, too, that she gave him as much pleasure as he gave her.

In the morning, Daphne, Wes and Hubert readied themselves to leave the Farway house at nine-thirty, giving themselves more than enough time to get to Logan even in the event of traffic tie-ups. Wes refused to go before Audrey left for her club.

"We'll pick you up at the club, Mrs. Farway. This afternoon, whenever we're done in Boston. Don't, under any circumstances, return here. No matter what. I'll try to call if we're hung up in any way. Whatever you do, don't come back here until you hear from one of us. And don't go off by yourself."

"Hey, sonny, look who's giving orders around here," snorted Audrey.

"It's for your own protection, Audrey," put in Hubert.

"I know, I know. Lord, the things I have to put up with!"

"We're pretty sure it's Greenburg, but just in case it isn't, I want you someplace safe," said Wes.

They watched her drive up the driveway and then followed in Daphne's car. It was a beautiful morning, as clear and cool as the previous day. The gulls seemed louder than usual, as if celebrating yet another respite from the summer's heat.

By the time they were approaching Boston, Daphne had been coached on exactly how to act. Wes and Hubert had gone over with her every possibility. If Greenburg tried something in the airport, she was to scream. It wasn't a likely event but one never knew....

"You're not to leave the terminal with him or go into any private areas. Restaurants are okay. No dark cocktail lounges," admonished Hubert.

"Just get his proof, whatever it is, if indeed it exists. That's all we want," added Wes. "Don't take any chances."

She was decidedly nervous, even though she kept telling herself nothing could possibly happen in a crowded airport. Greenburg had chosen it for both their sakes. Perhaps, then, he really was innocent.

They were far too early. "Say," suggested Hubert, "could we run by my place? I'd like to grab some clothes. Everything I own is dirty. And you never did get my racket. I had to borrow one."

"Sure," said Wes, turning west onto Massachusetts Avenue, "it's better than getting jumpy waiting at Logan."

Daphne and Weston waited in the Volvo. Hubert emerged from his house looking as white as a ghost. He came up to them, tottering as if he were a very old man.

"What's the matter?" asked Wes instantly.

"There was a message on my answering machine, Weston." Hubert closed his eyes tightly and then opened them. "It was Joe Marion, the man who's been blackmailing me." He swallowed. "Wes, he's threatened Dodie and her kids. Wes—" Hubert choked and his voice stopped.

"There was a message on your machine?"

"Oh, Hubert," said Daphne, forgetting her own anxiety for a minute.

Wes got out of the car. "I want to hear it, Hubert."

The message was clear, although the voice was disguised, muffled by a cloth or something. "You know who this is, Hubert. I don't like the way you've been holding out on me lately, and I've decided to take action. You know your daughter, Dodie? The one who lives at 117 Baskin Road in Lexington? And her three darling kids? How are they, Hubert? You spoken to your daughter lately? I think we better talk."

Hubert was slumped in a chair, his face ashen, one hand pulling at his Vandyke beard.

"Damn!" said Wes when the recording was finished.

"I phoned him, you know," confessed Hubert. "Told him I wasn't paying another cent. That's what did it."

"The voice was disguised. Could it be anyone else?"

"Who? Nobody knows but you two and Audrey." Hubert was dialing a phone number. "Dodie," he explained. The look on his face as he listened, intent, tortured, was awful to see. He seemed to grow paler with each ring, and his hand on the receiver shook as if palsied.

Putting the phone down finally, he whispered. "No one home." His head snapped up and his eyes were wild. "Do you think . . . ?"

"No. Calm down, Hubert. They're probably just out. We'll try again later," soothed Wes. "Look, we've got to go now or we'll never make it to Logan in time. Can you handle it?"

"Sure," Hubert said, but he was white faced and distracted.

"The minute this is over with Greenburg, we'll go after this Marion. I promise. Don't worry. He hasn't done anything yet."

But Daphne wondered, what if he had? What if he had actually done something—kidnapped Hubert's daughter and her children?

"Look, Hubert, this creep wants money, not more crimes on his hands. He won't do anything till he hears from you or he wouldn't have bothered going to all the trouble of calling," said Wes reasonably.

"Yeah, sure, I know. I know that," muttered Hubert.

The drive into the city was horribly silent. Daphne couldn't think of a single thing to say that would relieve Hubert's anxiety, so she stayed quiet, trying to remember everything she had to do when she met Greenburg. They had to take care of that first. Then they could look for Dodie and her kids.

Boston's Logan Airport was one of the most improbably situated airports in the world. It lay on a spit of land right on the Atlantic Ocean and was connected to downtown Boston only by two narrow, outmoded tunnels that caused endless traffic jams. The Callahan Tunnel led into Logan; the Sumner Tunnel went back out. At the approach to the exiting Sumner Tunnel, there were usually flower sellers stationed to take advantage of the hundreds of halted cars, so notorious was the stoppage.

The traffic wasn't bad that day going into the tunnel, and Wes remarked on their good fortune. But they could see that the road into the Sumner Tunnel was clogged, bumper to bumper, with cars that were honking and crawling, overheating, as they waited to get out of the airport. Daphne viewed the jam on the other side of the median and her mouth compressed into a line. Glancing sideways at Wes, she saw his frown.

"Oh, well," she said brightly, "sometimes the tie-ups disappear like magic. You never know."

No one bothered to answer.

Wes pulled up at the Outgoing Passengers entrance to American Airlines and put a card in his window, an official parking permit from the service.

"We'll be right behind you, Daphne," he said. "Just don't go anyplace alone with him."

· "I know, you already told me."

He turned around to the back seat. "Hubert, you all set?"

"As ready as I'll ever be," replied Hubert. "Let's just make this fast."

Daphne got out and entered the building prudently ahead of the two men. It was twelve-ten. Walter should be there. What did he have, she wondered, that could prove his innocence? Her mouth felt dry; what if he tried something violent? She wanted badly to turn around and see if Wes and Hubert were still behind her, but she knew she couldn't. Greenburg might be watching; in fact, he'd be stupid if he weren't watching her, and Wes had said he was very smart. Well, right now he was very rattled, as well, and could be desperate. Who knew what he might do?

She made her way past the mothers with crying babies, the brisk career women, the lobster-red sunburned tourists, the Japanese businessmen. The American Airlines counter spread along a wall, and there were long lines of patiently waiting travelers in front of it. Slowly Daphne strolled along the concourse, searching for a tall, thin man with red hair.

There he was. Her breath stopped for a heartbeat of time. He was pacing, his body practically jumping with tension. She was dying to look behind her, but Wes and Hubert couldn't get too close and maybe she wouldn't be able to see them, anyway.

She walked up to Greenburg; he stopped pacing abruptly.

"Okay," he said and then halted, obviously at a loss.

"Your proof, Mr. Greenburg," she said quietly.

"You'll have to come out to my car."

"That wasn't part of our deal." Daphne tried to suppress a twinge of apprehension.

"Look, my car's right outside that exit." He pointed to the last door on the concourse. "Right over there. There are people all around. What do you think I'm going to do, pull out a machine gun and spray the place?"

"All right." It wasn't a private room or anything; she guessed it would be okay. But what would Wes think when she started going outside with Walter?

She followed Greenburg's lanky frame to the end of the concourse, walking slowly so that she wouldn't outdistance her bodyguards.

"What is this proof?" she asked once again.

"You'll have to see it with your own eyes to believe me" was all Greenburg would say.

He held the door open for her, and she waited for him on the pavement. Two Greyhound buses were pulled up at the curb, disgorging luggage to a crowd of senior citizens who were clustered on the sidewalk. The people all wore hats that read Armchair Travelers and they were laughing and joking with one another, calmly ignoring the angry glances of others who were trying to get by them.

But Walter just skirted the mass of seniors and led Daphne to a car. She had a chance to turn and look swiftly behind her, toward the doors, but all she could see was an ocean of happy, wrinkled faces topped with brightly colored caps.

Walter opened the passenger door of his low red Honda. "It's there," he said.

"What is it? I don't see anything." Daphne was edgy and she kept trying to gain time. Were Wes and Hubert lost in that mass of oblivious, happy wanderers?

"You'll have to look in the back. I'm innocent, Miss Farway, believe me."

She snatched another look toward the terminal; now the oldsters were streaming into the building, blocking all the entrances. There must have been hundreds of them.

She looked nervously at Walter, but he stood well back and seemed more relaxed. She supposed it couldn't do any harm to just look, and besides, Walter might start getting suspicious if she delayed any longer.

Daphne stepped forward and craned her neck. There was nothing in the car, just two empty red seats. She started to back away, to turn and demand to know what kind of foolishness this was, but something hard pressed into her back.

"What?" she gasped, trying to whirl. But Greenburg caught her arms in a steely grasp and shoved her into the car, toward the driver's side.

"Let me go," Daphne rasped, struggling, sprawling onto the seat.

He was in the car beside her, the gun in his hand held low so that nobody outside could see it. Could she get out her side quickly enough? Her mind froze. She was too frightened. He could pull the trigger in a split second and he was desperate enough to do it.

Greenburg leaned over and jammed a key into the ignition. "Drive," he commanded, holding the gun on her with a hand as steady as a rock. "Drive! I mean it!"

Panicked, Daphne turned the key. The car roared to life, fed by too much gas. She ground it into first and jerked out into the traffic, searching frantically in the rearview mirror for Wes and Hubert.

Her kidnapping had taken maybe ten seconds. The sidewalk was still filled with milling armchair travelers, each one of their cheerful expressions an unholy rictus to Daphne. *Oh, God, where's Weston?* she thought frantically.

Then finally, with a burst of relief, she saw him break through the crowd. He stood on the edge of the sidewalk and stared after Greenburg's car. Then he whirled and disappeared.

He was going for his own car, she guessed. He'd follow. He'd get her away from Greenburg. Wes would find some way to manage it.

She almost hit a taxi, swerved around it and braked too suddenly for a family crossing in front of her. The gun was still trained on her midsection, a black, all-seeing hollow eye. She followed the traffic, trying to stall and buy time.

"Move," said Walter. "Faster!"

The approach to the Sumner Tunnel was still jammed with stop-and-start traffic. Walter made her cut people off to gain a few yards. Once she almost ran down a flower seller as she changed lanes abruptly. She wondered if a policeman would notice her erratic driving and stop them, but for once there were none to be seen.

"Go, damn it!" said Walter as the car ahead moved past the tollbooth and into the tunnel. Could she alert the attendant? But the booth was automated, and she was forced to toss in the coins Walter handed her and drive on.

The tunnel was dim and echoing and filled chokingly with car exhaust. They inched along. Nervous tension formed a lump in Daphne's throat. She kept swallowing, but it was stuck there and she felt as if she couldn't get a proper breath of air.

The awful slowness of the traffic was a blessing to her, yet it was also a curse, because Wes was held up by the dozens of cars behind them.

Hurry, Wes!

She seized a moment to look in the mirror again. Oh, thank God, there he was! His old green Volvo was there, weaving among the other vehicles as Wes tried to catch up to them. He was perhaps a hundred yards back.

Hurry, Wes! she screamed silently. If Greenburg's car reached the far end of the tunnel before Wes's, she was lost. There were half a dozen major streets that went off in several directions at the exit to the tunnel and the traffic dispersed there, speeded up and raced away on the various expressways to Maine and Rhode Island and New York. Wes would never find her then, never!

The circle of light that presaged the end of the tunnel grew in Daphne's vision like an apocalypse. Once she reached it she was as good as dead, murdered like Brady. It wouldn't matter to her anymore that her murder would be the final breaking of Walter Greenburg. Wes would find him and avenge her and Brady.

Stop, jerk forward, stop again. The cloying, suffocating atmosphere of fumes and smoke was unbearable, and Daphne's mind was suffused with the endless monotony of terror and waiting and hysterical hope. *Please, Wes, hurry.*

Then she saw Wes. He was on foot, running between the lines of stopped cars. He was gaining on Greenburg's car, slowly but surely. Hope burst within her. If she could just delay a little it would help. *Oh, Wes, hurry!*

She kept her foot on the brake when the line moved, but Walter jabbed the gun at her. She pulled ahead, slowly, marking time. Behind her Wes was racing, dodging cars. *Hurry!* Then suddenly, ridiculously, she was afraid for him, running like that with his head still so bad and his weakness and dizzy spells.

Sunlight glared into her eyes; when she looked in the rearview mirror, it was all dark behind her and she couldn't spot him. The traffic slid forward relentlessly. She was out of the tunnel, in full sunlight, half blinded.

"I can't see," she gasped, stepping on the brakes. An angry horn sounded behind her. In front of her, the traffic dispersed onto ramps and around corners, melting away.

"Go!" shouted Walter. He jammed his foot on the gas pedal, snapping Daphne's head back with the force of their acceleration.

She had no choice but to drive. Behind her, she saw the black mouth of the tunnel diminishing in the distance. Then Walter pointed and she had to turn a corner and the tunnel disappeared from view.

Tears of self-pity filled Daphne's eyes suddenly. It was too late! Walter would take her somewhere and kill her! Wes could never find her in time now.

She drove, not seeing where she was, nearly running into other cars.

"Please let me go," she finally pleaded.

"No. Not until I prove I'm not guilty," said Greenburg.

Laughable. He was still playing that ludicrous game.

They drove south along the shoreline of Boston Harbor. Wharves stuck out into the water, and factories belched smoke. Walter directed her to pull off onto an apparently deserted pier. There was an old wooden warehouse with faded writing on its side that she couldn't read. She drove into the huge opening and down the center of the derelict building. It was shadowed and silent and very, very private.

"Stop," said Walter.

She braked and turned the key off. Her heart pounded in a slow, heavy rhythm. *This is it, this is it.*

Greenburg turned to her, very serious, very intent on what he was doing.

Daphne swallowed. She knew she was quivering all over with terror.

"I'm sorry," said Walter Greenburg then, "but you left me no choice."

CHAPTER FOURTEEN

"GONE!" Wes choked out, sliding back into the car. "I can't see his Honda anywhere!"

He drove, weaving in and out of traffic like an Indy 500 racer, heading north toward the city of Charlestown. He pulled into the first service station he saw, jumped out of the car and raced to a telephone booth.

"Damn!" Weston's fingers shook as he leafed through the phone book. Greenburg, Arthur G., Greenburg, Brooks. Greenburg... Then he found him: Greenburg, Walter A. He ripped the page out of the book and hopped back into the car, pulling out onto the avenue with tires screeching.

"Take it easy," breathed Hubert, buckling his seat belt.

"If by some miracle Greenburg took her to his place," said Wes, "I'm going to be only seconds behind."

But when they pulled up in front of Walt's apartment house, his car was nowhere to be seen. Of course Wes checked the door, anyway, very carefully. Locked. He thought desperately for a moment. If Walt didn't know he'd been followed, he might be inside with Daphne. He backed off several paces and surged forward with his foot, slamming it against the door once, then twice, until the wooden frame splintered. Once inside, he crouched, his gun ready, but he was quickly swamped by a feeling of futility to find the place empty.

"Call the police!" he heard someone shouting in the hallway.

Wes barged back past the openmouthed residents and down the hall, taking the steps two at a time.

Hubert was watching the street. "Not there?"

Weston's lips pulled into a tight, unforgiving line. "How in hell are we going to find her!" he snarled, knowing that he was fast losing command of his emotions.

"Settle down and let's think," Hubert said, getting back into the car.

As they sped down the residential street, they passed a patrol car, siren screaming, obviously heading toward Walt Greenburg's place.

"I kicked his door in," explained Wes, shrugging.

"What do we do about Daphne now?" asked Hubert, unperturbed. "Contact the police?"

Wes finally pulled to the side of the road. He rested his head on the steering wheel and fought the nausea rising in his throat. "I don't know. God, Hubert, I feel so helpless." He pounded his fist on the dashboard.

"Yeah, well, that's not going to accomplish a blasted thing. Look," Hubert said, "there's a restaurant across the street. I've got Greenburg's license plate number. I'll call the cops. And while I'm at it, I'll check on Dodie and the kids. You just try to get your cool back, boyo."

Weston's head came up. "Damn, Hubert, I'm sorry. I forgot . . . Dodie."

Hubert smiled weakly. "Guess we're both trying to function on overload."

Ten minutes later, Hubert threaded his way back across the street and got into the car.

"Dodie?" Wes was careful to ask as soon as he saw Hubert's gray pallor.

"No answer."

Weston could see that the older man's lips trembled and that his fists were clenched into balls in his lap. He himself wasn't feeling much better. "What did the cops say?" he asked finally.

"They put out an APB on Greenburg's Honda. It's all they can do for now. The desk sergeant told me to bring in photographs of Daphne and Walt and file a formal complaint."

"Swell," muttered Wes under his breath. "By that time she'll be . . ." If she wasn't already, he thought in despair.

All afternoon Weston's mood flip-flopped. One minute he was consumed with rage; the next he felt dizzy with helplessness. Time and time again, he had to remind himself that he was a Secret Service agent, a highly trained select individual who was not supposed to panic when the going got tough.

But this was different. It was not as if he'd been guarding some stranger. No, this was Daphne, the woman who had lain beneath him on the moonlit beach. She'd offered her body to him—and her love.

And he'd betrayed her. He'd sent her out like bait on a hook and lost her. This was his fault—no one else's. It tortured him as nothing in his life had ever done. His fault, his fault. How despicable of him. He should have planned better, he should have known better, he should have second-guessed Greenburg. There was something he could have done to avoid letting Daphne out of his reach for those few critical seconds. But what? What could he have done? He went over and over the scene in his mind until he wanted to scream in anguish. If he'd stayed closer, if he'd realized, if, if, if . . .

What was Greenburg doing? Where was he? So clever. Wes never would have thought Walt could be so clever. But then, Greenburg was a trained agent, despite his youth-ful, innocent appearance. Oh, yes, he was good, too.

Obviously better than Wes.

Somehow, during those long, agonized hours of searching, Wes did keep control. He had to for Daphne's sake. He tried everything he could think of to locate her, drove to half the deserted alleys in Boston, checked sleazy hotels, bars, anything. He sensed in his gut that it was all a waste of time.

Hubert checked with the police several times. Nothing. He also called his daughter's twice more. "She can't be out shopping this long," he told Wes. "Look, I hate to ask, but would you drop me off at my place? I'm going to have to get hold of Joe Marion and find out what's going on. If he's got Dodie . . ."

"I'll drop you," said Wes, "but only if you promise not to do anything crazy. Chances are this guy is full of it, just trying to scare the hell out of you."

"I realize that," said Hubert, obviously fighting to keep panic from his voice.

"Dodie's no doubt got the kids at a picnic or gone to the zoo. Call the guy. Find out what's going on. If he really does...have Dodie," said Wes gently, "then he'll ask you for money and make arrangements for an exchange."

"I wasn't born yesterday," snapped Hubert. Immedi-ately, he said, "Sorry."

"It's all right. Believe me, I do know how you feel."

He pulled up in front of Hubert's. "I'll be in touch," he said, "just as soon as I have Daphne back safe and sound." Even to his own ears the absurdity of his state-ment was evident.

"I feel terrible leaving you like this," said Hubert. "I feel as if I'm deserting you."

"You aren't. There isn't much I can do right now. I'm going to check once again at Greenburg's," he said, "and maybe stop by the police station."

"There isn't a whole lot more you *can* do."

"Good luck," said Wes, "and I'll call."

"Okay. You take it easy, too. It's possible she's . . . all right, boyo. Keep believing it. Greenburg might just hold her, you know, and ask for safe conduct out of the country."

"He might," replied Wes, putting the car into gear. Of course he knew Greenburg wouldn't. Walt would see Daphne as the ultimate threat now that Brady was out of the way.

It was ten past five. Wes knew that if he was to catch the last ferry over to the Vineyard he'd have to rush. It crossed his mind to telephone Audrey at her club, but he knew he couldn't do that. And to stay in Boston, driving around helplessly, searching, made no sense. He'd stay with Audrey and telephone the Boston police from there. Just in case.

He drove too fast down to Woods Hole. He didn't care. The only thing in his mind was Audrey. What was he going to say to her? The truth—that there wasn't a chance in a hundred that Daphne was still alive? Or should he hold out hope to her, tell Audrey that her daughter might be held as a hostage for Greenburg's safe conduct out of the country?

As Wes drove down through the forested interior of Cape Cod, he realized suddenly that he and Hubert had raced all over Boston, called in the local police force, put out an all-points bulletin on Greenburg, and not once had either of them contemplated calling Jerry Gallent.

So that was another chore hanging over Weston's head: telling Gallent the whole story, apologizing for mistrusting him. He wondered, idly, if there would still be a place for him in the service. Wouldn't Gallent fire him immediately? Perhaps. But then Wes realized that he didn't care, not anymore, not after what had happened to Daphne. After what he'd done to her.

He flicked on the radio to clear his head. Later, when he was alone with Audrey, they would grieve together.

The news was on. Mention was made of the president's desire to meet the Russian premier that autumn at the bargaining table. A summit.

"The president is hoping for a warming in relations after the Gorvieski Labor Day visit to the United States," announced the newscaster. "Now on to the weather with Joan.

"This is Joan Delucey with the latest in weather. The National Hurricane Center at Coral Gables, Florida, has posted warnings tonight for the residents of Virginia Beach and northward as far as Atlantic City. Tropical storm Ethel has been upgraded to a full-fledged hurricane, whose eye reportedly carries sustaining winds of 120 knots. The tidal surge in those areas where the warning is posted could be as high as fifteen feet during the high tide, which is expected at 2:00 a.m. in Ocean City, Maryland. Residents all along the mid-Atlantic seaboard have been asked to evacuate low-lying areas. For residents of New York and Long Island, a hurricane watch is now in effect. Stay tuned. I'll return with the local weather after these messages."

To top it all off, thought Wes, a hurricane. It was far to the south, however, and the storms always veered out to sea before hitting New England.

"Joan Delucey back again. The forecast for Boston and vicinity is once again clear and sunny, with temperatures expected to reach into the middle seventies. But the humidity is expected to rise as Hurricane Ethel pumps moisture into our area later in the day. This station will keep its listeners posted as to the track Hurricane Ethel is taking and later in the hour, I'll have the coordinates for all you tracking buffs out there. Good evening from WBSL, your up-to-the-minute news station.''

Woods Hole was, of course, jammed. The tourists would not leave until after Labor Day and even then, weekends in the autumn could be crowded on the Cape. Wes parked and headed toward the ferry. He just made it on. Somehow he'd almost hoped he would miss it and not have to face Audrey. No such luck.

Already, in the early evening, a low mist was blanketing the ocean. It looked to Wes as if the ferry were drifting through a field of cotton, ethereal and dreamlike. He tried to clear his mind as he leaned against the rail and the mist swirled by below. But putting thoughts of Daphne from him was impossible. He'd see her face in the mist, soft and rosy cheeked, framed by curly short hair. He'd see her wide blue eyes and small straight nose, her mouth, curving nicely above a firm, obstinate chin, her heavy breasts and shapely legs. Daphne.

He couldn't stop the terrible question from forming in his head: had the end been quick? A knot clenched beneath his ribs, like a fist tightening, until the pain was almost intolerable.

He tried anger. Better to be angry than miserable. It drove away the pain for a moment, anyway. Anger he could deal with.

The problem was, he realized then, that she'd come to mean too much to him. He'd never known pain like this before and he asked himself if it would last forever. Was this the way Daphne had felt when news of Brady's death had reached her? My God, how had she borne it?

The mist lying on the ocean surface had thickened into a foggy wall, beckoning the ferryboat. Somewhere in the distance he heard the horn of another ship as it passed to the starboard. Then the island ferry was chugging into the bank, which obscured everything, causing the late sunlight to diffuse eerily and turn the silent world to copper.

Another foghorn sounded somewhere. Ships passing in the night, he thought. Like Daphne and himself. The idea was too lonely to contemplate. He'd always hated the expression, anyway.

He could hear islanders and tourists talking all along the port side, their voices muffled in the leaden air. He could see a face or two, an older couple, a child. Then they were gone in that golden veil. He saw a woman standing in a crowd up toward the bow. His heart jumped inadvertently in flashing hope and then calmed. She could have been Daphne. He supposed he'd see a lot of women who'd cause his gaze to rest on them for a minute. It was bound to happen. The pain would stop someday, wouldn't it?

Wes stared back into the fog as its color altered subtly with the setting sun. Now it was mustard yellow and murky, and he felt a sad hand squeeze his heart. He wondered how it would end.

THE *ISLAND QUEEN* seemed to take forever crossing to Vineyard Haven that evening. Daphne was the first person in line when the gangplank lowered, the first to rush off onto the dock. She had to get to a telephone. Wes must be half out of his mind thinking she'd been kidnapped and killed by Walter Greenburg. She couldn't forget the picture in her mind of Weston running through the tunnel trying to get to her.

There was a pay phone inside the ferry building. Hands shaking, Daphne called the club, her fingers crossed. When

Audrey answered, Daphne blurted out, "Has Wes called?"

"No, I haven't heard from him or Hubert. What's…?"

"I'm on my way to the club. If he calls, for God's sake tell him I'm all right."

"What's going on?"

"It's too complicated. I'll tell you later."

"Daphne, do you know there's a hurricane headed our way?" asked Audrey.

Daphne rolled her eyes in exasperation. "A hurricane. Oh, for goodness' sake, Audrey, they never get up here."

"They do sometimes."

"Look, I've got to go. Remember, if Wes calls, tell him I'm all right, that you spoke to me."

"How do I know it's really you?" said Audrey with asperity. "Maybe you're really somebody impersonating you."

"Goodbye, Mother," said Daphne in disgust as she hung up.

She turned away from the phone and started making her way through the crowds to where Wes had parked her car that morning. Had it really only been that morning that she and Wes and Hubert had gone to the airport? It seemed a lifetime ago. A lifetime of shocks and terror and tormented worry over what Wes must have been going through.

Sooner or later he'd contact Audrey even if he believed Daphne was… Her mind refused to finish the thought.

Tendrils of fog drifted between buildings, and the sea was completely blotted out by a yellowish haze. Even the sun, still relatively high in the sky on this summer's evening, was haloed and dimmed by fog. The glow gave the town an otherworldly aspect, like one of those cheap horror films that used a lot of dry ice.

She felt drained as she started up the hilly side street toward her car—exhausted and racked with worry and totally worn out. Around Daphne the tourists chirped and exclaimed and chattered like creatures of an outlandish species, one that had no relation to her own. She shut her mind to them and dragged herself up the hill. She had to get to the club.

Her trusty old VW was parked near the far end of a side street, hidden from her sight by the layers of mist rolling into the harbor. She made her way toward it, footsteps dragging, stepping around cars that pulled out of their spaces blindly. The fog parted for a minute and she saw her car.

There was someone getting into it! A car thief? "Hey," Daphne called, walking faster. "What do you think you're..."

She stopped short, frozen, and felt relief wash over her in a vast, cleansing surge. Her knees went all watery, and her heart gave a great glad bound. Then she was running toward him, crying his name.

"Daphne!" he said hoarsely, turning and seeing her, a look of incredulous, stunned relief on his face.

She ran into his arms, as if it were the most natural thing in the world to do, and he held her tightly, crushing her to him.

"Oh, Wes! Oh, thank heavens! I was so worried...!" She buried her head against his chest and felt the strength of his embrace. He said nothing for a time, but she could feel the thump of his heart against her cheek.

"I thought you were dead," he breathed into her hair. "I thought..."

"I know. I tried calling your place, but you were never there," she murmured.

"Oh, God. I thought you were dead," he said again, wonderingly, stroking her hair with one hand. Eventually he pushed her gently away from him and held her at arm's length. His face was shadowed with exhaustion and marked with anguish.

"It isn't Greenburg," Daphne rushed to say, her eyes searching Weston's face. "He let me go. He only wanted to prove he could have killed me if he was the guilty man. He handed me his gun and let me go. Wes, he even drove me down to Woods Hole to get the ferry."

Wes was silent for a moment. When he spoke his voice was husky. "You mean, he put us through all that . . ." He closed his eyes and swayed.

"Wes!" Daphne grabbed at him, terrified. "Are you all right?"

His eyes opened. "I am now. I wasn't."

"Oh, I know. I've been crazy all day."

Wes rubbed a hand across his eyes. "I looked everywhere, Daphne. I called the police. I was sure he was going to . . ."

She couldn't bear the torment she saw in his eyes. She reached out and touched his cheek. "I'm okay. It's over. Walter Greenburg is not the one and I'm fine, and now I'm going to drive you straight to the house, feed you and make you go to bed."

He wouldn't let go of her until she gently disengaged her hand from his and got into the car. He seemed to be still too stunned to think for himself.

"I'm driving home, Wes," she said. "We'll call Audrey from there. I'm too tired to pick her up."

The sun was brighter once they'd left the coast, and it shone down on the forests of tangled grapevines and old stone walls as Daphne drove. The convertible top on her car was down, and the wind felt cool and refreshing in her face.

Wes seemed to gather his wits as they sped along, and finally he turned to her and asked with some of his old spirit, "What happened? I want to know every detail."

She told him everything: how she'd tried to stall, how she'd seen him but it had been too late, how she'd been forced to drive to the deserted warehouse on the pier.

"And he had a gun on you all the time?" interrupted Wes.

"Yes. Steady as a rock. I was terrified."

"I can imagine," said Wes. "That son of a—"

"He was desperate. It was the only way he could think of to prove to us he was innocent." Daphne shuddered.

"It was effective," mused Wes.

"Then he just turned the gun around and handed it to me and that was that. I knew he wasn't our man then."

Wes nodded. "So we've narrowed it down." He shook his head. "A helluva way to proceed with an investigation."

When they got to the Farway house, much to their surprise, Audrey was outside, taping windows. "A hurricane's headed our way," she explained. "It hit the Chesapeake Bay area today and is supposed to get here sometime tomorrow."

"You were supposed to be at the club, Mrs. Farway," said Wes.

"I couldn't let my poor old house blow down, could I?"

"It's dangerous for you to be here alone," he said patiently.

"Well, I just got here and you're here now, so I'm safe," she snapped. "Where's Sam, anyway?"

"He's at home in Cambridge. Had a little problem to take care of," said Wes. "Did he call the club?"

"No, nobody bothers to let me know anything." Audrey sighed dramatically.

"Audrey, we've had a hard day," said Daphne. "Can we just eat and relax?"

"I'm not stopping you. Fix yourselves sandwiches. Just go on and take it easy. *I'm* going to tape my windows."

"Irritating, isn't she?" murmured Daphne as they went inside. "But she hates storms. It's the only thing in the world she's afraid of. Of course, they rarely hit us here. The last big one was in '38, like I said."

"Look, Daphne, would you mind fixing me some coffee and a sandwich? I've got to call Hubert. He must be a mess by now if he hasn't gotten hold of Dodie. And I'll try to get him back here as soon as possible. I can only go without sleep so long."

"Oh, Wes," Daphne said, "do you have to stay up tonight? You aren't really well and today was awful . . ."

"Somebody's got to, and I'm the only one here," he replied. "I'll manage."

He went to call Hubert and then came back to the kitchen, sat down at the old pine table and sipped the coffee Daphne had made.

"Well?"

"He was there. The poor guy's going nuts. He can't find Dodie or her husband anywhere. He went out to Lexington and spoke to one of her neighbors. The house is empty, car's gone." Wes leaned on an elbow, resting his head on his hand. "He can't locate Joe Marion, either. He said he'd try to get back here as soon as he can."

"Trouble seems to come in litters, doesn't it?" Daphne reflected, sitting down next to him at the table.

Wes gave her a lopsided smile. "Whatever can go wrong will go wrong."

"And I got you into this," Daphne said.

He shrugged. She sensed that he was disconcerted by the way he'd just reacted to her and was trying to withdraw from the intensity of his emotions. The closeness between them was fast dissipating. She knew it but couldn't do a thing about it. Wes was retreating into his shell of friendliness, leaving her outside, all alone. He needed time, she told herself. She'd have to try very hard to let him be.

Audrey came in, looking harassed. "I'm all out of tape and it's too late to go buy some. Damn. This is going to be a big storm, kids. I can feel it in my tennis elbow. Prepare to batten down the hatches."

"Need some help, Mrs. Farway?" asked Weston too eagerly.

"You bet your tushy I do, young man!"

Immediately, without saying another word, he left Daphne in the kitchen. It wasn't until a moment later that she realized that he hadn't had a chance to eat anything, nor had he even finished his coffee. She sank down wearily on a chair at the kitchen table and stared sadly at his untouched plate.

CHAPTER FIFTEEN

THE TELEPHONE RANG SHRILLY at nine-thirty that evening, startling Daphne. When she answered it her composure fled totally. It was Jerry Gallent.

"What the devil is going on?" he was yelling even before Daphne could gather her thoughts. "I'm at Weston Leroux's place! The window's broken, the door was open and there's a big spot of blood on the floor! Where is he? You know where he is, Miss Farway, and I want an answer right now!"

Her mind stumbled, trying to follow the man's angry words, trying to remember what she'd told him, how much she was supposed to know, how much he would know if he were indeed guilty.

"How should I know where he is?" she replied in an automatic attempt at evasion.

"Look, I'm not stupid. I got to thinking about all those things you said the other day. About someone in the office selling our itinerary to the Russians and Brady being murdered and all that." His tone was much calmer. "I was furious that day. Imagine me selling secrets to the Russians! And I pride myself on good security in the office. It's hard to take, Miss Farway, but there *could* be something to your allegations. It's just that it's not me, that's all. Whatever Brady told you was wrong on that score. I wanted to talk this stuff over with Wes, so I drove over to his place. And I found the scene of a crime, Miss Farway. Now what do you know about it?"

He could still be guilty. He could be just trying to feel her out. *Be careful,* she warned herself.

"Why on earth should I know anything about Mr. Leroux?"

"Come on, everyone knows that you had lunch with him that day and he was Brady's partner. Then, of course, he took that leave of absence. I wondered about that. And then the little costume drama you pulled the other day. Cute. It smacked of Weston's methods. Hell, I taught him those methods! It wasn't too hard to put two and two together. Now what's happened to my agent?"

"I have no idea." She wished Wes were there to tell her what to say. Gallent was so plausible, his logic so sound. Was he innocent or just a criminal who was superb at covering his tracks?

"I want you to know," Jerry Gallent was saying, "I called the police on this. I have old friends on the force and I pulled out every stop on this one. Unfortunately there's no body, no missing person report, no crime. There's not much they can do."

"You called the police?" Daphne asked faintly.

"Of course. Something's happened to Wes and I want to know what. I bet you could tell me, Miss Farway, but since you won't, maybe the police will find him for me."

The police. He'd called the police? A guilty man did not call the police in to investigate his own crime, did he?

She almost told him then. But the phone crackled horribly in her ear and she couldn't hear anything for a minute. Just long enough to reconsider, to doubt.

"You there?" Jerry Gallent was saying. "It's the hurricane. The wind's gusting pretty bad on the coast by now."

"I'm here."

"There's no time to waste, Miss Farway. If you really want to do something about this so-called assassination plot of yours, you'd better talk to me—and quick. I'm driving down to your place in the morning. I know damned well Wes is there or you know where he is. We've got work to do!"

When Daphne hung up she was shaking in reaction. Then she noticed that Wes had come into the room silently and was standing there, watching her, his face a study in reserve.

"It was Jerry Gallent," Daphne breathed.

"What did he want?"

Daphne felt behind her for a chair, sat down and repeated the conversation to him.

Wes listened impassively. "So he called the police?"

"That's what he said."

"It's easy enough to check out." Picking up the phone, Wes dialed a number in Boston and asked for Police Chief Daniels. After a few pointed, evasive questions, he hung up. "Gallent reported it," Wes said.

Later, when Daphne was getting ready for bed, Audrey came in to see her. "I hate storms," she hissed. "They scare the pants off me."

"It will probably die out. You know, like they all do," said Daphne comfortingly. "A little wind, some salt spray..."

"This one's a bad one. I can tell. I remember '38. I was a little girl but I remember. Listen to the wind out there."

Daphne listened. It *was* blowing hard; somewhere a loose shutter banged against the house in a restless cadence.

"It'll keep me up all night," muttered Audrey. "Tomorrow I'm going inland to the club. I can't stand this."

"That's where you'd be now if you'd followed orders."

"Orders! I don't like orders. Blast it all, I wish good old Sam was here. I could use a nice friendly argument to cheer me up."

"Hubert's got more to worry about than quibbling with you, Audrey," began Daphne.

"What's the matter?"

Daphne told her about Hubert's missing daughter.

"The dummy. He should have waited to call that filthy blackmailer! Boy, he's done it, hasn't he?"

"I hope not."

"Well, I guess he'll need some help, won't he? And Wes is occupied. You're occupied. I'll have to do it."

"Mother..."

"I wasn't born yesterday. I'll bet I could find that daughter of his."

"Stay out of it, Audrey," warned Daphne.

"Sure, sure," said Audrey, already thinking hard. "Wonder if the girl's run off with a lover?"

"With three little kids?"

"Yes, well, that does present a problem."

At 11:48, Daphne finally decided she just couldn't sleep. She rose, threw on a light robe and went downstairs. The house creaked and grumbled around her as if it were alive and protesting the wind that buffeted it. Even the muted roar of the surf reached Daphne's ears. She shivered inadvertently.

"Wes?" she called softly, seeing a light in the kitchen. "Wes?"

His head jerked up. "Who?" he asked, startled.

"It's me. I couldn't sleep," she said. "Do you mind if I stay here awhile?"

"Sure, it's okay. You can help keep me awake."

"Oh, Lord, I feel so awful. Couldn't you just lock the door and go to sleep?"

"There are dozens of ways to get into this old place. And tonight, with the wind, I wouldn't even be able to hear anyone trying to get in," he said.

"It's Michael Toth, isn't it?"

"It looks like it, Daphne, but I'm not ready to accuse him quite yet. Let's see what the chief says tomorrow."

She sat down at the table across from him. One old ceiling fixture was lit, dropping a cone of light on them. Otherwise the room—the house—was in darkness. Outside the wind sang and shook castinets of sand and hissed through the sea oats.

"They're calling her Ethel," said Wes, looking toward the window that faced the ocean.

"She'll veer out to sea. They always do. This isn't very bad," said Daphne.

"It's a helluva spot to live in," said Wes thoughtfully, "during a storm."

Sand and spray and rain tapped on the windows like ghostly hands.

"Felicity wants in," smiled Daphne.

"Ghosts. You believe in ghosts," Wes said, searching her face, his eyes serious.

"You're not talking about Felicity, are you?" she asked.

His silence was pointed.

"You're thinking about Brady."

"You won't let him go, will you?"

Daphne stared at him. How could he possibly still think that? She felt angry and hurt and insulted. Rising, she walked to the tall kitchen window and looked out, trying to form words in her mind that would refute Weston's statement. From the antique, whorled glass, her reflection stared back at her, distorted and pale.

Then she saw movement in the reflection and Weston came up behind her. Their likenesses wavered in the glass as the wind pressed against the window; they shivered, then steadied. She turned and searched his face.

"Is that what you really think?" she asked.

"I don't know. Sometimes I do. You must compare us all the time."

She sucked in a breath of irritation. "So? What if I do compare you? Do you feel so...so...inadequate?"

He didn't answer, but just stood there looking at her with those clear green eyes that gave away nothing. He finally spoke. "Go to bed, Daphne."

"No," she said stubbornly. "I'm not leaving you alone down here all night. I can't sleep, anyway."

A gust jolted the house then. Somewhere a heavy object fell with a rattle and a thud. "Oh!" said Daphne, starting, grabbing his arm unconsciously.

Her touch seemed to break down a barrier. Weston drew her to him slowly and bent his head to her upturned face. His mouth covered hers with a fierceness that surprised yet thrilled her.

She could feel his unshaven cheek rasp against hers, and the small pain of it felt good. His lips moved on hers, inflaming her senses.

Somehow they got to the couch in the darkened living room. Outside, the wind battered at the old house and the sea reached for it, licking at the dunes. The frenzy of the storm made Daphne feel as reckless as the elements. Her hands roamed over Weston's body, feeling, touching, learning every hollow and angle.

There were no words between them, only soft sighs of pleasure. Clothing fell to the floor. Weston's hands were gentle and then hard on her flesh. With each touch her breath quickened, her nerve endings tingled, the demanding ache in her belly swelled.

He nibbled at her neck, then down to her shoulder and arm. Each finger he kissed, before proceeding up to her breasts. She moved under him, awash with fantastic delight that surged in waves of pleasure over her.

She arched her back and felt electric bolts of sensation shoot through her body. Her hands twined in his thick, shiny hair and she pulled his head closer, wanting him near, wanting to be inside his flesh.

He was so warm and strong and he moved against her like smooth satin.

She pulled him up over her, throbbing, unable to wait, and he entered her, hard and hot and thrusting. They moved together as one being; there was no difference between them. Red hot upwellings rippled through Daphne and she felt herself being carried along, higher and higher, faster, until her mouth opened in a wordless cry and she felt her whole body convulse in a final paroxysm.

Later they lay together and her hand stroked Weston's hair, slowly, languidly. "Are you still there?" she asked softly.

"Barely."

"Listen to the storm," she whispered.

There was a sustained hissing roar outside, and it seemed as if the house shuddered. Water slashed at the windows—rain and sea spray mixed.

"The old girl's really going to town tonight," said Wes, running a gentle hand down the soft white flesh of her hip.

"I resent that, sir," objected Daphne, laughing.

He turned his head to kiss her ear and tickle it with his tongue. "I didn't say I was complaining, did I?" he murmured.

The morning sky was leaden and gray, swept by fierce internal currents of wind and rain. When Daphne went into the kitchen, she found Audrey huddled over a battery-powered radio. Her mother barely looked up. "She's headed right for us, damn her ugly heart to hell!" rasped Audrey, her profanity born more of fear than disrespect. "I don't know if I can take it, Daphne."

Outside the window, the surf was surging in great pewter-colored waves that towered up and up and crested, finally, in angry curls of foam before they ebbed, swirling on the sand, to build for another assault.

"Winds at 130 miles an hour, four hundred miles across. Long Island is really getting it right now. Oh, I hate this!"

Jerry Gallent arrived at about ten. When she saw his taxi, Daphne ordered Audrey upstairs and rushed to tell Wes, who immediately hid behind the Chinese screen. Then she took a deep breath and went to the door.

Gallent was pale green, windblown and soaking wet. "I hate boats," he growled as Daphne let him in. "They should build a bridge to this island! The waves were higher than the ferry, and there's no way I'm going back until this storm is over!"

She showed him into the living room, expecting him to sit down. But he stood in the middle of the room and looked around.

"Where is he?" Gallent asked.

"Who?"

"Leroux. Don't play games, Miss Farway."

"I haven't seen him in at least a week," she said. Gallent must think her alone, unprotected. Then he would feel safe to make a move against her—if he were the guilty man.

"You're here alone, then?"

"Yes."

"If you don't mind my saying so, miss, you're being pretty foolish. If you're right about this plot and if Brady was killed when he confronted the traitor, then you, my dear, are in distinct danger. If I could put two and two together, so could he." He walked toward the Chinese screen and then turned and looked out the window. "Filthy weather," he commented. "Sometimes I'd like to be back in Utah. It's a lot drier there."

Gallent turned suddenly, moving quickly for a heavy man, and made Daphne jump. "Look, I'm really worried about Weston. My agent must have been hurt. The police haven't come up with anything. I checked. I also—" here he gave her a fierce scowl "—looked into Brady's shooting a little more. Ballistics reported the bullet to be a .38, the kind issued to Secret Service agents." He shook his head sorrowfully. "Brady should have come to me. I would have listened. Then he'd still be here."

"Do you . . . ah, have any idea who the guilty man is?" asked Daphne .

Gallent didn't answer immediately. He came over to where Daphne sat and looked down at her, his short legs astride, his heavy, bushy brows drawn together, the lines on his face deeply etched and somber. "I think it's an agent named Michael Toth," he finally said.

Daphne drew in a breath. They were closing in on the guilty one. "Why?" she asked.

"I don't know why I'm telling you this," Gallent said. "But since that crazy Hungarian might just come hunting you, I guess you're entitled to know."

He paused and then went on. "Toth is a naturalized citizen. Now, I'm no bigot, but I'm a little leery of these Eastern Europeans. They're torn between the old country and the new. Toth had a touch of trouble getting his security clearance. Something about some organizations he belonged to in high school. Commie stuff. Then lately he's been bugging me to be on the liaison team during Gorvieski's visit because he speaks Russian. He's scheduled for the airport squad, not liaison. He knows that. It's kind of an odd thing for him to ask.''

"So you think Michael Toth is the man?"

"I can't be a hundred percent positive. But I'll find out, don't you worry. It's very possible that Toth is a Russian plant, a mole, and he could be working for that faction in the Kremlin that would like to see Viktor Gorvieski dead and gone."

Gallent scowled again. "But right now I'm more concerned with Wes Leroux. He seems to have disappeared off the face of the earth."

"Not exactly" came a voice from behind Daphne, "but close, Chief Gallent." And Weston stepped out from behind the Chinese screen into full view of his superior.

"Well, I'll be damned," exclaimed Jerry Gallent. "You don't pull your punches, do you, Leroux?"

"I had to be sure," said Wes.

"So what happened to you? I'll tell you, Wes, when I saw that blood on your floor..." The man whistled through his teeth.

"Somebody took a potshot at me."

"I take it he missed."

"No, he hit me but only a glancing blow. I was lucky. Dingy for a couple of days, but real lucky."

"Did you just get up and walk away?" asked Gallent.

"No, not quite. Daphne—Miss Farway—found me on the floor and got me back here."

Gallent's square face swung around to Daphne, and he eyed her with intense interest. "She did, huh? Well, now..." Then he turned back to Wes. "So he knows you're on to him," said Gallent soberly.

"He?"

"You heard me before. It's got to be Toth."

"What about Greenburg?" suggested Wes.

"What about him? You tell me."

"I can tell you he's eliminated as a suspect as far as I'm concerned, but maybe you know something I don't," said Wes carefully.

"You mean the Russian girl, don't you?"

Daphne looked at Wes in surprise, but he was staring steadily at his boss.

"Sure, I knew about that," said Gallent genially. "So did his superior, Rex, out in Frisco. We decided to let it go when he transferred. I really don't think Walt could handle being a double agent, do you?"

"Not anymore, I don't."

"So, who's left with the clearance to get his hands on the itinerary?" asked Gallent. "Me, you, Hubert Samuels, maybe."

"It's not Hubert," said Wes tightly.

"Where is he, by the way? He told me he was sick when I called him in to replace you. Hubert sick? He's never been sick, far as I can remember."

"He was here, working with me. Right now he's...well, he's at home. He's got a problem, a family problem."

"So you've been watching over Miss Farway here all by yourself?" He clucked and shook his head. "Getting a bit tired there, Wes?"

Wes sat down and rubbed a hand over his face. "A little."

"Well, good thing I showed up. Now we're going to set up a plan to catch Mr. Toth and I'm going to call the office for backup. No one needs to know anything at all about what's going on down here—the guys they send are just bodies." He turned to Daphne. "May I use the phone for a minute, Miss Farway?"

He made the call while Daphne went to sit next to Weston on the couch. "You trust him?" she whispered.

"More and more each minute. He wouldn't call for backup if he wanted us dead."

Gallent was talking loudly; the connection must have been bad. "Yeah, and if that hellish ferry isn't going, go straight to the Coast Guard station at Woods Hole. Tell 'em you've got clearance from the White House if necessary." He paused, listening.

"No, don't call Hubert. He's busy, but get some of the guys from my list. And hurry it up, Tommy. I'll give you directions to the house. It's out in the middle of nowhere." He gave the directions and repeated his order to hurry. Then he hung up.

"That was Tommy Taylor, Wes. He'll send some guys down here fast. Now why don't you get some shut-eye?"

"No, not yet. I want to hear what kind of plan you're considering. Will you call Washington?"

"Not yet, Wes." Jerry Gallent paced the room, hands clasped behind his back, square bulldog head thrust forward. "Toth will only get alerted and go underground. He'll run and we'll never know what information he gave them. There'd be no time to dig him out and no time to rethink the whole itinerary. We've got to get him red-handed. We need their exact plan. You know what a stickler Washington is these days."

Daphne watched the chief. It was fascinating how the man just took over. Nothing rattled him. He was as solid as a rock, mentally and physically. She was terribly glad and relieved he was there, on their side.

"You know, we pulled the same thing with Toth as we did with you," said Wes finally. "He's set up already. I think he'll try something soon."

"You did? Well, well. Maybe we'll just wait it out, then. This storm might stop him, anyway, at least for a while."

"I want to apologize for putting you through the wringer," said Wes. "We just didn't know which one it was. We had to eliminate each man as best we could."

Gallent nodded. "You did well. And you *did* find out. That was the hard part, Wes. Your Miss Farway did a great job. Very convincing." He broke into a broad smile. "Maybe I should hire her."

"Wes, can I talk to you a minute?" said Daphne. "Excuse me, Mr. Gallent, but this is kind of private."

"Sure, go ahead. I'll wander around and check the security in the place. Go on." He waved a hand, dismissing them.

Daphne drew Weston into the kitchen. "I want you to go to Hubert," she said. "Now that Gallent's here and has sent for some more men, you're free to go help him."

"I can't, Daphne."

"You can. I'm perfectly safe now. And you'd better hurry because if Ethel really does hit, the ferries will stop running and you'll be stuck."

"Daphne..."

"Hubert needs you. And he's almost like your father, Wes. There's no one else in the world to help. I'm really worried about him myself."

"I don't know. I think the chief is okay, but I'd feel a lot better being here myself."

"You're too tired to do anything now, anyway. Fresh men are coming, Wes. I'll be perfectly safe."

"Safe," he said wryly, "with a crazy Hungarian after you and a hurricane trying to blow you off the island!"

"Perfectly safe," she repeated lightly, "like I said." She took his hand and brought it up to her lips. "Go on, Wes. I know you want to."

"Maybe... Let me check with the chief," said Wes, frowning. "We'll see what he says."

Gallent was all for Weston going. "Get outta here, Leroux. I can handle it."

"When will the backup get here?" asked Wes.

Gallent checked his watch. "By two, Tommy thought, even with the storm."

"I'm not sure..." Wes said.

"Look, I don't know what Samuels's problem is and I don't want to know, but if you're that worried you'd better go. I've got this place all under control." Gallent gestured to a window that was streaked with silvery rain. "You'd better get going if you want to make it. If the winds hit ninety, the State of Massachusetts is closing down—no cars on the road, no ferries. A real war zone, Wes. Get on outta here."

Daphne ran upstairs to her mother's room to find out whether there were any men's raincoats in the house. "He's going to help Hubert," Daphne explained.

"Poor Sam," mused Audrey. "By the way, can I come downstairs now?"

"Sure, it's okay now. And we know it's Mike Toth. Mr. Gallent is going to stay and guard us."

"Us? I'm going to the club if it gets any worse, and from what the radio says, it's heading right up the coast."

"The raincoats, Audrey?"

"Sure. In the hall closet, stuck somewhere in the back. All sizes," she replied distractedly.

"You can use my car," Daphne said to Wes a moment later, helping him into a yellow slicker. "The convertible top leaks a little, but never mind. Give our best to Hubert and find Dodie for him. Try to call, okay? Of course the lines may go down in this storm so if I don't hear..."

"You sound like my nursemaid," grumbled Wes.

"I don't feel like your nursemaid," Daphne said, smiling impishly. "Now hurry. The ferry leaves at eleven-fifteen."

"I hope I'm doing the right thing," Wes said.

"You are, really."

"Be careful, Daphne. Toth could be here on the island somewhere, waiting."

"Hey, I'm safe. Isn't your boss here? Come on."

He pulled her into his arms. "If anything happened to you and I wasn't here...," he said fiercely.

She silenced him by pulling his head down and kissing him. Slowly, reluctantly, his arms went around her waist. "There. Now don't worry," she said breathlessly, leaning back in his arms.

"Hey, you two, cut the romance," said Audrey loudly. She stood in the hallway in her slicker and sou'wester, a small overnight bag over her shoulder.

Wes dropped his hands from Daphne as if he'd been scalded.

"Well, young man, are we going or are you going to play kissy-face all day?" demanded Audrey.

Wes looked at her blankly.

"I'm going with you," Audrey said very distinctly. "I'm getting off this island before the hurricane gets here and I'm going with you to help Hubert. We can take my car. And that's that."

Wes looked at Daphne helplessly.

"Well?" said Audrey impatiently.

At the front door, Wes turned to Daphne one more time. "Stay away from the windows and keep everything locked up tight and do what the chief says. Don't worry. We'll get Toth, Daphne.''

And then he and Audrey dashed to her red Saab, splashing in the mud, propelled by the savage wind, soaked by driving rain.

Lightning flashed in a long jagged streak, illuminating the scene, and then came the reverberating crash of thunder. By the time it died away, Audrey's car had disappeared up the drive and Daphne realized she was standing in the open door, lashed by rain and wind, wet to the skin.

Swiftly she slammed the door shut and locked it. Then she turned to find Jerry Gallent standing right behind her.

CHAPTER SIXTEEN

"You're not so hot at checkers," said Daphne, laughing. "Would you rather play cards?"

Jerry Gallent smiled. "Maybe gin rummy is more up my alley."

Daphne rose from the card table where they'd been playing and went to get a deck. She wondered just how long they could entertain themselves and kill time without going completely stir-crazy. Her worry over Hubert and Wes was never far from the surface of her mind.

"When do you think your backup team will get here, Mr. Gallent?" asked Daphne as she returned with the cards.

"It's Jerry. I told Wes I thought around two. But I suppose it depends on this weather," he replied. "I'd say pretty soon, anyway."

"I hope the ferry keeps running." She broke the seal on a new deck and began shuffling the slippery cards.

"Our main problem, of course," he said, "will come if Mike Toth does try something before they get here."

"But, really, wouldn't he have tried already?" asked Daphne while dealing.

"Not necessarily. I assume you gave him a story similar to the one you told me. Chances are he really believes you're after money from him. In that case, he'll bide his time until he feels it's safe to come after you."

"If it were me," said Daphne, listening to the shutters bang against the house furiously, "I'd use the storm as cover."

"How's that?" Jerry placed his cards in his hand one at a time, eyeing each carefully, his face expressionless.

"You know," replied Daphne, "use the storm somehow to make my... my *demise* look like an accident."

"It's a possibility. Toth is a very sharp man."

"He might even be on the midafternoon ferry." Daphne discarded.

Jerry looked at her discard casually and then picked it up, throwing out a queen.

Daphne picked up his queen and grinned. "I suppose I should be scared," she said, "but it feels as if I've been in danger all my life. It's beginning to feel normal."

"You never should have put yourself in this position. You should have told me the truth in Boston that day."

"I know that now." She picked up a queen from the deck and discarded a five. "But back then I didn't know who I could trust."

"You trusted Wes Leroux."

"*Brady* trusted him."

"I see." He picked up her five.

Daphne drew from the deck. A queen. She tried to keep the smile from her lips, discarding a six. "So what would you do if Mike burst through that door right now?"

Jerry patted the bulge under his suit jacket. "I'm ready if he does."

She picked up the nine that Jerry discarded. "Gin!" She laughed, pleased.

He grimaced. "I wasn't paying attention. Next time," he said, mock-brusquely, "I will."

"Is that a challenge?"

His thick head bobbed up and down slowly.

They played and talked, mostly about Mike Toth. Daphne did her best to avoid the subject of Hubert and his "family problem" and thankfully Jerry never asked.

Daphne fixed tuna sandwiches for lunch while Jerry checked the taped-up windows one more time.

"Mike is probably sitting at home in Boston," commented Daphne, "waiting out the storm."

"Not at home," smiled Jerry. "More likely in a beer-slinging pub."

"Well, don't you think that makes more sense than his coming down here in this weather?"

"You've asked me that six times."

"I have?"

He nodded, wiping mayonnaise off his chin with a napkin, indicating that his mouth was full. When he'd swallowed, he said, "More like a dozen times. Relax, Daphne. I can handle Toth if he tries anything. Wes wouldn't have left you in my care," he teased, "if I weren't any good."

Daphne blushed. "Of course," she said sheepishly.

Having Jerry Gallent there was like having a father around. He was easy to talk to and had an alert, dry sense of humor. He seemed to enjoy when she baited him and Daphne found herself doing that often. "Are you sure your gun is loaded? When was the last time you were on a stakeout?"

It helped having him there. It took her mind off poor Hubert and Wes and her worry that someone had actually harmed Dodie. Surely Hubert's daughter was just off someplace with the kids. Still, Daphne fretted from time to time, wondering, anxious that Hubert and Wes and her impulsive mother might be in danger.

"I wish Wes would call," she said aloud once.

"He will." Jerry smiled reassuringly.

They turned on the radio often and listened for updates on Hurricane Ethel. The storm, at one o'clock, had passed Long Island and was battering the Connecticut coast, seemingly bouncing in and off shore. The eye was threatening to hit land near New London around four.

"On her present course," the announcer's voice informed them, "Ethel will move inland north of New London and miss the Cape Cod peninsula. Of course, Ethel has been moving erratically and could easily track back offshore and gain momentum. The residents of Cape Cod, Nantucket and Martha's Vineyard have all been warned to evacuate in the event that Ethel takes an eastwardly course."

Gallent got a very serious expression on his face. "Maybe we should evacuate. I mean, here you are right on the shore."

"I wouldn't," said Daphne calmly.

"Your mother left. And it *is* getting pretty bad. You might be smart to consider it."

"First of all, hurricanes never hit us here. I'm sure Ethel will go on out to sea now. In the second place, Mike Toth might come. If no one's here, our whole plan goes down the drain."

"Daphne, my dear, brave young lady, if the storm inundates this house, it won't matter if Toth arrives or not."

She set her chin stubbornly. "I'm not leaving. We islanders don't leave." Then under her breath, she added, "Except my mother."

Gallent lifted his bushy eyebrows and spread his hands, giving up. "Okay, be a stubborn Yankee. I guess if this old place hasn't washed away for a hundred years, it won't now."

Daphne smiled benignly in victory.

They decided to drive to Beetlebung Corner to load up on groceries. "Audrey left in such a hurry," explained Daphne, "that she didn't even leave milk."

"Will the roads be open?"

Daphne laughed. "I hope so. If they're not, we're in real trouble."

They took her VW bug. Rain, carried on a sixty-mile-an-hour wind, slashed at it. The convertible top leaked.

"What, exactly, is Beetlebung Corner, by the way?" asked Gallent. "Or is it dumb to ask?"

Daphne smiled. "It's just a crossroads with some stores. But there's a very old grove of tupelo trees there and their wood used to be made into barrel plugs called beetles, or bungs. So, beetlebung. It's very simple, actually."

"Of course," said Jerry, wiping away the water that dripped from a hole in the canvas top. "I haven't been in one of these for years," he called over the roar of the wind. "Are you sure it'll stay on the road?"

Daphne strained to see through the windshield while the wipers did all sorts of crazy things. "I'm not sure of anything. Maybe we should have forgotten the milk."

"Should we turn around?"

She shook her head. "Just passed the point of no return. It's Beetlebung or bust!"

Jerry Gallent shot her an incredulous glance. "I think you're enjoying this!"

"I am. It's exciting. We islanders like a good challenge." In truth, Daphne was a little frightened. Already there were branches strewn over the road and deep puddles in low places. The water was lifting off the surface of them in a steady spray from the driving wind. The trees were nearly bent to the ground. Where the ocean could be seen from the road, it was a solid wall of froth and fury, flinging itself against the dunes, wave after wave.

Jerry looked out his window. "What holds the sea back?" he asked rhetorically.

"Not much," replied Daphne under her breath.

The tupelo or black gum trees were there at the crossroads—slashed by the wind. They got out of the car, hopping over puddles, and rushed into the store. It was jammed. "Everyone must have had the same idea," panted Daphne.

"Doesn't *anyone* plan on leaving the island?" asked Jerry.

A hurricane update came over the radio that sat propped on top of the vintage cash register. A hush fell over the shoppers.

"Hurricane Ethel has stalled south of New London, Connecticut. It's impossible to predict her next move. At this time the winds surrounding the eye are reported to be 120 knots. The residents of all low-lying areas within a hundred-mile radius of the eye are being advised to evacuate. For information about the evacuation center nearest you, call the Connecticut State police. Stay tuned for the next update."

Daphne bought milk and bread and butter and things they could eat out of a can, if necessary. "Not a great diet," she told Jerry, "but if we lose power..."

The drive back was even more treacherous. The road was impassable in places, but Daphne merely stepped on the gas and forced the little VW over the sandy shoulders. "If we get stuck," she called, "we may have to go on foot." She eyed the man's bulky frame and felt a surge of security—he'd get her there.

It broke her heart to see the damage the wind was doing to the island's lovely foliage. And what if the storm really did start moving eastward? It could strike the Vineyard with tremendous fury; the only thing between New London and Martha's Vineyard was water.

She and Jerry raced for the house. He went first, "To check inside," and she carried the bag of groceries, having been instructed to wait in the vestibule until he'd checked out the whole place.

It took him fifteen minutes, and Daphne was beginning to lose patience standing there, her yellow rain slicker dripping, the water puddling around her feet. She couldn't hear him, so steady was the trainlike roar of the wind as it buffeted the old Victorian mercilessly.

It was eerie listening for footfalls she couldn't hear, and imagining Toth lurking somewhere in one of the shadowed corners of the rambling house.

But finally Jerry appeared from the living room. He snapped on the hall light. "All clear."

"Are you sure?" she asked breathlessly.

"Positive." He took the groceries from her.

Daphne fixed them both hot tomato soup, while Jerry sat in the kitchen reading one of her cook books. "Key lime pie?" He raised a doubtful brow. "Thought that was from the Florida Keys."

"For shame!" admonished Daphne. "Didn't you know that they stole that from Martha's Vineyard? The limes were kept under lock and key in those days, so . . . *key* lime pie." She went on to tell him about how Felicity Hawthorne had been about to prepare lime pie when news of her husband's death had reached her.

Jerry Gallent inadvertently glanced at the ceiling in the direction of the guestroom. "Boloney," he declared.

"No," said Daphne, "pie."

She talked a lot over the hot soup. The lights kept flickering on and off and Audrey's radio squawked with news of Hurricane Ethel, still stalled just off the Connecticut coast.

"Tell me about the Secret Service," she suggested. "Anything."

"Nervous?"

"Some. Between the ocean hitting the top of our dune out there and then wondering about Mike Toth..." Her voice drifted away into anxious silence.

"Well," he began, smiling in understanding, "mostly we try to nab counterfeiters or bust some of these gangs that steal Treasury checks. We guard diplomats..."

"No, I mean *real* stories. Surely something crazy has happened to you in...how many years?"

"Twenty-four."

"So tell me."

"Well, I'll keep it on the light side. No breaching of security or anything like that."

"Of course not."

"I was stationed years ago in Texas, at Lyndon Johnson's ranch, and got myself in some real trouble once. It was about two in the morning and raining like there was no tomorrow. The president appeared at his bedroom window and handed me that blasted mutt of his and told me to walk him."

"He asked *you* to do that?"

"I told you, Daphne, our lives are not always so glamorous. At any rate, I walked the mutt for a good ten minutes. I was wet and mad and the stupid dog was covered with mud. The president's window was still open so I threw the dog in and it landed right on the president and Ladybird's white bedspread."

"Oh, my..."

"Exactly. I guess I lost my head for a minute. Anyway, Johnson appeared at the window with the mutt in his arms and told me that from now on, I would not only walk the dog but towel him off afterward." Jerry Gallent shrugged, remembering.

They finished their soup, and Daphne did the dishes in the flickering lights. It wouldn't be long before the power went off; she found candles in a drawer and put them on the table. Then she and the chief went upstairs and filled the five bathtubs in case they lost water pressure.

Outside, the fringe of the hurricane tormented the island. From a third-floor window, Daphne stood looking out over the ocean. The sea was dark and ferocious, flinging itself against the innocent dunes and tearing at the precious sea oats that Audrey so carefully cultivated. The foamy whitecaps could be seen all along the horizon, mountains of salt water. At least ten-foot seas, Daphne thought.

"Quite a sight," observed Jerry Gallent from behind her.

Daphne's hand went to her throat. "Oh, my gosh, you frightened me."

"Thought I was Toth?"

She nodded. "For a moment."

"He's not going to harm you," said Jerry in a curious voice.

Was he as worried as she? And why hadn't Wes telephoned?

"Let's go downstairs," he said in that familiar, kind tone. "I'll teach you how to play a real man's game. Poker, my dear."

Daphne followed him down the dim hallway. "You do have your gun, don't you?"

He paused on the narrow steps. "Yes, Daphne, it's loaded and ready," he said patiently.

She tried to smile. "Sorry, I was just checking," she said and trailed him down into the darkened house.

CHAPTER SEVENTEEN

WESTON'S EYES felt grainy and heavy lidded. The wipers on the car swished back and forth, right to left, again and again. A strong wind buffeted them, rocking the Volvo. The sky was so dark. The few cars on the road had turned on their headlights. Hurricane Ethel must be nearing.

And then Wes was watching the wipers, not the road, and just for a second his lids closed. Just for a second...

"Wake up!" came Audrey's shrill cry in his ear. "Wes!" She grabbed the wheel. "Are you crazy!"

"I've got it," he said, adrenaline pounding through his veins.

"Pull over," she commanded, "I'm driving."

He relented. She was right, of course. He pulled over to the side of the road and stepped out into a puddle.

Audrey slipped over into the driver's seat. "That's better," she said. "Now just sit back and relax and I'll have us in Cambridge before you know it."

The rain was still falling heavily, and there were tree limbs on the streets when they drove up to Hubert's house.

"Hey, Sam!" called Audrey cheerfully as she walked in through the garage door.

Hubert appeared from the back somewhere, an expression of astonishment on his drawn face.

"Thought we'd come and give you a hand. Did you find Dodie?" asked Audrey.

"No, not yet," stammered Hubert.

"Well then, let me have your address book and I'll begin calling every number in it," said Audrey. "Your daughter has to be somewhere."

"You haven't located Joe Marion?" asked Wes.

"No." Hubert looked haggard. There were circles under his eyes, and he wore an old bathrobe. "I was trying to get some rest. Didn't sleep all night."

"Hubert, Gallent's out on the island with Daphne," Wes said quietly.

Hubert looked at him hard. "He's okay, then?"

"Yes," said Wes firmly. Then he filled Hubert in on the events of the past twenty-four hours.

"So he's got men coming and you're sure it's Toth," concluded Hubert. He stroked his Vandyke thoughtfully with one hand.

"I figured you needed help and Gallent's there."

"Thanks, Wes, but I'm not sure what you can do. Or Audrey there."

"Mrs. Farway had ulterior motives. She wanted off the island until Ethel expires."

"Ah, so there's something she's afraid of. I was beginning to wonder."

In the background, they could hear Audrey's voice asking questions on the phone, pausing, then talking some more. She put her hand over the mouthpiece once and yelled to Hubert, "What's her last name, Sam?"

"Stoddard, Dodie Stoddard."

"Thanks, Sam." To the unknown person on the phone, she repeated, "Dodie Stoddard, Hubert Samuels's daughter. No? Thanks, anyway."

Hubert fixed coffee, and he and Wes hunched over big steaming mugs at the kitchen table, both tired, both worried, both torn by harsh emotions.

"I tried to call this morning, but I couldn't get through," said Hubert. "The whole East Coast is a mess. I suppose everyone wants to find out how relatives on Martha's Vineyard are."

"It's wild out there. Frankly, my sympathies lie with Mrs. Farway. Daphne *likes* it, I think."

"Daphne. How're you two getting along? I mean, you were pretty upset yesterday," said Hubert casually.

"Anybody would've been," said Wes offhandedly. "Come on, Hubert, you know me. She's a nice girl." And even while he said the words he knew he was lying. Daphne was much more than a nice girl.

"Sure, boyo," said Hubert dryly. "Why don't you give in a little? Some nice girl's gonna come along someday and want to take real good care of you. Maybe you already found her. And if not, you can sure give it the old college try."

Wes was about to make a sufficiently cool riposte to Hubert's fatherly advice when Audrey's shriek echoed from the other room. Both Wes and Hubert snapped their heads around in tandem.

"Sam! I found her!" Audrey yelled excitedly.

Hubert leaped to his feet, knocking over his mug of coffee. "What? Where? Is that her?"

"Just a minute!" Audrey held up a restraining hand and listened for a time. "You say she left this morning? Yes, it must be the storm. Well, thank you. Oh, I think it's awful, too. Goodbye."

Hubert was practically jumping up and down as Audrey hung up, a smug expression on her face.

"That was Mrs. Owens, the housekeeper for a certain Mr. Theodore Stoddard..."

"Ted Stoddard, I remember him," breathed Hubert. "Some rich old coot in Dave's family. He was at the wedding. But where's Dodie?"

"Now calm down and listen," ordered Audrey. "Dave and Dodie and the kids arrived a couple of days ago down in Newark where this Ted Stoddard lives, having been told he was dying and wanted to see them."

"What?"

"Yes, so they got there and he wasn't sick at all. A practical joke, they decided, but not very funny."

"But where's my daughter?"

"They left this morning to drive home, but New York state and Connecticut declared emergencies because of Ethel, so they must be stuck somewhere in a motel or something."

"She's all right?" asked Hubert.

"She was perfectly fine when they left this morning, Sam."

Hubert sat down abruptly. "Who would have done such a thing? Who would have told them Ted Stoddard was dying? What about that message from Joe Marion? I don't understand..."

Wes had the oddest feeling that he was missing something, something important. Daphne on the island, Dodie called away on a false emergency. Marion's message to Hubert... An idea hit him suddenly with the force of a mule kick to the gut. His eyes flew up to meet Hubert's horrified gaze.

"Daphne," whispered Hubert.

"Daphne," concurred Wes.

Audrey stood in front of them, hands on hips. "Somebody wanted you off that island, both of you," she said agitatedly. "Daphne's in danger!"

"Toth!" said Hubert hoarsely.

"Goddamn it!" rasped Wes, grabbing the phone and dialing the Farway house. His heart pounded in fear. Toth had neatly lured them all off the island. Thank God for Gallent, but he was alone...

"Maybe the guys from the office got there," suggested Hubert.

"In this weather? They probably stopped the ferries hours ago," said Audrey, then to Wes, "Is she there?"

Wes heard the phone ringing. *Pick it up, Daphne!* he shouted silently. *Pick it up!* It rang once, twice.

"Maybe they've evacuated," suggested Hubert.

It rang again.

"Never! Not my daughter," said Audrey emphatically.

Four rings, five. *Answer. Come on, answer!*

"The lines could be down," Hubert offered.

"Not if it's ringing. Is it ringing, Wes?" asked Audrey.

He nodded. It was ringing, all right. Again and again and again.

Finally he hung up. "No answer," he said softly.

"Oh, dear Lord in heaven," cried Audrey, "could something have happened already?"

"They could have gone somewhere. To get groceries or candles in case the electricity goes out," soothed Hubert. "Or bottled water."

"Yes, yes, they could have..." agreed Audrey hopefully.

"I'm going back," said Wes harshly.

"You'll never get there. The state police are about to shut down the roads, and the ferries aren't running," said Hubert.

"I'll get there," Wes insisted. "I can always say it's Secret Service business. There's the Coast Guard if the ferries aren't running."

"We'll call again in a while," Hubert replied. "Wait a bit."

"I'm going, Hubert. This is all my fault. I should have figured it."

"It's *my* fault," said Hubert sadly.

"Listen. You can do something," said Wes. "Try to locate Toth. Call the office, check his home. Go down to Dorchester if you have to. It could be that he isn't on the island."

Hubert looked skeptical.

"I know it's a remote possibility, but if you could find him..."

Hubert nodded.

"I'll call you from Woods Hole. Leave Audrey here to answer the phone and let her know what you find out. If the lines are down, well, too bad. I'll try to call, anyway." He pulled on his still wet raincoat. "Keep trying Daphne. If you get her, tell Gallent what's going on. He'd better be careful."

"He's careful, Wes," assured Hubert.

"But there's only one of him and if the crew from Boston can't get there..."

"Take it easy," warned Hubert.

"Sure."

"No heroics."

"I knew I shouldn't have left!" said Wes tightly. Then he opened the door and raced out to his car through the driving rain.

He got stopped twice by state police on the Southeast Expressway and had to show his Secret Service ID. It was hard to see the road because of the torrential rain, and his car was pushed around by the wind as if it were a toy. He crouched over the steering wheel like a wild beast, his hands claws, his shoulders aching with tension. The car radio spewed information about Ethel, ordering evacuations, giving wind speeds. The eye was nearing Boston.

The wind and rain got worse as he approached the coast. Long jagged lightning streaks split the sky and thunder shook the ground. Crossing the Sagamore Bridge, Wes almost got blown against a guardrail.

The ferry pier was closed up, deserted. A sign hung, blowing and banging, on the gate: Ferry Shut Down Until Storm Passes.

Once more his car splashed through puddles and slid around corners, throwing out rooster tails of water. Branches blew onto his windshield and fouled the wipers. How much worse was it on the island, he wondered.

The U.S. Coast Guard office was a beehive of activity. Wes finally located the commander, a harried-looking middle-aged man.

"Secret Service," snapped Wes, flipping open his identification. "I'm on a job. I have to get to Martha's Vineyard."

"You crazy, man? We're still trying to get the last few stragglers off the place!"

"I'll call the White House if I need to, sir. This is a priority matter," said Wes coolly.

"I'll send you out there on the next cutter *if* the captain thinks he can make it. That's the best I can do," replied the commander. "You'll have to wait till he gets here."

"How long?" pressed Wes.

"I don't know, with the wind and all. Maybe half an hour."

"Damn." So long! And then the crossing, the drive to Daphne's house . . . "Let me use your phone."

"Sure. Lines are down to the island, though. They just went a while ago."

Wes swore again. He made his way to the phone. Coast Guard men were everywhere in the small building. On phones, on radios, yelling, dashing in and out. Phones rang ceaselessly and red lights blinked on consoles. The needle of the wind speed instrument zigzagged crazily on its roll of paper.

He dialed Daphne's number. Static. His heart fell. If he couldn't get there...

He called Hubert's house. Audrey answered breathlessly. "Sam just called! He's in a Hungarian bar in Dorchester and Mike Toth is there, drinking beer and singing Hungarian folk songs, waiting out the storm!"

"He found Toth?" Wes asked blankly.

"Yes, he's in Dorchester. Can you hear me, Wes?"

"Yeah, I hear you. Thanks." He hung up, puzzled. Toth in Dorchester, singing folk songs? A cold chill seemed to grip Weston. Something was terribly wrong.

His hand reached for the phone again. He dialed the number and listened to it ring. Janie Kelly answered. "Secret Service."

"Tommy still there? This is Wes."

"Sure, we're all stuck here. Hang on, Wes."

"Agent Taylor," said the familiar voice.

"This is Wes. Tell me, Tommy, when did you send out those guys to Martha's Vineyard?"

"What guys? You nuts, Leroux? In this weather? Say, is this some kind of joke?"

"Chief Gallent didn't call this morning and ask for backup on the Vineyard?" Weston's voice was very careful, very controlled.

"Of course not. He's in the hospital getting a hernia fixed. Why would he call for backup? Wes, are you okay?"

"Sure, I'm fine. Thanks, Tommy." He stared at the phone for a long time before his mind could fit itself around the finality of it.

Gallent had never called for backup, at all.

CHAPTER EIGHTEEN

JERRY LOOKED AT DAPHNE with thoughtful, hooded eyes and her heart thumped heavily. Then he made his move, slowly and deliberately, and she knew he'd tricked her. All along he'd played on her weakness and not once given himself away.

She looked down at her hand. "I should have known," she said.

"I'm sorry," he replied, and she could almost believe him, "but I've got aces over sixes." Then a taunting grin split his lips.

Suddenly she laughed. "Is that all?" She spread her cards on the table. Three tens. "Don't three of a kind still beat two pair, Jerry?"

"Why, you bluffed me!" he sputtered.

Daphne shrugged eloquently. "Me? Certainly not. I really thought you had something better. Guess it's not your day."

"Sure," he grumbled.

"I suppose I ought to shut up and deal, right?"

In the background Audrey's radio barked and hissed and crackled in time to the bolts of lightning that were splitting the afternoon sky with more frequency.

"You sure this house is going to stand?" asked Jerry nervously over the roar of the storm.

"She'll take the wind—" Daphne glanced toward the porch door "—but the ocean . . ."

"You think the ocean's going to get worse?"

She could see beads of sweat forming on his upper lip and in between folds of skin under his chin. Neither of them had ever felt such a low barometer. "I think the dune will hold the waves," she said without enough conviction, realizing that each wave pounding and tearing at the sand was weakening it. How long could the dune hold back the surging tide?

"I suppose it's too late to evacuate," said Gallent wistfully.

"Yes, I'm afraid it is."

Jerry looked at his cards, sliding them one by one into place in his hand. "When's high tide?"

"About one this morning," she said. "If Ethel is past us by then we should be all right."

The house seemed to sway on its foundation. Lightning split the sky over the frantic ocean. The lights in the house flickered and went out.

"Blast it," said Jerry gruffly.

"It was bound to happen." Daphne reached for the flashlight. "I've got candles. We'll be okay." Even though it was only a little after five in the afternoon, the sky was so dark that it might as well have been night.

The house seemed to be rocking as she went into the kitchen to fetch the candles; everything was a little topsy-turvy, and the ceaseless roar of the wind was enough to drive the most stalwart islander mad.

And Wes. Why hadn't he called earlier, when the lines to the mainland were still up? Although he might have when they'd been at the store. Automatically she checked the extension phone in the living room. "It's still got a dial tone," she reported to Jerry. "But I'm sure it's only local and not for long."

Weston's chief was obviously anxious. He had been ever since the report had come over the radio late that afternoon that Hurricane Ethel was on the move again. He never stopped asking Daphne questions, either. Could the waves reach the house? And if so, where would he and Daphne go for safety?

"Upstairs," she replied, "and hope the foundation holds."

The phone rang. Daphne's heart lurched. It must be Wes! But then she realized that it couldn't be. He was in Boston and the lines had been down to the mainland for hours.

She picked it up. "Hello?"

It hissed and crackled. "Thank God, Daphne! Don't say anything!" commanded Weston. *"Nothing."*

She opened her mouth to answer, but shock kept her silent.

"Just listen closely and do exactly as I tell you."

The connection was terrible and her heart was beginning to beat too heavily beneath her ribs. "Okay," she managed, half yelling into the receiver.

"Can you hide somewhere? Give me a simple yes or no." The line hissed for a long moment. "Daphne? Are you there?"

"Yes, I'm here."

"Can you hide?"

"I...sure, yes." An ugly sick fear was beginning to crawl in her stomach. Her thoughts spun. Wes was on the island somewhere. He was having her speak in monosyllables. Why?

Hisss. "Daphne. Don't react at all when I tell you this. For God's sake, play it cool. It's Gallent."

"What?" she whispered.

"Daphne?"

"I'm . . . here."

"It's Gallent!" he was yelling. "I'm on my—" *hisss,
crackle* "—way! Stall for time. Hide. I'm hanging up now.
For God's sake, get away from him!"

All Daphne could hear then was the snakelike hiss on the
line and finally the semblance of a dial tone. She was
rooted to the spot in terror and disbelief. Behind her stood
Jerry Gallent, so near that she could almost feel his breath
on the bristling hairs of her neck.

Think! her mind screamed, unable to assimilate the
knowledge. *It's Gallent. Think!*

She still held the receiver in her hand. Her lungs felt as
if they were bursting from the fist tightening inside her
chest. "Oh, yes, Mary," she croaked hoarsely into the
phone. "Sure, we're all right here. How's your place
holding up?" Daphne paused. "Good, good. Well, I guess
I'd better go." Carefully, she replaced the receiver on it
cradle. She knew she had to turn around. She had to face
him sometime. With tremendous effort, she managed to
put a smile on her face, but felt as if she were wearing a
mask.

"That was Mary," she said too brightly. "A neigh-
bor." Didn't he see that her lips were frozen, as stiff as
boards? How could he fail to notice the quaver in her tone,
the trembling of her chin, the sweat pouring out of her oily
palms?

It was Gallent.

His eyes were riveted on her, pinning Daphne as if she
were a doe in the headlights of a car.

"Funny time to call," he said briskly into the silence.

Why had he waited? Why hadn't he already killed her?
She had to answer him. "She was scared. Mary lives
alone."

"Your friend, huh?"

"Yes . . . yes. We went to school together." Daphne began to walk toward the card table. Hide. She had to hide. And Wes. He was coming. Yes! But, she realized in horror, how was he going to get there? The hurricane, the roads . . .

She had to stall for time. "Why don't you shuffle and deal?" She turned to face Jerry. Her knees were like rubber, her smile wooden. "I'm going to use the bathroom. I'll be right back." She knew that her voice was coming out all childish and too cheerful. She knew he must see clear through her ruse. He nodded, glanced at the cards and then back to her face. "I'll be right back," she said. "Maybe I'll fix us something to eat then."

Shut up, her mind screamed at her. *Get away, hide*.

Daphne took the steps slowly. Her knees actually did buckle near the top. She righted herself, leaned against the wall for a moment and swallowed several times convulsively.

Hide.

Where? She craned her head and searched down the long, dim hallway. It seemed to shiver and waver with the uncertain shadows. A flash of lightning hurled a pattern of brilliant white squares onto the floor, making Daphne's heart leap.

No, this floor was too easy to search. The unused third floor was better. *Hide*, her mind screamed.

Just then the whole house seemed to lurch on its foundation as a vicious gust of wind struck it. There was a loud report, like a bullet shot, that made Daphne jump out of her skin. But it was only one of the doors, one of the bedroom doors, slammed shut by some freak wind devil. It was the door to Weston's room. Felicity's room.

Daphne stopped short. Something about a bullet shot. What was Felicity trying to tell her? The gun! Weston's gun! It was still in the drawer of her night table. She'd almost forgotten it.

Daphne hesitated only an instant before making her way down the hall and into her room. Her hand was pressed to her heart, as if willing it to slow its painful thumping against her ribs.

She reached into the bottom drawer of her night table, pushed aside the magazines and nail polish and felt cool metal touch her fingers.

Then, starting toward the door, she had a sudden idea. She went into the bathroom and flushed the toilet, in case he could hear. Finally, cautiously, she took the steps to the third floor. Lightning illuminated the hallway for a moment, chasing the black shadows back into corners. Then it was unearthly dark again.

She'd forgotten the flashlight, but it didn't matter. Daphne knew the six rooms by heart; she'd played in them hundreds of times as a kid.

She moved down the hall to the last room on the ocean side of the house. A bolt of lightning again rent the nightlike firmament, followed by several charged flashes that chased one another like white neon wires twisting grotesquely in the sky. Her breathing was shallow and her mouth cotton dry as she pushed open the last door and stood there, thinking, wondering if this was to be her final act.

Cobwebs stuck to her face as she moved into the room. Relentless lightning tore at the island, illuminating the dusty old hat boxes and Christmas decorations and trunks that had belonged to her grandmother. Daphne made her way to a corner behind an old steamer trunk, replacing the boxes she'd displaced to block Gallent's path. The air was oppressive, heavy with mildew and dust and mothballs.

She knelt behind the trunk and felt the wall at her back. It was trembling as Ethel's fierce hand prodded the house.

Daphne sucked in a few deep breaths and settled in to wait. Thoughts batted at her, some too horrible to hold on to, some inane. Why hadn't Audrey, the neat freak, tidied up the third-floor rooms? How had Wes found out it was his chief? How had Wes gotten to the island? And then she'd see Jerry Gallent in her mind's eye, his fatherly face, the bull-like head and neck. Why hadn't he tried to kill her already? Was he waiting for Hurricane Ethel to strike in her fullest fury and cover his tracks? Could it be that he was reluctant to do her harm?

He did like her, Daphne thought. Crazy as it seemed, as she crouched there, drenched in cold perspiration, with cobwebs glued to her hair and a heart that threatened to leap from her chest, she knew he liked her.

Lightning played nasty tricks with her vision. There was an old stand-up hat rack in a far corner and the blasts of light coming in the window made the rack come alive, humanoid and otherworldly.

Where was Gallent? Still waiting below in the living room or checking her bathroom? How long did Daphne have until Wes got there? How long had it been since he'd called?

She looked down at her two oily hands and stared at the gun. It felt cold and slippery. Could she use it? Could she point it at him and pull the trigger?

The house creaked and moaned in the surge of the storm and Daphne sat waiting, envisioning the movements of Brady's killer, of a man so clever that he had duped them all, lured Wes off the island, pointed a finger in Toth's direction, a man who was smart enough to have moved them all like pawns.

And she was wondering if she could pull a trigger on him?

Outside, the hurricane approached the island with ungodly fury and, below, Gallent must have been getting curious.

WES HUNG UP THE PAY PHONE and fought his way out of the storm-tilted enclosure. The furious wind was bending the island to the earth, ripping at the trees in Vineyard Haven, carrying papers and loose boards along with it like missiles. Horizontal sheets of rain slashed him out of a lightning-torn sky; stinging pellets that plastered his shirt and trousers to his skin and his hair to his head. Where in hell had they parked Audrey's car that morning? And, even if he found it, would the keys be in it?

He finally located the car on a hilly side street. He tried the door. Nothing. It was locked, then, and the keys were in Audrey's purse. A string of oaths tore from his lips and was lost on the violent wind.

The island, from what he could see, was deserted. It looked ghostly, like Felicity's island the night she'd lost her husband, Wes thought, as he searched frantically up and down the streets near the wharf.

There! Over near an old brick house, a vintage pickup truck. Wes almost grinned to himself as he staggered and swayed, fighting the ruthless wind, barely making headway along the street.

Assuming the door locks probably hadn't worked in years, he headed for the battered vehicle. An old green Chevy pickup. He yanked on the door, pulled it open, stepped up into the windless haven of the cab and sat on the torn seat. He shook his head like a dog that had come in from the rain and wiped the water from his forehead. Then he bent, reached up under the dashboard and felt around in the mass of wires. Yes, those two. He pulled them loose with a gentle tug, pressed his foot on the accelerator several times and held the two wires together. She turned over immediately. He patted the steering wheel affectionately and put her in gear. Then he smiled to himself grimly; in his youth he'd stolen cars just to go for joyrides. Now, at last, all his ill-gotten experience was paying off. Maybe there was a purpose in everything.

Purpose, he remembered. Daphne's life.

He knew the way, but everything had changed since that morning. Branches lay strewn in yards and in the roadway, making the going slow. The sturdy tree trunks seemed to be twisted, fighting the wind with a sort of human pride.

The wipers swished the rain away and away futilely. The road was flooded in spots, and he had to gun the old truck and drive around on the sandy shoulders. In West Tisbury, there was an enormous, once-majestic tree across the road. Wes pulled into a driveway, tore across a marshy lawn and skirted the century-old patriarch, coming off the curb with a metallic crunch.

Daphne, he prayed, *hold on. Use your head.*

The road followed the south shoreline. Wes could barely see the ocean, but he had an impression of a dark mountain of water to his left. No dunes there to bar its relentless drive. He'd never seen anything like it—a gigantic, seething mass of water cresting and swelling and cresting again to plunder the land. Had he really crossed that only a short while ago? He thought fleetingly of the captain of the cutter, at that minute recrossing the channel. The young man deserved a medal. And when this was over, Wes was going to make darn good and sure he got one.

Another stretch of flooded road lay ahead. There was no way around it this time. Wes gunned the old engine and plowed into the water, praying it was only on the surface.

The Chevy made skidding progress, like a tank grinding, and moving sideways. And then it seemed to lurch, to sink onto its side. The motor sputtered then died.

Wes swore, pounded the steering wheel and climbed out on the passenger side to stand in three feet of water, the bright late afternoon sun striking him in the eyes.

His thoughts were solely on Daphne and the mile or so between him and the house. It wasn't until he'd made his way through the flood and onto drier land that he stopped short, panting.

Sun. The goddamn sun was out! He stood catching his breath, his hands on his hips, and surveyed the sky. The sun, yes, and a brilliantly blue sky overhead. As he turned in a circle, mesmerized, he could see black whirling clouds on all horizons. So the island was in the eye of the storm. Amazing.

He caught his breath and began to jog down the slick road, conserving his strength, as it was becoming painfully obvious that the storm was heading in fast again from the southwest. Before he reached the Farway house, the storm would once more be unleashing its fury on the island.

It was eerie and too hushed. The clear sky was surrounded by a black mass of swirling clouds and rain and howling wind. And then sweat started to pour from him and the evening sun felt like a gentle hand on his back. It was windless, a vacuum, and all the air was spinning around him in a huge circular maelstrom. Wes gasped, wondering if his bursting lungs were getting any oxygen, wondering when the storm would descend on him, and knowing there was no way to beat it.

He recognized a bend up ahead. The road rose and curved, and then straightened for perhaps a quarter of a mile before it reached the Farway drive. At a crest of the road, he could see the ocean to his left. For maybe five hundred yards sunlight struck the frothing wall of sea and tipped the myriad waves golden. Beyond that was the charcoal gray boiling water churned up under the onslaught of Hurricane Ethel.

Wes slowed for a minute, leaning over and sucking in air while he rearranged his shoulder holster, and checked his gun. Just how wet was it? Too wet to be useful?

The house. He could see the third floor from the road. He ran harder. His mind was becoming oxygen starved and his thinking unclear. Daphne, Gallent, Daphne. Was she still alive? Was he driving himself only to burst through the door and find he was too late?

A sadness rushed into his pounding heart, leadlike, unfamiliar. *I love her,* he thought. But it was too late.

A wind was nudging his back. Then his shadow on the road ahead disappeared. The air darkened and the wind began to butt him along, faster and faster, until he was certain his lungs were going to burst. Then rain. It began to spatter his head. Then it pelted him. The storm lashed the south end of the island suddenly and violently and tore at Wes, but he barely noticed; in his mind was a single thought: he loved Daphne and he had to get to her.

THE SUDDEN SILENCE was nerve shattering. Daphne couldn't account for it for a time, thinking it was her own terror making her hallucinate. Then she realized—the eye of the storm!

Dust motes danced in the stripes of uncanny yellow light that stabbed in through the window. Daphne's heart hammered in her chest so hard that she was sure Jerry Gallent must be able to hear it. Straining her ears, she listened for his footsteps. He must be searching for her by now. He must have guessed what she'd heard over the telephone.

Wes. Where was he? How far away? Was Hubert with him—or Audrey? She sat hunched in her corner, sweating, quivering, listening.

The banners of light faded, and the room darkened again. The eye was passing. A little shiver of wind rushed against the window. Then it started again in full force: rain, thunder, lightning, the freight-train roar.

Where was Gallent?

She almost screamed when the door swung open. Adrenaline burst terribly, painfully, inside of her. She was cornered.

She felt automatically for the safety catch of the gun with one hand. Could she really shoot him? Her eyes were staring toward the door as if she were hypnotized. She couldn't see him but she could hear boxes being pushed aside.

"Come on, Daphne. I know you're there. I won't hurt you." His voice was warm and convincing, and she had to fight a powerful temptation to believe him.

"Make this easy on yourself, Daphne. Come on out. I can explain everything."

She steadied the gun in her two hands, as Weston had showed her. Her mouth was so dry that she couldn't swallow. Terror welled up in her like a gush of hot tears.

"Please, Daphne. Let's talk," Jerry Gallent was saying in a wheedling tone.

Boxes crashed and scraped across the floor. Lightning illuminated the room whitely for a moment, and then it was dusky again. Pinpoints of light danced in front of Daphne's eyes, and she blinked madly. The trunk in front of her was shoved aside.

"Daphne," he said sadly and she did believe him then, but it was too late.

Inadvertently she scrabbled crablike backward, into the wall behind her. The gun in her hand scraped across the floor uselessly. There was another flash of lightning that flickered bizarrely on Gallent's squat form. They stared at each other and in that instant Daphne saw his gun trained on her forehead, saw his finger begin to squeeze the trigger slowly, ever so slowly.

The room went black and the low rumble of thunder commenced. Blindly, Daphne snatched up her gun, pointed it at his afterimage and pulled the trigger.

WES DIDN'T PAUSE to try the door. He ran at it, leading with a shoulder, and crashed through it, not even feeling the impact. He pulled his gun and crouched, ready, but no one was there.

He flattened himself against a wall and prepared to burst into the kitchen.

A sound grabbed at him. A gunshot! Upstairs! He raced for the steps, taking them two at a time and sucking air into his tortured lungs. Fear blazed in his brain.

The third-floor hall was as dark as a tomb. There, at the end, he spotted a blacker rectangle, an open door. Light winked obscenely from it for a stop-action moment. Lightning.

Panting, Wes ran down the hall and burst into the room, careless of all precautions. *Daphne,* his mind shrieked at him, *Daphne!*

There was a noise, a scratching sound, a low moan that was spectral against the din of the storm. In the corner.

Lightning flared again, shimmering on a body on the floor. Weston's heart burst in his chest.

It was Jerry Gallent. He was groaning and trying to get up, but there was a red stain on one side of his shirt, a spreading blot of color.

Automatically, Wes kicked the gun away from Gallent's limp hand. His heart thudded in his ears. Outside, the tempest raged on in mindless wrath.

"Daphne," Wes called in a hoarse rasp. "Daphne."

CHAPTER NINETEEN

"SO YOU REALLY WANT to do it?" asked Audrey, her hands firmly on her hips.

"I have to," answered Daphne steadfastly.

"Heaven knows why. I think you're cuckoo. Let the man alone."

"I don't know why, either, but it's just something I have to do," replied Daphne stubbornly.

"I'll drive, then," sighed Audrey, rolling her blue eyes.

"You don't have to, *Mother*."

"I'll drive," snapped Audrey and that was that.

When the skyline of downtown Boston appeared, Daphne couldn't help but recall the day she'd driven in to confront Jerry Gallent, the day she'd met Wes, the day that had started her relationship with the Secret Service—and with Wes.

And then the awful, nightmarish culmination of the affair. Everything had happened so quickly. The storm had raged and flashed and Gallent had lain on the floor moaning. Wes had pressed a rag to his chief's shoulder, they'd waited until the local police could make it through the tail end of the storm, and then they'd both slept in exhaustion. Audrey had arrived back the following day and Wes, of course, had left almost immediately to return the old Chevy truck and head for Boston and all the explanations and red tape.

It was a lovely, warm Indian summer day in Boston when Audrey pulled up in front of Massachusetts General Hospital. The leaves of the trees along the Charles River were edged in color, just barely beginning to turn, and the sculls were out, scudding across the broad surface of the river.

The venerable old hospital was huge. It took Daphne nearly half an hour to even locate Jerry Gallent's room.

The policeman on guard let her enter. She pushed the wide door open and tiptoed in. Two weeks had passed since that awful day that Ethel had assaulted Martha's Vineyard and Jerry Gallent had tried to kill her. It was hard to believe it had even happened.

Chief Gallent—she'd always think of him by that title—lay on the hospital bed with his eyes closed. He looked pale and thin, a wraith, not the bull-necked powerful man who had tried to kill her and Wes and had almost succeeded.

"Chief Gallent?" she asked timidly, feeling horribly uncomfortable. Why had she come, anyway?

His eyes opened and he stared at her for a moment with a dark, penetrating gaze. Some of the fire was still there. "Well, well, if it isn't cute little Daphne," he said quietly. "Come in, sit down."

She smiled shakily and pulled a chair up to his bedside—not too close. "I wanted to see how you were," she said. "I mean, after all, I . . ."

A wry lopsided smile caught at Gallent's mouth. "Yes, you shot me, didn't you?"

She looked down at her hands. "Yes," she whispered.

"Your aim was terrible. Only nicked my brachial artery and broke my collarbone."

"I'm glad my aim was terrible," Daphne said. "I was only trying to protect myself."

"And most effective you were, too." He looked at her for a minute. "Why on earth are you here? Even my wife doesn't visit me here."

"I feel responsible. Brady would have come."

"Ah, Brady, yes, I'm sure he would have." A moment of silence followed. "I'm sorry about Brady."

"Yes." She looked at her hands again.

"He found out everything, you know. He called me to his apartment that night. God, it was hot out. And there was nothing else I could do."

"Why?" Daphne whispered.

"A traitor, a Russian spy? He'd have ruined my life. I needed the money so badly. I had no choice."

"You always have a choice."

"Yes, I suppose so," Gallent said slowly. "In a way, this is easier. Now I truly have no choice."

"I'm sorry," said Daphne quietly. "I liked you."

His face softened a little. "I liked you, too. Hey, I still do. I just want to know one thing. Where in hell did you get that gun?"

"Wes gave it to me. It was in my bedroom."

"Smart young man, Wes. And you, too. You were both too clever for me." He paused for a minute. "You know, I got the feeling that you and Wes, well, there was something going on between you."

"There was." Daphne blushed. "But it's over."

"Well, none of my business." He paused. "I've been reading in here, following my case. My lawyer says maybe I'll be out in time to see my grandchildren graduate from college."

She couldn't stand it. Pity and a sense of justice battled inside her. "I . . . I brought you something." She fumbled in her big straw bag and pulled out a box of candy. "I couldn't think of anything else."

"Well, thanks, Daphne. I've always had a sweet tooth."

She stood. There was an awkward moment. "I hope things go well for you," she said.

"Sure," he replied lightly. "You too."

"Well, goodbye, then." Daphne gathered up her bag and turned to leave.

"You know, you're really quite a girl, Daphne Farway," said the chief. "Wes Leroux is a fool if he doesn't grab you."

She felt her cheeks redden again. "Wes is busy these days."

"Yes, so I hear. A well-deserved promotion. Say, on the way out, send in that big lummox of a cop, will you? He's not a bad poker player. Not as good as you, of course, but it helps pass the time."

The corridors passed her as if Daphne were on a moving sidewalk. She hurried to get outside, to the sun and the fresh air and the crisp smell of autumn. It was only when she stepped through the front doors that she took a deep, lung-stretching gulp of air.

Freedom. She closed her eyes for a moment and thanked God fervently for her blessings.

There was only one thing missing, the single item that would make her life perfect: love.

DAPHNE SAT BACK in her chair and tapped her pen on her teeth. The first draft of her latest cookbook was finally complete, and only needed the usual revisions. Of course, it was a month late, but she'd called New York and explained everything to her publisher and he'd understood. He'd even enthusiastically urged her to attempt an outline on her "adventures" with the Secret Service.

"But I don't write novels," she'd tried to explain.

"Oh, you can handle it—part truth, part fiction. It'll be a smash."

"I'll try." She'd finally given in, knowing that he was right, that she had filed in her mind all the ingredients for a true thriller.

She could hear Audrey below in the kitchen rattling pots and pans, preparing for the Big Weekend, as her mother had dubbed the upcoming three days when Hubert and his family were due to arrive for a visit. Hubert, Dodie and her family and, Daphne thought uneasily, Weston had been invited down, too. By Audrey, and without Daphne's consent.

Wes had called a couple of times right after Gorvieski's successful trip to Boston, and he patiently answered all Daphne's questions: Jerry Gallent had been receiving money from the Russians to cover his gambling debts, and he'd set Mike Toth up to take the fall in his place. He'd exploited each person's weaknesses with consummate skill. Greenburg's Russian girl, Toth's ties to Hungary, Hubert's involvement with the blackmailer, which Gallent had known about for years. It had even been Gallent who had cleverly lured Hubert off the island by telephoning Hubert's daughter with the story of her husband's rich and sickly uncle in Newark.

"Naturally," Wes had told Daphne on the phone, "he hadn't counted on Brady telling you so much or my getting involved. But even then, all he had to do was keep throwing red herrings at us until after Gorvieski was assassinated."

"We were too clever for him, then," she'd replied.

"Not really. It was Hurricane Ethel. Gallent had called Toth and told him to get down to the Vineyard, but Mike couldn't make it because of the storm. I guess the chief was waiting for him, though, to make it look like Toth killed you. Then, when Mike didn't arrive, Gallent got desperate. The storm saved your life." Then he went on: "Now look what Gallent has to face—public disgrace, a trial, a jail sentence, at the very least."

Daphne had cringed. "I feel sorry for him."

"Don't. He's a murderer and a traitor to his country. He's a user. There wasn't anything in his office he didn't know. He ran his own campaign of fear, Daphne, biding his time, bluffing when he needed to. Like calling the police about my missing body."

"He turned everything to his own advantage," Daphne had reflected. "Even when he found out that you weren't dead."

"Exactly. When something went wrong, he simply shifted gears and put another plan into effect."

And then, a few days later in early September, Wes had called again. "Hi," he'd begun. "Sorry I haven't been in touch more."

But Daphne had known why: Wes was no longer interested in her. It was over. "That's all right," she'd said, trying to sound cheerful. "I know how busy you've been. The office must be in a turmoil."

"Well, now that Gorvieski's gone and we've got our new boss in from Washington, things are quieting down."

"And you?"

"I'm fine. I got a promotion. Second in command," he'd told her offhandedly.

"That's wonderful. How's your family?" The conversation had become small talk like "how's the weather?"

"I had dinner with Jim and Nancy last night. They asked about you, in fact."

"Tell them hi for me."

"I will. How are Audrey's sea oats?"

"A mess. The storm tore down half the dune. It'll take years to rebuild. And our trees..."

"Well, guess I better get back to work. How's your cookbook coming along?"

"Good, almost done." It was over, Daphne kept thinking. "Wes? Do you think you might make it down sometime to visit?"

He had hesitated and her heart had cried silently. Then he said, "I'll try. Maybe in October. I've got a lot of catching up to do at the office."

He hadn't called back. And for the past three weeks Daphne had been miserable, trying to lose herself in her work, helping Audrey clean up after the storm, merely killing time until the pain in her heart abated.

She felt certain that a part of Wes had come to love her, but obviously he was keeping that barrier of his firmly in place. She'd been foolish to believe for even a moment that she might be the one to get through to him. But time, she reminded herself, was a good healer.

Then Audrey had stirred it all up. She'd been planning on Hubert and Dodie's visit for a week and then gotten it into her head to call Wes and invite him, too.

"You didn't!" Daphne had cried.

"Sure I did. I won't have my daughter moping around here when she could be happy."

"I could throttle you! You're making me out to look like an idiot! A pathetic, heartsick schoolgirl!"

"Oh, pooh! Wes agreed that you two had to talk."

"What, exactly, did you tell him?" Daphne had demanded hotly.

"That you were miserable." Audrey had shrugged. "Did you want me to lie?"

And now, in a little more than an hour, Wes and Hubert and the whole crew would be there. What was she supposed to say to Wes? Damn her interfering mother!

She got up from her chair and went to her bedroom. She hated to do it. She hated to think that she was dressing for Wes, and so she told herself it was for Hubert and Dodie and her family.

"Chin up," she told the mirror as she slipped into a light wool skirt and a crisp plaid shirt, topping it off with a bulky sweater. She used the curling iron on her bangs and put on makeup and—oh, what the heck—perfume. For Hubert, of course.

Audrey pulled into the drive with her guests right on schedule. Daphne stood at her window upstairs, anxious, unwilling to greet them at the door, feeling childish and wounded and afraid.

They piled out of Audrey's car—Hubert in natty checked slacks, Dodie, attractive in a smart blue wool dress, with prematurely gray curly hair, a tall husband and three cute small children in tow. And Weston.

He stood beneath the big tree, dappled sunlight playing on his sandy head and straight shoulders, his hands in his trouser pockets, a smile lighting his face.

He looked well, and as appealing as ever. He was wearing a soft suede flight jacket, khaki slacks, a sport shirt. He seemed relaxed as he helped with the bags. He kept smiling and talking as he walked toward the house.

And then he glanced up. He never broke stride, but there was a pause in his movement as their gazes met for a moment. He nodded slowly, the smile fading, the light in his green eyes dimming before he strode out of her vision. Then there were voices drifting upstairs from the foyer, and Daphne felt tears burning behind her eyelids. She closed them for a minute and sighed. It was no use hiding; she might as well go on down and face them.

"Daph-nee!" called Audrey. "Oh, Daphne, they're here!"

Taking her time, Daphne walked down the stairs and was greeted by Hubert, who kissed her cheek and then introduced his daughter and her husband and his grandchildren. Wes was there, too, of course, but he stood off to one side quietly.

Finally Daphne turned to greet him officially.

"Daphne," said Audrey, interrupting the moment, "why don't you show everybody to their rooms? Oh, and Wes, be a good boy and carry up the bags?"

"Sure, Mrs. Farway," he said, but his eyes rested on Daphne.

When everyone was settled in—Dodie upstairs changing diapers, Hubert in the kitchen arguing with Audrey about the possibilities for a superpower summit, Wes surveying the damage to the dune—Daphne stepped out onto the porch.

She saw Wes standing there, looking out to sea. His back was to her and Daphne stood quietly, studying him. From inside voices drifted out to the porch. Audrey and Hubert were still arguing. Daphne wondered if that was why her mother had invited Hubert down—to argue. To stir things up, to get her blood boiling with commotion. Anyway, she decided, Hubert seemed to like her mother, and Audrey was quite obviously fond of him.

She took a deep breath and decided to approach Wes and explain to him that it was okay for them to be friends. Why spoil the whole weekend avoiding the issue?

When she walked up behind him and said softly, "Penny for your thoughts," his body snapped taut.

"I didn't hear you coming," he explained, but she could see the stiff set of his shoulders and the alert look in his eyes.

"My turn to startle you." Daphne smiled, trying to convey to him that it was all right, that there would be no tears, no recriminations.

He turned his head and gazed down the beach. So that was the way it was going to be, she thought, feeling a sinking sensation in the pit of her stomach.

"Why did you come, Wes?" she asked impulsively.

"Let's walk," he replied, avoiding her question.

They made a path down the broken dune. Wes commented on the deep gouge the ocean had made in the sand.

She wondered if he had the slightest idea of how sore she was inside, or if he even cared. And she wondered why she was with him, why she was rubbing salt into her wounds. She must be a masochist.

When the Victorian was no more than a rooftop over the dune, Wes finally stopped walking. He turned to face her, the sun to his back. She couldn't read his expression in the shadows, but she saw the dark plane of his cheek and the muscle working in it. She shielded her eyes with her hand and observed the thin line of his lips and his slightly flared nostrils. Something was eating away at him.

"What is it?" she urged gently. "We're friends, aren't we?"

"Friends," he said harshly. "Of course. Problem is, I haven't slept in a month, and I feel like hell."

She stared at him blankly.

He ran a hand through his hair. "I can't stop thinking about you, Daphne."

She took a quick breath, feeling the blood throb in her veins. "Are you telling me that you . . . care for me?"

"That's what I'm saying." His eyes fixed on her apprehensively.

"Oh, Wes," she said, knowing it was so hard for him, and realizing that he might put up that barrier against her at any moment. "You're afraid, aren't you?"

"I guess that's what you'd call it."

"But you don't have to be...or maybe, for a while, you do. It's okay. I'm afraid, too. But it's worse to be alone. It's twice as scary, don't you see?"

"I'm starting to." He traced an imaginary line in the sand with the tip of his shoe. "What I've been going through..."

"Wes," she whispered, hope springing in her breast, "do you want to try?"

"I do," he replied quietly. "But what if I chicken out? What if I break both of our hearts?"

"Mine's been breaking for weeks," she confessed.

He merely nodded, his head bowed.

"So where do we go from here?" she ventured.

"I want you, kids, everything."

"Me too."

"But do you trust me? I mean, I'm not Brady. I'll never be as open."

"I know that. You'll have to learn to trust yourself, though. You'll have to work at marriage. Everyone does."

"You're so down-to-earth." He reached out then and touched her cheek with his fingers. A flame ignited in her. "You're everything I ever dreamed of having. Secretly, of course." He smiled. "But it was always there. I just can't believe I could be so lucky."

No one had ever said anything so lovely, so sweet to Daphne. Her heart raced in joy. "That's one big compliment. I hope I can live up to it."

"You already do." His head came down slowly and an arm reached out to pull her to him. Their lips met gently, searching. Then an urgency built between them and his hands moved up under her sweater and kneaded her back, crushing her to him.

When they broke apart, he said, "You don't know how long I've wanted to do that! God, I feel so great." He hugged her to him. "You're going back to Boston with me on Monday. Don't you dare say no. You can write on the kitchen table while we search for a new place. Then we'll start a family right away."

"Do you think we should get married first?" She smiled, her head resting on his chest.

"Oh, yeah. This weekend. Right here."

"Blood tests, Wes."

"Oh, then next weekend. At your house. Jim and Nancy can come down and stand up for me and all that. And Hubert . . ."

"I've got an idea." Daphne held back a chuckle. "Why don't we dump the wedding plans in Audrey's lap and hide out in Boston, living in sin and making a baby and driving her crazy?"

He lifted her chin up with a hand. "That's mean. You're as bad as she is."

"Hey," said Daphne, "I owe her one. She asked you here without my consent and look what's happened."

"What's happened?" asked Wes lightly. "You got a proposal of marriage. I realized how much I love you. That's all."

"That's all?" she asked, laughing. "Isn't that enough for you?"

His mouth covered hers again and he whispered against her lips. "It's enough for me, Daphne, forever and ever."

Harlequin Superromance

COMING NEXT MONTH

#234 THE FOREVER PROMISE • Meg Hudson
Fourteen years ago Claire Parmeter left King Faraday at
the altar when she discovered that another woman was
carrying his child. Now King and Claire meet again.
Mutual desire draws them together, but the ghosts of
their past threaten to separate them once more....

#235 SWEET TOMORROWS • Francine Christopher
Valerie Wentworth thinks she's put Wall Street behind
her forever. But that is before an irate financial planner
waltzes into her antique-doll shop. Not only is Cutter
the most gorgeous man she's ever seen, but he has the
formidable wits to match her own, and their bodies,
well . . . they fit together perfectly.

#236 HALFWAY TO HEAVEN • Pamela Bauer
Designer Rachel Kincaid can't afford to fall in love with
sexy department store magnate Cole Braxton III. She is
still holding out hope that her missing fiancé will return
home. But Cole isn't about to wait around forever.
Faced with a barrage of difficult choices, Rachel finally
realizes the answers lie within her heart....

#237 CHILD'S PLAY • Peggy Nicholson
Snatching a small boy from under his bodyguard's nose
is no mean trick, even for Tey Kenyon. She can't let
Mac McAllister interfere with her plans, but interfering
with her heart is another matter!

ATTRACTIVE, SPACE SAVING BOOK RACK

Display your most prized novels on this handsome and sturdy book rack. The hand-rubbed walnut finish will blend into your library decor with quiet elegance, providing a practical organizer for your favorite hard-or soft-covered books.

Only
$9.95

Approximately
16" x 8"
when assembled

Assembles in seconds!

To order, rush your name, address and zip code, along with a check or money order for $10.70 ($9.95 plus 75¢ postage and handling) (New York residents add appropriate sales tax), payable to *Harlequin Reader Service* to:

In the U.S.

Harlequin Reader Service
Book Rack Offer
901 Fuhrmann Blvd.
P.O. Box 1325
Buffalo, NY 14269-1325

Offer not available in Canada.

BKR-1

Can you keep a secret?

You can keep this one plus 4 free novels

Janet Dailey
Americana

Don't miss a single title from this great collection. The first eight titles have already been published. Complete and mail this coupon today to order books you may have missed.

Harlequin Reader Service

In U.S.A.
901 Fuhrmann Blvd.
P.O. Box 1397
Buffalo, N.Y. 14140

In Canada
P.O. Box 2800
Postal Station A
5170 Yonge Street
Willowdale, Ont. M2N 6J3

Please send me the following titles from the Janet Dailey Americana Collection. I am enclosing a check or money order for $2.75 for each book ordered, plus 75¢ for postage and handling.

_____	ALABAMA	Dangerous Masquerade
_____	ALASKA	Northern Magic
_____	ARIZONA	Sonora Sundown
_____	ARKANSAS	Valley of the Vapours
_____	CALIFORNIA	Fire and Ice
_____	COLORADO	After the Storm
_____	CONNECTICUT	Difficult Decision
_____	DELAWARE	The Matchmakers

Number of titles checked @ $2.75 each = $_____

N.Y. RESIDENTS ADD
  APPROPRIATE SALES TAX $_____

Postage and Handling $ .75

                          TOTAL $_____

I enclose _____

(Please send check or money order. We cannot be responsible for cash sent through the mail.)

PLEASE PRINT

NAME _____

ADDRESS _____

CITY _____

STATE/PROV. _____

BLJD-A-1